Grottos of CHINATOWN

by Arthur J. Burks

Off-Trail Publications

Elkhorn, California

Thank you, Larry Estep!

Front cover artwork by Rafael De Soto
from *Thrilling Detective*, November 1934

GROTTOS OF CHINATOWN
THE DORUS NOEL STORIES
Copyright © 2009, Off-Trail Publications
ISBN-10: 1-935031-08-2
ISBN-13: 978-1-935031-08-6

OFF-TRAIL PUBLICATIONS
Elkhorn, California
offtrail@redshift.com

Printed in the United States of America
First printing: March 2009

CONTENTS

All stories from *All Detective Magazine*

ARTHUR J. BURKS
(1898-1974)

"There is more blindness per square yard of bonehead in the writing business than in anything I know anything about."

Arthur J. Burks and *All Detective*
John Locke

THE AUTHOR

ARTHUR J. BURKS (the J. was "just there for the hell of it") is best remembered now for his reputation as a speedy and prolific pulp writer, and less so for the enduring quality of his fiction. He produced many hundreds of stories for a variety of pulp magazines, in most genres:

> I could write anything except love and western stories. I couldn't write those. I'd sold a few, but I still couldn't write them, you understand. My westerns were homestead stories and my love stories were "ghosted" to be run under the bylines of women, in magazines that "Burks" could never hit. ["Folks, I'm Bleeding," *Writer's Digest*, March 1939]

From late-'24 forward, he was a constant presence in detective and adventure pulps. He had early success in *Weird Tales*, and its companion magazine, *Real Detective Tales and Mystery Stories*. When new genres appeared on the scene—the air pulps, the gang pulps, weird menace—he was quick to join in. He came a little late to the science fiction pulps, making his first appearance in the April '30 issue of *Astounding Stories of Super-Science*. He wrote boxing stories for *Fight Stories*, *Sport Story Magazine*, and others. Though his output fluctuated in later years, he appeared in the pulps through their demise in the late-'50s.

The near-indefatigable Burks was more than a pulp writer, though. His first book, *The Splendid Half Caste*, was published in 1925. His first novel, the well-reviewed *Rivers into Wilderness*, came out in 1932 under the name Burke MacArthur, probably to spare his pulp readers false expectations. In 1934, he published a family history, *Here Are My People*, of which the *New York Times* wrote, "If there is any virtue inherent in homely honesty, then this book by Arthur J. Burks has a great deal to recommend it." Throughout his career, Burks co-wrote or ghosted many books, most of which remain unidentified. The subject matter ran far afield from his own interests as suggested by some of the titles: *Creating Hooked Rugs* by Vera Bisbee Underhill (1951); *Chicken and the Egg* by William H. Wilson, everything there is to know about chickens and their eggs, including prize-winning recipes.

Burks was born in 1898, on a ranch near Waterville, Washington. He joined the Marine Corps in 1917, and was commissioned in 1919. He remained a Marine until '28, then served a second time in WWII, rising to Lieutenant Colonel.

Burks began writing in 1920. His first published story was a 1200-worder, "The Vagrant's Dream," which appeared under a penname, Estil Critchie, in the *Globe and Anchor* of San Domingo City, West Indies. He earned $4.57 writing that first year, $1.58 the second from a single sale to the *Los Angeles Examiner*. In 1923 he enrolled in a correspondence course with the Palmer Institute of Authorship in Hollywood. His knowledge of the writing game developed. In 1924, he made his first "real" sale to *Weird Tales*, for $15 (presumably "Thus Spake the Prophetess," November '24). For the first couple of years, all his sales were to *Weird Tales* and *Real Detective*. Then he began to branch out.

The first time he was identified for his prolificacy was an interview in the August '28 *Writers' Markets and Methods*, Palmer's magazine, titled "Arthur J. Burks—Speed-King of Fiction." In 1936, his well-known abilities earned him a 700-word profile in *The New Yorker*:

> Average daily output of the Burks Underwood is four thousand words. In emergencies Burks can do three or four times this amount. Once, for example, *Sky Fighters* called him at ten in the morning and ordered three stories, a total of some twelve thousand words. It got them by six in the evening and Mr. Burks made two hundred and fifty dollars for his day's work. ["Burks of the Pulps," February 15, 1936]

In later years, Burks bragged that he'd "once appeared on a dozen magazine covers simultaneously." It wasn't much of an exaggeration. While he didn't receive a cover credit in every case, Burks appeared twelve times in ten pulps dated December '35:

1) *Detective Tales*, "Snoops"
2) *Dime Mystery*, "Death—The Tempter"
3) *G-Men*, "Steel Vests and Brass Hands"
4) *Horror Stories*, "Murder Brides"
5) *Horror Stories*, "Living Nightmare" (as Spencer Whitney)
6) *Popular Detective*, "The Knockover"
7) *Sky Fighters*, "The Gun Dodger"
8) *Terror Tales*, "Slaves of the Blood-Wolves"
9) *Terror Tales*, "Death's Masterpiece" (as Spencer Whitney)
10) *Thrilling Detective*, "Corpse Whispers"
11) *Thrilling Mystery*, "Devils in the Dust"
12) *War Birds*, "The Flying Mongol"

If he had a better month, we've yet to discover it. Early on, though, he pointed out the contradiction between quantity and quality. In rebuttal to the interview, he wrote:

There's money in writing, but not all of one's produce is salable, and that which is written so rapidly that the typewriter has to be changed frequently to keep it from going up in smoke, is usually not worth writing. [" 'I Confess,' " *WMM*, December '28]

We inherently understand the contradiction, which makes the tales of speedy pulp-writers both amazing—and amusing. Both aspects come forth in this anecdote from the March '35 *Writer's Review*:

Burks was writing regularly for Clayton's *Astounding Stories*, then edited by Harry Bates. Bates, in a verbal session with Burks, gave him to understand that if he intended to write for his magazine, he should put more time in on his stuff, and not reel them off first-draft in literally as much time as it took to type them. Burks said "O.K.," went home and dashed off a three-part serial, *Earth, the Marauder* [July-September '30], in three days. However, he held on to it for a little over two weeks, and then submitted it. Bates looked it over and decided to accept it, although with some minor revisions. In a later conversation with Burks—after Arthur had cashed the check—which ran into four figures—Bates commented on the "marked improvement!"

Burks' productivity took a toll, though. In the March '39 *WD* article, he wrote of his eventual burnout:

Whatever title I selected, it seemed to me that I had used it a dozen times before. Every word, sentence or paragraph, I had done over and over again. I hadn't, of course, or fans would have raised hell—they're sure spotters of things like that—but it *seemed* like that to me. I was sick, tired, of doing formula, and only formula fed the kitty. Some of the formulas were so cut and dried that the slightest deviation from them meant a reject, and to stick to them drove me nuts.

A sampling of his titles verifies the problem: "Wings of Amazonas," "Wings of Chaos," "Wings of China," "Wings of Ebony," "Wings of Gallantry," "Wings of Hatred," "Wings of Disaster," "Wings of Judgment," "Wings of Revolt"; and also, "Blizzard Wings," "Dead Man's Wings," "Fearless Wings," "Ricochet Wings," "Speed Wings," "Storm King's Wings," and the unforgettable "Weird Wings." Despite his anguish, Burks continued to write and publish, though his output decreased, particularly during his WWII service. The 1944-47 period shows very little published work, book or magazine.

After first leaving the Marines, Burks "came to New York in 1928 to spend two weeks; and spent fourteen years." He was an early member of the American Fiction Guild, and served as its president for two years. A fellow member was love-story writer Walter Marquiss. In the last of the Dorus Noel stories, "The Blood Screen," Burks offered his friend a subtle tribute:

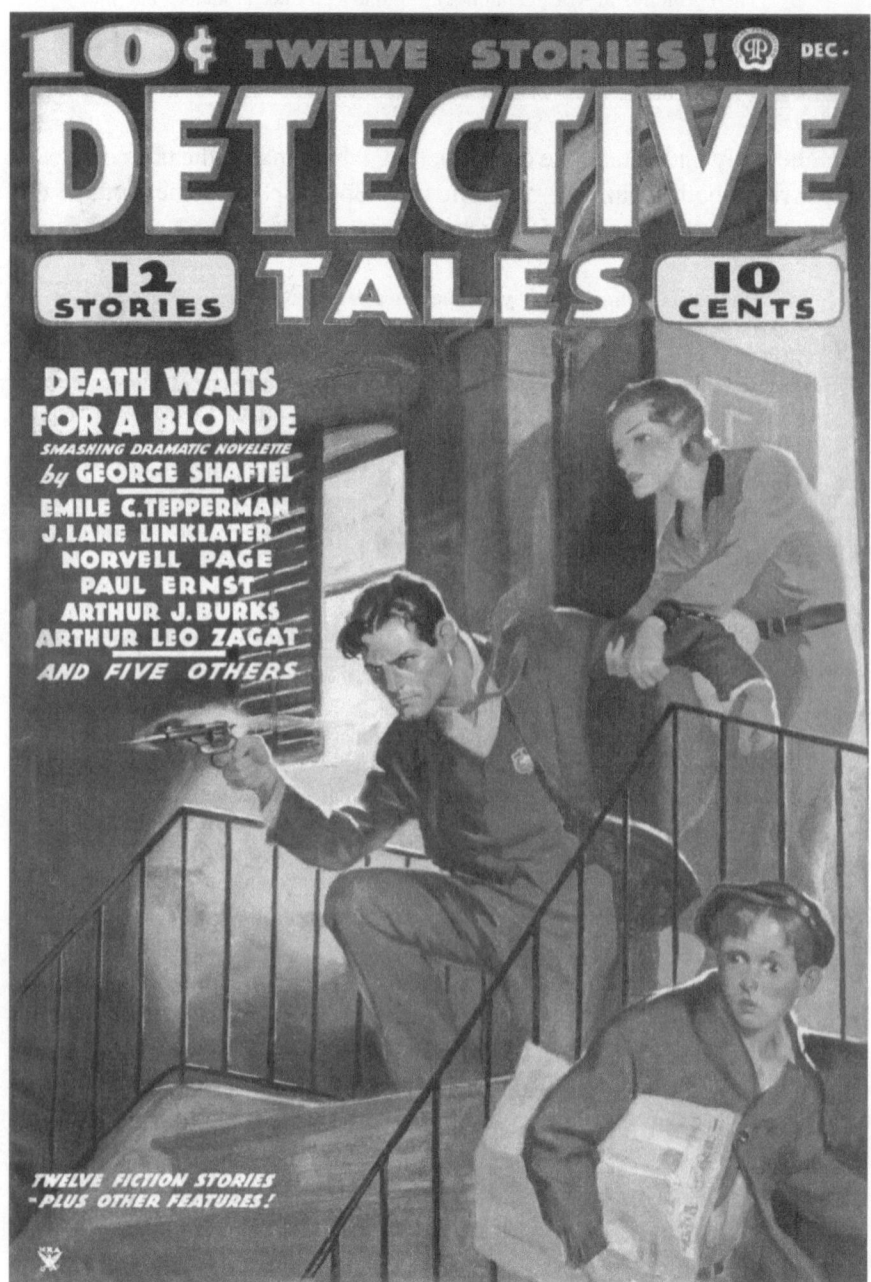

December 1935   Cover art by John A. Coughlin

December 1935 was a very good month for Burks. He placed twelve stories in ten pulps, including "Snoops" in Detective Tales.

> Thaddeus Courtin had died in bed. Noel, on viewing the corpse, was struck by the alabaster whiteness of the skin. His eyes narrowed thoughtfully. The lieutenant in charge of the investigation regarded Noel with a certain degree of animosity.
>
> "It's a queer go, all right, Noel," he said, "but I figure I can handle queer cases as well as the next one."
>
> "Maybe," said Noel. "Nobody denies your ability, Marquiss. What does the coroner say?"

Beginning in the late-'30s, Burks became interested in paranormal phenomena. He published some of his views in the book *Who Do You Think You Are?* (Orlin Tremaine Co., 1939). He believed himself to have ESP, healing hands, and other mystical abilities. He gave public performances and lectured. He published many books and pamphlets in the field, with titles like *Sex the Divine Flame* (1961), *Our Lives Behind Sleep* (1965), and *En-Don: The Ageless Wisdom* (1973). In 1970, he wrote former pulp editor Leo Margulies with a book proposal, in which he described how his life had changed since the old days:

> I've been doing better all these years than I did my best year, financially, as a writer. Lecturing and "doing readings," which came about by accident in Arizona in 1958, have since required all my time. I've traveled the nation nine months a year, finding it exciting and interesting. I do on the conscious level what Edgar Cayce did under self-hypnosis. I've done some thousands, including for people in Hollywood, and one state governor, now a United States senator. . . . I'm in NYC maybe twice or three times a year, always so busy doing the hour-long readings that I get up at six am and tumble into bed at 11, dog-tired.

It seems he was destined to work with great energy at any task he undertook.

His stories generated little interest after magazine publication. A handful of his science fiction and weird menace tales have been anthologized. A 1954 collection of six fantastic stories, *Look Behind You* (Shroud; Buffalo, NY), was published with a print-run of 650 copies. He received his best recognition with *Black Medicine* (1966), an Arkham House collection of his early *Weird Tales* work, which Vincent Starrett, in a *Chicago Tribune* review, described with loving nostalgia as "a collection of off-trail tales guaranteed to keep restless readers up nights." This present volume appears to be the first book-length collection of Burks stories since *Black Medicine*.

Arthur J. Burks died in 1974 while residing in Paradise, Pennsylvania.

THE MAGAZINE

1932. IT HAD BEGUN TO SINK IN: the Depression was no short-term problem.

Industries were under severe financial stress; customers were short of pocket change. The pulps, selling entertainment, a staple of the imagination but not the belly, were far from immune. Publishers struggled to find answers. Carson Mowre, Executive Editor of Dell Publications, attacked the idea that the pulps were dead (*Writer's Digest*, August 1932):

> The pulps are in the doldrums. Circulation has fallen and many are the dire predictions concerning their future. Remedies are suggested. Expensive experiments are being indulged in by publishers. Students of publishing make searching analysis and tell us that the pulps are breaking their old cocoon and merging into another form of butterfly. They sourly tell us that the pulp as we now know it is doomed. That present publishers will fail and a new group with a new idea will usurp the field long held by the pulps.
>
> Hooey!

Mowre had faith in his customers' devotion, while deriding their intelligence:

> The fact is that the buyers of pulps have been hardest hit by the depression. They look longingly at the money they formerly spent for a magazine. Many of them don't have it. Had they the money they would buy the same magazines they always did. Their tastes have changed only slightly; the readers of pulps represent a distinct section of our population. Morons, if you like. They will always be with us.

Never underestimate the loyalty of a moron. The problem was not the product, merely the price. In the following issue of *WD*, Mowre dropped hints about the company's plans, for anyone who could read between the lines:

> We have an immediate market for detective stories in the shorter lengths. Short stories of around 4000 words in length and a few short novelettes of about 8000 words.
>
> These stories are for our new magazine, the title of which is yet unannounced, and should be of the action type rather than the deductive type. The lone wolf type detective story will also be considered. Color and locale should be authentic and the author should strive to insert something of the O'Henry twist in his stories. Avoid the stereotyped detective yarns.
>
> One thing that will cause an immediate sale is the different type of story.
>
> *All Western Magazine*, which has formerly been a bimonthly, will now be published monthly and is in the market for the same type of story that has been used in the past. [September 1932]

The first clue was "shorter lengths." The second was the acceleration of *All Western* to a monthly, which bucked the trend of the shrinking market. In this same general period, major titles like *Detective Story* went from weekly to monthly; *Top-Notch* and *West*, twice-a-month to monthly; *Adventure* went from twice-a-month to monthly in June '33; many other titles were discontinued and the entire Clayton chain collapsed. There were successes too in this period—*The Shadow* went from monthly to twice-a-month in late-'32, likewise *Dime Detective* in '33—but the overall picture suggests turmoil and transition.

Dell's answer was revealed on the newsstand with two pulps bearing November cover dates. *All Detective Magazine* debuted as a thin 64-pager with a radical cover price of 5¢. *All Western* had come out in October '31 as a 10¢ bimonthly, and now re-emerged as a 5¢ monthly companion to *All Detective*. One of the key elements would be shorter stories, to maintain variety. The first issue of *All Detective* had six, one of which was the first installment of a serial. The page-lengths of the stories: 13, 8, 5, 7, 22, and 2, leaving a few pages for ads and miscellaneous. In most pulps, stories under 10 pages would be considered filler material, which explains Mowre's emphasis on "different" stories and O'Henry twists. Readers would not keep buying a pulp full of filler—at any price. They would need stories with a memorable jolt.

In the first issue, Mowre laid out the plan in a one-page announcement:

> With this issue ALL DETECTIVE makes its bow to readers. It is a magazine of fascinating detective and mystery stories. The best authors procurable will be represented on its pages.
>
> ALL DETECTIVE will be honest with its readers. There will be no long pages of description and flowery language. Every story will have something to say and will have that elusive quality that will make you remember it long afterward as a "different" story.
>
> Magazines of this class are known as "pulp-paper" magazines. It is sometimes used in a sneering manner. We are proud of that name. It is another way of saying value. Many of the greatest authors of our day have appeared in the pulps. Many of our greatest men have read them.
>
> Naturally we cannot give you a magazine with as many pages as one costing four times as much—we will give you a magazine that is the biggest value money can buy. In hard times quality and price are first considerations. ALL DETECTIVE will give you those qualities.

He touches on all the key themes: short, efficient stories; fascinating, "different," quality stories; low cost. And he even devotes a paragraph to flattering the tastes of his moronic readers, some of whom are "our greatest men."

If the 5¢ gambit paid off, Dell intended to promote the pulps to weekly publication, the clue hidden in the increased frequency of *All Western*. As *Writers' Markets and Methods* noted, the experiment would be "watched with interest by writers and publishers." One keen set of observers were the good folks at Metropolitan Publishers of Chicago, well out of nose-punching range from Dell in New York. Metropolitan quickly reworked their existing pulps into blatant imitations of Dell's. *Popular Fiction* became *Nickel Detective*, and *Two Gun Stories* became *Nickel Western*. Similarly, they were 64-pages and 5¢. They hit the newsstands with January '33 dates, which meant that Dell enjoyed a mere two-month grace before the vultures landed. In retrospect, Mowre's caginess in unveiling Dell's plans reflects a justifiable paranoia. In the pulps, few ideas—good, bad, or otherwise—went unpilfered.

If it was a duel on the newsstands, Dell was the one to cry uncle. After four issues, both *All Detective* and *All Western* doubled cover prices to 10¢ and increased length. The *Nickel* twins didn't fare any better. *Nickel Western* folded after four issues, while *Nickel Detective* lasted six before changing title to *Strange Detective Stories*, a memorable short-run which lasted four issues as a 15¢ 160-pager. Dell's experiment would probably have failed in any event, but Metropolitan's poaching may well have accelerated the final result.

All Detective's new length was 96 pages, essentially a nickel for the first 64 and another nickel for the remaining 32, a worse deal for the reader. With the November '33 issue, *All Detective* expanded to the standard 128-page length, where it remained for its run. The 10¢ cover held, though, until the October '34 issue, when it jumped one last time, to 15¢.

While the magazine changed size and price, the emphasis on the "different" remained. Mowre refined his demands for contributors, as demonstrated in this blurb from the January '33 *Author & Journalist*:

> *All Detective* is especially interested in stories with unique and different ideas. . . . The purely deductive story is not wanted, neither is the gang drama. Stories with glamour, strong suspense, startling development, their setting in unusual and out-of-the-way places, get a fast reading and checks. Unusual crime methods, accompanied by a well-characterized hero, a logical solution of mystery, and a dramatic plot, will ring the bell every time. Horror and exotic stories are used occasionally.

Mowre was following the trend toward weird detective stories already established by *Detective-Dragnet*. These eventually became labeled as "menace" stories:

> *All Detective*. The "menace" type of detective story is now being favored by Carson Mowre, editor. [*WD*, September 1933]
> *All Detective*. Make your ideas as unusual and outstanding as possible. And keep to the action type of detective work. Nobody seems to like the easy-chair detective these days. Blood and thunder, menace and murder are the rule. [*WD*, January 1934]

January 1933   Cover art by Eugene M. Frandzen

Dell caught the industry's attention with new, 64-page nickel pulps.
Following the trend toward weird detective stories, many of All Detective's
covers featured unusual themes.

The definition of Mowre's needs continued to expand:

> *All Detective.* "Our crime stories must have a direct emotional appeal for the reader. The first way of gaining this end is the creation of a hero with whom the reader would like to and can identify himself. Once he is living the story vicariously, the most primary play upon his emotions is suspense. Work toward that sensation of something about to happen, the mounting fear. Menace is the strongest method of creating suspense. Draw the antagonists of the hero as such resourceful, diabolical characters that the reader fears the outcome; draw the crimes of the antagonists so vividly, stressing the physical horror, that fear of this fate grows in the reader. Make him *feel* the crime, not as plot development, but as the ghastly reality. Color helps suspense: characters and situations which in themselves are exciting to the emotions. The bizarre is another aid: freakish, monstrous, fantastic criminal actions given an aspect of plausibility. Criminal actions which could but don't happen. Avoid the stock in character and situation." [*A&J*, April 1934]

The covers of *All Detective* caught the eye with vivid depictions of skeletons, skulls, sarcophagi, hooded men, devils, nooses, and, of course, beautiful women under grave, often bizarre, threat. The groundwork was being laid for the weird menace genre. The descriptions of the stories on *All Detective* contents pages were often lurid:

> "The Mad Cracksman," by Frank Richardson Pierce: *When the witches' fire got too hot Jerry sent to the madhouse for a twisted brain—a perfect cat's-paw to confound the law.* [March 1933]

> "Enter the Killer," by Frederick Painton: *To those who dared the night* The Thing *dealt a strange death. When the dawn caught it abroad a greater power than its own evil collected the dues of the Devil.* [September 1933]

> "The Racketeer Rajah," by Warren Hastings Miller: *King-pin of the Singapore underworld, he fathered the evil hatched in that festering Malay port; then reached out for a white man's ship.* [November 1933]

> "Hands Down," by Hugh B. Cave: *He escaped from the living dead to be marked by the doublecross, but he had a mark he could make himself in the slime of a death that crawled.* [February 1934]

> "Croaker's Cart," by Jay J. Kalez: *He cheated the chair and turned a young police interne against his kind; but ghostly hands drove the wheel which turned the ambulance of escape into a wagon of stiffs.* [April 1934]

As time went by, *All Detective* featured an increasing number of series characters, "the creation of a hero with whom the reader would like to and can identify himself," as Mowre's blurb had it. Ted Tinsley's Scarlet Ace was the first of these, in the fourth issue. Burks' Dorus Noel soon followed, in the sixth. Others included Erle Stanley Gardner's Bob Crowder; Lester

Dent's Fade, Spectacularist of Crime; Earl W. Scott's Ex Avery, Border dick; and Frederick Painton's Captain Lansing Colt, super-salesman for munitions makers.

The July '34 issue introduced Doctor Death, a criminal mastermind, and, we trust, the antithesis of the type of character the reader would identify with. Doctor Death featured in four novelettes, and died with the magazine. The bad Doctor is killed off in the last issue of *All Detective* (January '35). A new title, *Doctor Death*, took the place of *All Detective* with a February date. It featured a revamped Doctor Death, a mad scientist.

Dell was in fact making a double-move to join the burgeoning ranks of the hero pulps—or in the case of Doctor Death, the "villain" pulps. February '35 marked the last issue of Dell's remaining air pulp, *War Birds*. It reemerged in March as *Terence X. O'Leary's War Birds*, headlining an old favorite from Dell's war pulps. Both experiments were a failure, as neither *Doctor Death* nor *TX* made it past three issues. *War Birds* returned later in '35 and ran nine more issues through '37. *All Detective* never returned. Weathering the storms best of all, *All Western* appeared monthly through August '38, and sporadically into '43.

THE STORIES

IN "SWEAT SHOP," a July '35 *Writer's Digest* article (reprinted in full in *Pulp Fictioneers*), Burks told this story:

> Once I got twenty rejects in a row from a house which had been worth almost $2000 a month to me. I thought I had lost my grip, was finished at thirty. Letters of rejection said that I no longer had the right slant. I began to wonder. I submitted a story under another man's pseudonym. Back came a letter with a check. The letter said:
>
> "We are pleased that you have the freshness we want, that you have so admirably caught our slant."
>
> They'd rejected better stories under my own name. Later I found out the reason. I had said something to a writer about branching out to new markets. He had carried tales to the editor, who had said:
>
> "He'll come to me on his knees before he'll sell another story to the house."
>
> As things happen I didn't go to him on my knees. I never went back. I landed with another house at better rates. Then and there I made this resolution: never to give any one house the chance to make me go hungry for an editor's whim.

Burks was too professional to fill in the details: "I've made it a rule not to mention names here." However, armed with a deep record of his pulp appearances, thanks to the extensive indexing that has been done in recent years, we can deduce the houses in question, and the editor who took umbrage.

Born in 1898, Burks would have been "finished at thirty" in 1928. Around that time, he was completing his lengthy record of sales to two magazines, *Weird Tales* and *Real Detective Tales and Mystery Stories*, with only a handful of appearances elsewhere; and he had just started a long and diverse run of sales to Fiction House. For several reasons, however, this does not make a plausible point of the breach. *Weird Tales* and *Detective Tales* had started as twin titles in '23 for a single company, The Rural Publishing Corporation of Indianapolis, with Edwin Baird editing both. But by the time Burks started selling to both magazines, Farnsworth Wright had become the editor of *Weird Tales*, and *Detective Tales*, with Baird remaining as editor, had split off into a separate company and given the longer title. Both magazines paid meager rates, which make them unlikely candidates to fulfill Burks' $2000 monthly income. Additionally, in a March '29 article (*WMM*, "Are Editors Human?"), Burks had extremely kind things to say about both Baird and Wright. So, in all probability, Burks had simply outgrown the pay-rates of the two magazines; and the "finished at thirty" remark represents either a misremembering or a round-off.

Before the run at *Weird* and *Real Detective* had concluded, Burks made his first (known) appearance in a Fiction House pulp, grabbing the only cover credit and the cover art for the August '27 issue of *Air Stories*. This was no mere air pulp, though; it was in fact the *first* issue of the *first* air pulp, making Burks a pioneering author in this new air-age genre. Burks probably leaped at the chance to strike out in a new direction that utilized his military background and traveling experience. He probably typed the story in rapid response to the inaugural *Air Stories* solicitation in the July '27 *Author & Journalist*:

> *Air Stories*, 271 Madison Avenue, New York, is the newest member of the Fiction House group. The editors write: "You writers can turn your eyes skyward now and shoot us some he-man, action-adventure yarns dealing with any phase of flying; Zeppelins and balloons are not barred if the story holds up, but naturally the faster-moving, zooming, loop-the-loop airplanes will provide the larger field for dramatic stories. Love interest is permissible if not overdone. Nothing morbid or glorifying criminal use of planes. No war stories. Right now we need a goodly supply of shorts—4000 to 6000 words long—and a half dozen novelettes—9000 to 12,000 words. We are pretty well stocked up on 40,000- to 60,000-word serials at present, but can stand a couple of complete novels—20,000 to 30,000 words. Remember to start your stories with a bang and keep up the pace all the way through—in other words, apply the formula for *Action Stories* to yarns that have an aviation angle. Keep away from the trite plots of smugglers and dope runners. Give us something fresh!" Robert A. Carter is managing editor. Payment is at 1 cent a word upon acceptance. All serial rights are purchased.

August 1927   Cover art by Frank McAleer

Quick to take advantage of a new genre, Burks made the cover of the first issue of the first air pulp.

The offered pay-rate would have been a nice raise from the half to three-quarters cent that *Weird* and *Real Detective* were paying. Burks' 18-pager would have met editor Carter's need for novelettes; and since Carter featured the story, "Jerry the Hawk," he must have been impressed. So, too, must other Fiction House editors have liked the newcomer. From 1928 forward, Burks made many appearances in *Aces*, *Action Novels*, *Action Stories*, *Air Stories*, *Fight Stories*, *Soldier Stories*, *Wings*, and several others. He made only scattered sales to other markets; and those may have been Fiction House rejects.

And so it went through 1929.

Burks showed a little more house diversity in 1930. He sold a series of Kid Friel boxing stories to Harold Hersey's *Gangster Stories*. Their hardboiled gangland slant may have made them unsuitable for Fiction House or *Fight Stories*. He placed a few stories with Clayton, first to *Flyers*, then to *Astounding Stories of Super-Science*, the first of many sales he would make to the science-fiction pulps. Other sales included Hersey's *Flying Stories*, Street & Smith's *Air Trails*. Burks was clearly branching out, as he had preached to the gossiping writer. All the while, Fiction House had been publishing his work. Until October '30, that is—when Burks was not to be found in any Fiction House pulp. According to our records, his September appearances in *Action Stories* and *Fight Stories* mark the end of the run. His byline did not surface in another Fiction House magazine until 1936, about the time that Jack Byrne, Managing Editor since late-'28, resigned to join Munsey. (Fiction House had limited activity during some of the intervening period, but that began with their 1933 suspension of publications.) All variables considered, Fiction House is the only plausible candidate for the company that gave Burks the silent sendoff, with Byrne the offended editor.

Burks had suddenly found himself without a primary market for his prodigious output. Candidates for replacement would most likely come from the secondary markets he'd already established. Dell, for instance. Our earliest record of Burks in a Dell pulp is "The Devil's Court" in the November '29 *Sky Riders*. Dell, with its variety of war and air pulps, looks like it would have been an ideal place for Burks to land. In fact, with *War Stories* debuting in November '26, Dell had as great a claim as Fiction House to launching the war/air boom that gave Burks so many new opportunities. Burks' next Dell appearance was in the July '30 *War Aces*. Then, in late-'30, with Burks now on the outs at Fiction House, the Dell appearances start with greater regularity: *War Aces* (November '30), *War Birds* (December '30, February '31), *All-Fiction* (December '30, January, February, March '31). These may have been from the pool of Fiction House rejects. Other Burks markets of this time include *Far East Adventure Stories* and Ramer's *Airplane Stories*. The Dell appearances then dry up, according to current records, until a couple of *War Stories* appearances late in '31.

And then, springing into existence, came the Thrilling chain, a new line of cheap, colorful pulps launched by publisher Ned Pines and editor Leo Margulies. Despite the fact that many early issues were filled with low-paid house writers, Burks started appearing in *Thrilling Detective* from the third issue (January '32), and in *Thrilling Adventures* (March '32), also the third issue. Burks remained diversified, but Margulies was a former literary agent who wouldn't have been bothered by his sales to other houses. Burks' sales to Thrilling increase in frequency, especially through 1934. He continued as a regular in *Thrilling Detective* and *Thrilling Adventures*; he also became a regular, naturally, in Thrilling's air pulps, *The Lone Eagle* and *Sky Fighters*. Burks hadn't sold much to Popular Publications, a chain which originated in late '30, a year before Thrilling came onto the market. But when Popular became the cornerstone of the new genre of weird menace, Burks sold heavily to its three titles, *Dime Mystery*, *Horror Stories*, and *Terror Tales*, from '35 forward. By the time he wrote "Sweat Shop," Burks was appearing almost exclusively for the two publishers, Thrilling and Popular.

All of this is really just a longwinded way of setting the context for the Dorus Noel stories. Burks' flurry of sales to Dell in late '30 and early '31 never gave him roots at the house. He didn't sell again to Dell until the Noel stories starting appearing with the April '33 issue of *All Detective*. Outside of several subsequent sales to *War Birds*, Dell did not become Burks' new home. In fact, the *War Birds* appearances soon gave way to a run of stories in George Bruce's new air pulps, *Contact* and *Squadron*, which came on the market in mid-'33 and lasted about a year.

Therefore, since the sales to Dell were relatively few in number, and scattered over time, and since the run at Popular did not establish itself until 1935, the house that Burks "landed with" after Fiction House could only have been Thrilling. Thrilling was known as a penny-a-word market; the fact that Burks cites his "better rates" with the new house suggests that he was popular with readers and was paid a premium. The "Sweat Shop" anecdote makes it sound like Burks made the leap from the one house to the other in short order, but that's another case of rounding-off; the gap would have been more than a year.

Now, for the stories themselves. Burks did on occasion use repeating characters, though as a rule series were not his forte; he never fell into the hero-pulp domain like Walter Gibson and other super-producers. As far as we can tell, these eleven Dorus Noel stories constitute Burks' longest run with a single character. Kid Friel appeared in six novelettes in *Gangster Stories* and *Gangland Stories* (1929-31), but the combined wordage is about

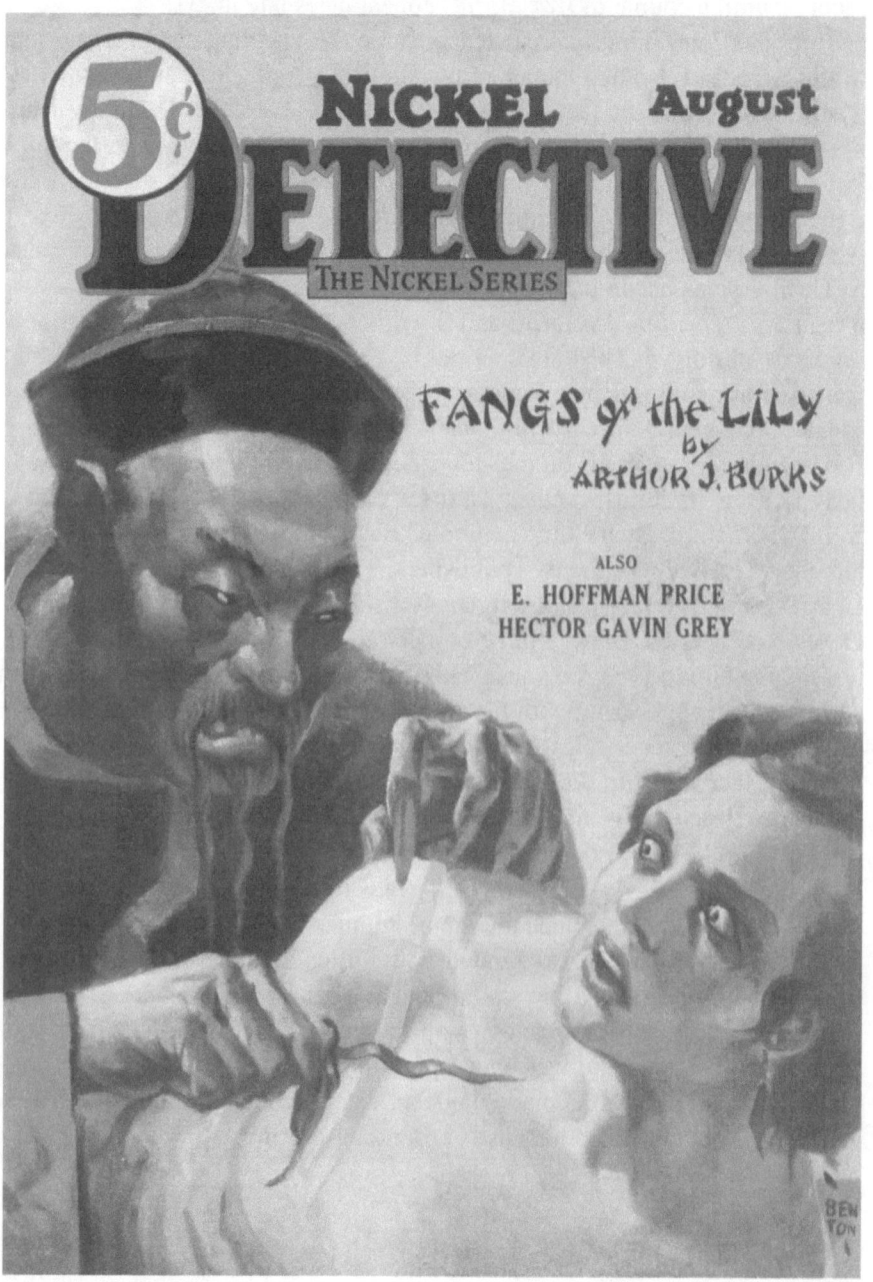

August 1933   Cover art by C. Benton

Of the lessons to be learned from this cover: No idea—in this case, the nickel pulp—goes unpilfered. Oriental villains were commonplace in this period. Burks was everywhere, with another story set in Manhattan's Chinatown.

50% more than the Noels. There were several other characters who appeared in three or four story sets; and there may be other minor series buried in the Burks canon yet to be unearthed.

The editor's introduction to "Folks, I'm Bleeding" listed many of the places Burks had visited: "China, Japan, Philippine Islands, Hawaii, Formosa, Manchukuo, Canada, Bermuda, Mexico, Nicaragua, Cuba, Santo Domingo, Haiti, Panama." Most of the traveling owed to his first eleven years in the Marines. He visited China in 1927 while serving as an aide to Brigadier General Smedley D. Butler, whose mission was to safeguard American interests during some momentary turbulence. That same year Burks co-authored a juvenile book with Butler, *Walter Garvin in Mexico*. Later, Burks wrote an action-packed two-part biography of Butler for *Thrilling Adventures* (August, September 1934), titled *The Fighting Leatherneck*: "He Led Men Through the Very Fires of Hell—And He Made Them Like It!"

Burks' many travels provided rich material for his writing, as the same introduction indicated: "Uses places he has actually visited for background, except pseudo-scientific yarns; he's never been to Mars or Venus, though may make it before he dies, and comes close sometimes when he's taken a few extra drops of Porto Rican rum."

The Noel stories are rich in Chinese lore. As the first story opens: "China had left her mark upon Dorus Noel." Quite literally. We soon discover that the twenty-six-year-old Noel bears torture scars from his time there. But the double meaning is obvious. The second story provides further details on Noel's background, also reflected in the furnishings of his Chinatown apartment:

> There were feather screens and lacquer screens. The place was China, and to Dorus Noel, China was home. In color he was white; in inclination he was a yellow man, because his many years in the Far East had inoculated him with the virus of the ancient land. So was he fitted for the strange part he was to play in the criminal annals of Chinatown. Sometimes, even, in the solitude of his sleeping room, he dressed in the splendor of China in the days of the Empire, and then even his eyes seemed to take on an almond shape.

As Burks moves from story to story, we don't really deepen our understanding of Noel. He's an undercover detective in Chinatown, and his experience confronting weird crimes and criminals is the main event.

In that first story, Burks is quick to establish his respect for the Chinese:

> "You'd die to avenge a Chinaman?"
> "He died for loyalty to me, sir," said Noel sternly. "How could I do less? And let me tell you something: a Chinese is not a Chinaman, he's a Chinese!"

By the third story, however, Burks' discipline breaks down, as he has Noel explain to his anonymous superior: "I know Chinks better than most." Burks' true attitudes are buried beneath such apparent contradictions.

But in story after story, Burks creates great atmosphere through his descriptions of Chinatown, Chinese people, Noel's Chinese collections and furnishings, and the infusion of Chinese history into the middle of an American city. One would then assume that Burks' experience in China was long and ample. However, in a March '47 *WD* article, "What's the Answer?," wherein Burks disputed the old writers' axiom, write what you know, he gave as one example:

> I made a trip from Tientsin, China, to Mukden in Manchuria. The whole trip, going, staying, returning, lasted five days, more than three of it on the train. I wrote about it for five years, novelettes mostly, one serial, innumerable story stories. Could that have been because I "knew" the country?

His five years is another case of round-off, as the Noel stories fall a year or two outside that range. But the lesson is clear: Burks could turn an iota of experience into a parade. The downside was his inability to go deeper into the subject matter.

As we know, Burks had been living in New York City for several years when the Noel stories were written. For pulp writers, it paid to be near the center of the publishing world. For Burks, it had the added advantage of putting him into proximity of another useful setting, Manhattan's Chinatown. Noel's apartment is near the intersection of Pell and Mott Streets, where Chinatown originated in the 1870s. By the time of the Noel stories, the Chinese population numbered well into the thousands. Chinatown is located near the bottom of Manhattan, forming part of the Lower East Side. To the west is Tribeca and Soho; to the north is Little Italy and the Bowery; a few blocks south is the Brooklyn Bridge. Bowery street bisects Chinatown north-south, while Canal Street cuts through the middle east-west. Off the main avenues, the narrow streets are turned into claustrophobic canyons by the four-, five- and six-story buildings. Many of the older buildings have fire-escapes built down the front façade, all the better for infiltrating the apartments of the unwary. No doubt, a simple visit to the district would have recharged Burks' mind with new story ideas.

In an August '49 *WD* article, "Inside a Writer's Brain," Burks demonstrates his thinking process as he conjures up a new story idea:

> "Marines? Marines? Now, let's see—eighteen years in the marines, active and reserve, with travel to many lands. Shall I write of the baseball game between marines and Japanese in Tientsin? Written in one way, I can sell it to Leo Margulies for his baseball magazine. Since marines are in it,

if he bounces it, *Leatherneck* will take it. Or should I write a slick story about a fragile, delicate, jade-like Chinese girl, picked at random from among the exquisite ones I saw in China—those gorgeously gowned gals whom the marines, with due irreverence, referred to as 'bosomless wonders'? No, typewriter keys, that won't do, for few of the readers for whom I wish to write today ever visited China. But I could switch the story to New York, couldn't I, and weave a delicate story around a cloisonné vase discovered in a Fifth Avenue shop? Or I can remember court gowns of the Manchu Dynasty, of which I have seen so many, and fictionally fill them with Manchu court ladies—no, that won't do, so few people know what Manchus are without too much description. Let's just take something simple, the sort of thing anybody finds around the house, or even around the typewriter."

And that describes, as well as anything will, how specific Noel stories germinated. Burks was famous for generating entire plots out of simple objects—and the shops of Chinatown were packed with objects. But, after reading the Noel stories, note again the requirements that Carson Mowre spelled out for *All Detective* contributors: "color and locale should be authentic," "stories with unique and different ideas," "setting in unusual and out-of-the-way places," "menace and murder are the rule," "freakish, monstrous, fantastic criminal actions," etc. Burks merged his brief China experiences, Chinatown, and Mowre's needs with uncanny precision. It's a perfect illustration of why Burks became one of the best-selling pulp-writers of his day.

DEATH OF THE FLUTE

Dorus struck the deathly flute from the boy's hands.

Not Always Does the Past Bury its Dead. Out of the Yellow Waters of the Pei Po Came a Strange Vengeance to Single Out Dorus Noel in the Tangle of New York's Chinatown.

CHINA HAD LEFT HER MARK UPON DORUS NOEL. He thought of that now as he sat musing, in his house on Mott Street, in New York's Chinatown. From somewhere out in the street, or perhaps in a store next door, a clock sounded the hour of three in the afternoon. At the same time some of his own priceless clocks began to strike. One of them he especially loved because it always gave him a smile. It was a beautiful gem incrusted thing which had been given to Emperor Ch'ien Lung by Louis Fifteenth of France . . . and when it struck the hour, eight tiny human figures in blue came out on its top and danced a tinkling minuet.

A second clock was all of glass, save for its works, which were surrounded like a serpent by a circular staircase. When this clock struck three it did it in odd fashion. A gold ball came through a hole in the fourth step and rolled down three steps, making a tinkling noise. At four o'clock the ball fell a step further, taking the additional hour to travel back up the circular stairway.

Now the one clock danced the minuet, the other rolled its golden ball down the three steps, thus striking the hour. Dorus Noel sighed.

"Thank all the gods," he murmured, "that Chu Chul is dead. He must be. With my own eyes I saw his clutching yellow hand sink under the muddy waters of the Pei Ho at Tientsin, and I waited for two months for his resurrection, which did not transpire. My work here in New York will be easy compared to the years-long game of hide and seek with The Cricket."

Noel had formed the habit of talking to himself because he found it easier to think, and he did not speak in Chinese because, in China, anybody who listened might have been a minion of Chu Chul. Now he rose from his desk and strode to a mirror on the wall, threading his way through the many treasures which filled his study. He passed the red lacquer screen with its decorations of tiny bird feathers. He circled the crooked screen just inside the door, which kept out evil spirits because they could only travel in a straight line.

He faced the mirror, before which his "boy" Liu Wong had placed two burning joss sticks for some strange reason of his own. Noel leaned forward, staring at his own handsome face, which looked far too old for his twenty-six years. He had lived three lifetimes in that age, and Chu Chul was responsible for most of his aging. His brown hair, almost red, should, he decided, have been gray. He lifted his hands, one of which was oddly twisted—memory of Chu Chul's pincers of torture—and pulled the shirt away from his chest, exposing it.

Then he stared long at the mark on his white skin. It was three parallel, horizontal bars, perhaps an inch in length, crossed by a diagonal transversal. They were the Chinese character "wong" which means "ruler," or "master of men." They were not Noel's chop. They had been burned into Noel's skin on the one occasion when Noel had fallen into the hands of The Cricket, in the cat-and-mouse game they had played. Even now Noel could remember every word The Cricket had spoken to him in Tangku when he had wielded the branding iron:

"So that you shall never forget, Dorus Noel, that The Cricket is your master, your ruler . . . as he is master and ruler of many men . . . and women. If it happens that you live you will go through life bearing my mark. And never, alive or dead, will you ever win over me. I never forget or forgive . . . and I pay my debts of vengeance!"

Right now Noel could hear the singsong voice of The Cricket speaking. He shook himself to dispel the fancy.

"Thank God that's over, and The Cricket is dead."

Noel returned to his desk . . . thinking back . . . recalling, planning on how he should perform his secret tasks in Chinatown. Here he must learn all over again. Here he would have what he had always hoped to have; contact with China, however slight, and contact with his own kind.

He didn't realize how the hours had fled until his stomach told him it was time for dinner. The two clocks struck. The eight little figures danced their minuet. The golden ball rolled down from the eighth step. It was seven o'clock . . . and vague shadows were creeping into the study. Liu Wong should long since have summoned him to dinner. Oh, well, perhaps the "boy" had forgotten that dinner was at six-thirty instead of nine as in Tientsin. He would remind him. Liu Wong should long since have summoned him by making his strange music on the "wooden fish"—a hollow fish made of wood, suspended from the kitchen ceiling, and used as a gong.

But only silence came from the kitchen. Noel did not even smell the enticing odor of food. Strange, strange indeed. In China the circumstance would have put him instantly on guard. But this was the United States. He started to rise. Then his hands fell back from the desk and he sat bolt upright in his chair. All the color drained out of his face. Perspiration beaded his forehead swiftly. His eyes went wide, mirroring horror, a premonition of disaster . . . for at last there came a sound from the kitchen. It never should have come from there, yet it came . . . and it sounded a tocsin of warning to the brain of Dorus Noel. For the sound which came was the note of the five-note Chinese flute. How well Noel remembered the five-note flute! Two Chinese musicians who knew the flute and the secret code of the Classics, could even talk with one another on their flutes, in a weird telegraphy which no "foreigner" could ever hope to understand.

It had been the telegraphy of Chu Chul! God!

But still Noel sat as one transfixed . . . and his mind named each of the five notes as he heard them, names that would have meant nothing to an American, even when translated, yet which in themselves gave a note of mystery, as the five-note flute ran its weird scale. Noel's lips shaped the names of the notes: *hung, ssu, chang, chur, fan*, and his brain translated their senselessness into English: *labor, four, top, measure* and *reverse*. He kept repeating them over and over again, while inside him the still small voice of warning began to cry out louder and louder.

"Don't concentrate on the five-note flute. Don't concentrate on the five-note flute! Don't speak the names of the notes, either in Chinese or English!"

With a distinct effort of will, for it seemed almost as though he were being gradually fastened to his chair, Dorus Noel leaped up and raced to his kitchen. There, beside a cold stove, his eyes set in a fixed stare, his face streaked with oily sweat, sat Liu Wong, his "boy." Liu Wong did not hear him come. He did not look up. His lips caressed the end of a flute Noel had never seen—or had he? Liu Wong swayed from side to side . . . and his lips ran the five-note scale without emotion, as though the lips had been dead, or the man himself had been performing in some strange hypnosis, or were a puppet pulled by strings in the hands of an invisible prompter.

At Liu Wong's feet was a brazier from which rose a thin spiral of yellow smoke, writhing and twisting like a nightmare snake as it rose to curl its tendrils about the face and head of Liu Wong. The smoke from incense powder, Dorus Noel knew instantly . . . and something more. He put his face over the smoke, inhaled a little, merely sniffing. His senses reeled. He staggered back. Then he jumped in, struck the flute from the hands of Liu Wong, jerked the boy away from the brazier, pulled him to a window which he flung open. Then he began to slap the boy on either cheek with his open palm.

Even as he labored with Liu Wong, Dorus Noel's lips shaped words in Mandarin:

"*Sheng Huang!*"

It was the name of a poison which could be administered in burning incense powder. A little of it stupefied; much of it killed. Noel struck the boy until Liu Wong's face was almost a livid bruise. Dully, his eyes looking far away, his face empty and stupid, Liu Wong began to regain consciousness. Noel darted to a taboret and brought a small drink of rice wine. Liu Wong gulped it and gagged, but his brain was reacting.

"You strike me, master," he said, his voice dull, lifeless, but no longer stupid. "Why?"

Dorus Noel whirled the boy around.

"Look!" he said.

Liu Wong looked at the flute and the smoking brazier. His face showed instantaneous fear. Then it became stolid, expressionless. One who did not know Chinese would have thought him unconcerned. Noel knew that inside Liu Wong strange fires were raging. He knew what Noel knew; that here was warning of impending death, both to Liu Wong and to Dorus Noel.

"So," said Liu Wong softly, "Chu Chul is not dead! He is here, in New York. He always said he would have revenge, master!"

"Yes," said Noel. "It is either The Cricket or one of his advance agents."

"How could he enter the United States?" asked the boy, but the answer didn't really matter, though Liu Wong waited for it.

"Who is there," said Noel, hopelessness in his voice, "to prevent The Cricket from entering anywhere? What happened? How did it happen?"

Liu Wong shrugged.

"I do not know," he replied. "I became sleepy. I slept. I wakened, and it was like swimming up from a deep well, to find my master slapping my face."

"You were swaying over the yellow smoke," explained Noel, "and you were playing the flute of five notes. I heard it in my study. I listened, unbelieving. I almost lost, Liu Wong, do you understand? He almost had me. I might have become unconscious . . . had I listened to the five notes long enough . . . and then Chu Chul could have entered, and . . ."

Liu Wong straightened.

"It is a warning," he said. "It is like Chu Chul. It pleased him to try to destroy you by using me, who worship you! It is Chu Chul's way of jesting."

Liu Wong held the burning brazier under a water faucet. He moved like a man under the influence of liquor. His face was blank, still sweating. When he had quite finished and the room had been fanned clear of the stifling fumes, Liu Wong spoke to his master.

"I shall seek Chu Chul," he said. "I shall slay him before he touches my master. I go to the house of the joss to pray for good fortune."

Noel placed a sympathetic hand on the shoulder of the boy.

"You know you are helpless, Liu," he said softly. "He has but to see you to command you . . . even to returning to slay me, your master! He ruled you too many years with his will."

"I shall go to the joss house and burn candles and make a prayer," insisted Liu Wong. "Then I return to make food for you, for never must you take food from any hand save that of Liu Wong."

"And while you are gone?"

"Chu Chul will not hurry. It pleased him to warn you. Now he will leave you to grovel in fear until he strikes again. It is Chu Chul's way."

Liu Wong stepped out onto the street and Noel watched him walk down Mott Street toward the nearest joss house.

"Poor devil!" muttered Noel.

He returned to his desk, his back against a wall, to await the return of Liu Wong. Now that he was warned he had no fear. He had crossed mystic sabers too often with Chu Chul to really fear him after the first shock of discovering that the evil genius of North China was not dead, but living. His thoughts were busy.

The eight little figures danced the minuet.

The golden ball rolled down eight steps. Liu Wong had been gone almost an hour. Fear for his safety at last broke in upon Noel's musings. Had Chu Chul regained control of his onetime minion? Would his next attack on Noel be in the shape of a rush by Liu Wong himself, knife in hand? It was not possible. Noel looked toward the door, but it was masked by the twisted screen which kept out evil spirits. Even as Noel looked, however, he heard dragging steps on the pavement outside and the screen fell into the room with a crash.

And crashing down atop the screen, Liu Wong fell on his face.

From his lips he poured out his soul in Mandarin.

"He tried to send me against you, master, but he failed. For this once, the will of Liu Wong was stronger than the will of Chu Chul!"

Noel jumped to the fallen man, turned him over. At the same time, out on Mott Street, a police whistle sounded shrilly. Somebody had seen this thing which now rested at Noel's feet and had notified the police. Far away a siren began screaming. But Noel scarcely heard it. Curious Cantonese who must have followed Liu Wong from the joss house had entered and were standing all around Noel and the supine man. Noel looked quickly at their faces. All were extremely "American," though all were Chinese. Chu Chul was not among them, nor any of his minions, Noel was sure.

Now he looked down into the face of Liu Wong. The man was suffering agonies and was trying not to show that he suffered. His face was a bloated horror. His body writhed and twisted in spite of all he could do to prevent it. His face was mottled like a bird's egg . . . and it had been savagely slashed to the very bone by what might have been the talons of an evil night bird of prey. A fighting cock, with steel spurs on every toe, might have made such marks . . . provided his legs had had the strength of a strong man's arms. In a matter of seconds, Liu Wong would be dead, of horribly administered poison.

Dorus Noel's face was hard, as expressionless as that of any Chinese face around him.

He spoke in quick Mandarin to the dying man. The Cantonese audience looked at one another. None was likely to know Mandarin, so widely different from Cantonese.

"What did it, Liu?" Noel whispered.

"*Nang tze*, the two-edged knife," came writhing through the puffed blue lips of Liu Wong. "It happened—it came out of nowhere—when I fought the spell and refused to turn against my master."

"Who did it? Chu Chul?"

"Not Chu Chul. Another . . . a minion of The Cricket . . ."

Then, with a great convulsive writhing, Liu Wong was dead. At that moment two uniformed officers entered, trailing a man in plain clothes who smoked a cigar and stared with arrogance at the circle of yellow faces around the dead man. The Cantonese exchanged glances which meant nothing to

Detective Lieutenant Hamas, but spoke volumes to Dorus Noel. Said the glances:

"Here this pompous fool is back again, trying to unravel one of our mysteries. Smart as he thinks he is he can't see his two hands in front of his stupid face."

All this and more Noel could read in the glances.

"Who are you?" the plainclothes man snapped at Noel.

"Dorus Noel."

"What-cha doin' in Chinatown?"

"I live here."

"Hell of a place to live. No place for a white man who don't know Chinks. Better move out. Takes fellows that knows these birds to get along with 'em. Who killed this jaybird? Did you?"

"No. He was my servant."

"Don't look like any Chinks I know."

"He's a Tientsin man."

Hamas stared at Noel, plainly uncomprehending. Noel didn't think it necessary to tell him that Tientsin was a city in North China. Obviously it would have been news to Hamas.

"Yeah, or, yeah," said Hamas, nodding. "I thought so! What killed him, did you say? Or do you know who done it?"

Noel spoke the two words Liu Wong had just used.

"*Nang tze!*"

Hamas whirled on the two officers.

"Go out an' scour this rabbit warren until you grab a guy named Nang . . . Nang . . . well, his last name sounds like a bee buzzin'. You may have to handle some Chinks rough, but get me this Nang . . . Nang . . . whatever his name is. This is the fastest I ever wound up a case!"

He knelt over Liu Wong.

"Lord, certainly carved him, eh? Never saw anybody bloated an' lookin' quite so awful as this. Hope we can sweat outa this Nang . . . Nang . . . what he used. The newspapers will eat it up, if it's Oriental enough."

"You'll need me?" asked Noel. "I live right here. Just moved in. If I may go?"

"Oh, sure, this is simple. Dorus Noel? Fine. I'll send for you if I need you. Better take my advice and get outa here. Gotta know Chinks to live among 'em."

Noel didn't answer. He donned his hat and strode down Mott Street, hoping that he could follow the back trail of Liu Wong, feeling all the time how futile it was to try, since Chu Chul would come to him if he gave him time.

"Chinatown knows him!" Noel thought. "He's already cast his spell over the Cantonese. I can't expect any help from them, not even if I give away who I am. He will rob them blind, bleed them of all their wealth, and they won't open their mouths. It's up to me, and I have to travel alone. But that's best. See what Liu Wong got for his loyalty to me. I can never again ask anyone to share my feud with Chu Chul. But how to find him?"

This was Chinatown at night. Lights showed dimly behind smoke blackened windows. Sprawling characters indicated the type of business which went on behind those windows. Noel knew the characters . . . for characters did not change with different dialects . . . China had but one written language. He read the names of shops, "delicious fragrance," "fragile willow tree," "graceful longevity," "gorgeous good fortune"—it was almost like being back in China.

Dorus Noel stopped dead in his tracks. People bumped into him. He didn't mind, didn't feel them. Would Chu Chul dare, here in the United States, to do the things he had done in China? Would he dare, actually, to destroy and torture a white man, almost in the heart of New York? Noel knew he would, but he must take a chance somewhere. He hadn't yet had time to learn the rabbit warrens of Chinatown, if indeed he would ever be permitted to learn them. Here he wasn't known, because he was under cover, save to the man, far out on Park Avenue, who had given him his police job in Chinatown. Of that man on Park Avenue he knew only that he was connected with the police, a very high connection, too. He had given Noel a telephone number, to be called in case of grave emergency.

Noel hurried to Canal Street, crossed it, strode west to Lafayette, already in New York, in contrast to Chinatown—and entered a cigar store. He called the secret number, that of his secret police superior, on Park Avenue. The voice he remembered answered. Noel spoke his name by way of identification, and was answered.

"If," said Noel, "I have not been heard from by you within twenty-four hours from this moment, turn Chinatown upside down to find me. Remember I told you of The Cricket?"

"Yes," the far voice was low and soft, but with a hint of steel in it.

"He's in New York, in Chinatown. He or one of his men has just killed my servant, Liu Wong. I'm going after him, in my own way. Know Detective Hamas?"

"Yes."

"Let him play with the Liu Wong case. He can't do any harm. I know how it was done . . . all of it but not, exactly, by whom. I shall discover that, or die."

"You'd die to avenge a Chinaman?"

"He died for loyalty to me, sir," said Noel sternly. "How could I do less? And let me tell you something: a Chinese is not a Chinaman, he's a Chinese!"

Then Noel, the ghost of a smile on his face, clicked up the receiver. He took a deep breath, turned back into Chinatown. He locked his doors, and windows, with the exception of one window—the window by which someone had entered his house, lighted the poisoned brazier at the feet of the sleeping Liu Wong and thrust the five-note flute into the "boy's" hand.

Noel, in his eyes a dreamy, faraway expression . . . sat down on the stool which Liu Wong had occupied, on which he had sat to play with senseless lips the flute of his erstwhile master, Chu Chul.

"A strange manner of returning to China and ways that are dark," thought Noel, "but it's one way to get to Chu Chul. Wouldn't this puzzle Hamas?"

But he didn't smile. He talked to himself at random, mustering his courage. Then he placed the flute to his lips and began to run the five-note scale. As he did so he rose to his feet and moved softly, like a sleepwalker, to the window which gave onto darkness. Far away he heard the banging of a gong in some joss house. From next door came the chattering of many Cantonese, busy with chopsticks and rice wine. He heard the shrill, high-pitched laughter of young girls.

Back, carefully. He would never know how to "talk" on this flute; but he knew that somebody would hear it.

"What is this sound?" the Cantonese would say . . . and eventually the word would reach someone, maybe several, to whom it would have meaning. In his mind's-eye he could see skulking figures come forth from behind secret panels . . . sent out by the man who had burned that mark on the skin of his chest. Dark alleys would disgorge the minions of Chu Chul. They would approach the sound of the five-note flute. Then . . .

All at once he had his answer.

It came from somewhere beyond that window of his, which opened on blackness and an alley that ended on a cul-de-sac at either end. His answer came in the same sounds he was making . . . the voice of a five-note flute. Only the answering flute made a sound like ribald laughter. It was jeering, sneering . . . almost demoniac. While he listened Noel could almost hear the queer, chattering laughter of Chu Chul . . . could almost hear it in the voice of the second flute. Chu Chul and his queer laughter . . . people who heard it might think The Cricket mad. Perhaps he was, but he had a brain that, mad though it might be, was one of the greatest, trickiest, Noel had ever encountered. The man was genius. A genius who was mad for power, a man who possessed strange knowledge not gained from books, even though he was a master of the Classics, and could repeat by heart whole sections from the Book of Changes.

Chu Chul was a dreadful menace. Once he had all but held North China in the hollow of his hand. He would have, but for Noel. Now he was here, in America . . . and Americans would be like babies in his hands. He would be able to create an organization which would control the city . . . the nation . . .

if the whim seized him. So Noel was fighting for something more than mere vengeance for the slaying of Liu Wong.

But still he hesitated, wondering what he should read into the voice of the second flute. The sound of it was approaching, apparently over the housetops. Sometimes it seemed in the alley outside, sometimes atop Noel's own house, sometimes in the room with him . . . but always coming nearer. What was its message? Noel remembered how he had almost been tricked when he had listened to the flute as played by Liu Wong, how he had fought off the numbing hypnosis. Now he would deliberately court it.

Chu Chul would not slay him . . . until Chu Chul, inexpressibly vain, had had his opportunity to gloat over his victim. He would be in Chu Chul's power, and whether he got out of it again, depended upon himself.

He sat down and ran the five notes twice again. Then he placed the flute beside him on the floor and bent all his will to reading some message into the five notes of the second flute—which now was no longer approaching. His brain caught the names of the notes, ran them through again and again. *Hung, ssu, chang, chur, fan—hung, ssu, chang, chur, fan*. Over and over he named the notes as the unseen flutist played them, until the Chinese names—he thought now in the Mandarin which was as much his language as English—became like a soothing litany. He knew his limbs were becoming numb, that his will was going out of him—out through the window, into darkness.

He sat, eyes wide open, staring at the open window.

Five minutes passed. The flute still played softly, but he did not hear it. He seemed to hear nothing. He did not seem to see the two evil faces which lifted above the window sill, nor the two shadows which seemed almost to flow across the window sill, into the room. He did not appear to feel it when one of the shadows snarled at him, and kicked him viciously in the ribs. He merely shook a little on the stool, and continued to stare straight to the front. They picked him up and carried him to the window . . . and he was still in the sitting position, knees drawn up. They dropped him to the alley below . . . and still he was in the sitting position, though he fell on his side . . . and remained there, motionless.

They carried him to the end of the cul-de-sac opposite the boarded end of the alley where the street was. A panel opened. Two shadows, carrying between them a figure which sat on air, as though it were Buddha, passed into utter darkness . . . moving down a flight of steps.

On a roof two houses removed from Noel's, a crouching third shadow chuckled. A yellow hand tucked a flute into a long sleeve. The shadow darted across the housetop, dropped over the edge . . . and darkness swallowed it. A pale yellow face was touched for an instant by a ray of vagrant light, before it vanished.

But Dorus Noel, who sat in midair in a Buddha-like posture, was not unconscious, not under the spell of any hypnosis. He had fought back from it at the last moment. Perhaps he could fool Chu Chul into believing him a victim of hypnosis—"power-over-you"—and then he could remember every twist and turn of any labyrinth through which he might be taken.

The two who carried him stopped in the darkness, in the midst of a dank smell—and rapped lightly on the panels of a door. The door was swung open, and over Noel's ears, all about him, poured the chattering laughter of Chu Chul. There was no mistake then, and Chu Chul was in New York, gathering strings of terror into his hands.

"Take him to the brazier," said Chu Chul in English. Since Chu Chul did not speak Cantonese he had to use English, for the Cantonese of Chinatown spoke but the two, English and Cantonese. It was odd that Chinese must address Chinese in English.

Then Noel knew that he hadn't fooled Chu Chul with his fake hypnosis. However, perhaps the man just would not chance it. Noel decided to continue the trick, even when, sitting on the floor in the position he had assumed and had never changed, his head was thrust into the yellow smoke which he could see through his widely staring eyes. It was almost impossible not to blink, but he managed even that.

And Chu Chul laughed.

"Fool!" he said. "Do you think to trick Chu Chul so easily? This time I shall give you something to remember!"

To get it over with quickly, Noel inhaled the *Sheng Huang* . . . and darkness filled with bobbing lights flowed over him. He did not even know it when he was lifted again and borne away.

He came to himself with his head throbbing. In his nightmare, preceding his awakening, he had heard the golden ball on one of his clocks roll, down four steps . . . three o'clock in the morning. Now his wrist-watch, on the hand directly before his eyes when he began to come awake, assured him that it was three in the morning. He did not even puzzle over the seeming coincidence. To one who knew the mysteries of China, that his dream coincided with the fact was trivial, of no consequence.

Chattering laughter. He turned his head dully.

Sitting at one end of a long room, on a dais, dressed in the royal robes of China—a travesty of empire—was Chu Chul, The Cricket! He was small enough to be a Cantonese. His skin was yellow, pitted with smallpox scars. His black eyes seemed to have no pupils. His hands were like claws. He was beardless. He sat leaning forward, stoopingly. It was thus he walked, too . . . a twisted caricature of a man.

"So, we meet again, Dorus Noel," he said. "Did you think I would be so foolish as to think I could gain power over you across the housetops as I could Liu Wong? You were smart, as usual, but not smart enough—also as usual. I thought it better to put you out entirely, in order that you might not, if I allow you to escape, remember the way back here with the stupid police who, stupid though they are, are still too strong for Chu Chul—at least yet! When will you learn that you are a baby in the hands of Chu Chul?"

Noel said nothing. Let Chu Chul enjoy his gloating, while Noel recovered his wits entirely, after his dose of the *Sheng Huang*. Noel was husbanding his strength. His side hurt where he had been kicked. His dull eyes studied Chu Chul's retainers, all Cantonese but one! There were a dozen of them. Yes, Chu Chul had started an organization. It would specialize, if Chu Chul remained Chu Chul, in murder, robbery, kidnapping—everything that would bring terror to men and wealth to the coffers of The Cricket.

"I thought you were dead," said Noel.

"No Dorus Noel will ever slay Chu Chul," replied The Cricket. "I decided to change for a while. I came here. Strange that you should follow. I like it here. There are greater opportunities."

"Who killed Liu Wong? Oh, I know that you ordered it. Who did it?"

Chu Chul smiled. His eyes played over the faces of his minions. They shifted uneasily. Noel watched the traveling eyes of Chu Chul, which rested for a fleeting moment on the face of one man. Noel spoke quickly in Tientsinese.

"He's the only North Chinese with you," he said . . . and saw by the larger man's face that he had understood. "In the United States, when a man slays another human being, he dies. What is his name?"

He saw sweat break out on the fellow's face.

Chu Chul, enjoying the by-play, answered.

"Sung Liao!"

The body of the North Chinese jerked at mention of his name as though he had been pricked with a needle. He was larger and darker than his Cantonese brethren. Noel rose to his feet.

"Well," he said, "what are you going to do with me?"

"I'm not going to kill you," replied Chu Chul. "Not when I know that within twenty-four hours of your death the police will turn Chinatown upside down to find you! Let's see, these were the words you said over the telephone to your plainclothes superior who lives on Park Avenue. . . ."

And Chu Chul gave the telephone number and the exact words that had passed between Noel and his employer. Noel's heart sank.

"You've already got to the police with your bribes," he said bitterly. "So they've tapped Mr. Blank's telephone wires? Well, what are you going to do, then?"

Chu Chul laughed, the laughter breaking off into a chuckle.

"One can be electrocuted for a slaying," he said, "but when one puts out the eyes of an enemy one cannot be so severely punished . . . and one is then forever free of the danger of being spied upon by a man, little and insignificant though he is, Noel, who can be so irritating. So, I shall put out your eyes . . . and let you find your way out of here and out of Chinatown!"

Noel's face did not change expression at all. For he still had an ace in the hole. There was one thing about him Chu Chul did not know . . . that he was the master of the art of *ta chuen*, Chinese equivalent of *jujitsu*.

"Bind him and bring him to me!" snapped Chu Chul.

The Cricket leaned forward over a burning charcoal brazier at his feet. It was the one un-Chinese thing in a room decked out with true Oriental splendor—for the charcoal burner was a Japanese *hibachi*. Chu Chul lifted from the coals a pronged piece of steel. The tips of it were white-hot. They would pass easily astride his nose. The tips of white-hot steel would put out the world's light for him forever, in the batting of an eye.

"Jump quickly, the man is tricky!" snapped Chu Chul.

The Cantonese, while Sung Liao held back fearfully—wondering what manner of white man this was who spoke the Tientsin dialect—jumped in at Dorus Noel, who waited until the last moment, and went into amazing action. He was still loggy from the *Sheng Huang*, but his strength, coupled with his knowledge of *ta chuen*, placed on his side the element of surprise. A hand reached for him. He grabbed the wrist with his left hand, thrust his right under the elbow, reached up over it, caught the wrist he held—and bore down swiftly with all his strength.

The Cantonese squealed in agony as his right arm snapped. He fell back, screaming . . . and from the hand of Chu Chul darted a black, gleaming thing. It struck the Cantonese of the broken arm in the side . . . and in a trice he was down, writhing as Liu Wong had writhed—while the black streak which had struck him returned to the hand of Chu Chul.

Chu Chul laughed.

"I do not like failures in my organization, new as it is," he said.

To Noel, fighting now against the remainder of the Cantonese, that black streak meant much. It was a knife, fastened to a rubber about the wrist of Chu Chul. The knife had been suspended above a brazier in which *Pi Hsuang*—a poison resembling spun candy or glass—had been burning, mixed with any sort of fat which would congeal into a coating of grease, on anything touched by the poisoned smoke.

After such treatment the knife—the *nang tze* which had tortured and slain Liu Wong—would be black with the grease, and the grease filled with *Pi Hsuang*.

• • •

Sight of what had happened to their fellow spurred the Cantonese to greater effort. They attacked Noel with the desperate fury of wild beasts. Noel broke another arm, and the man came in still fighting, with the arm dangling grotesquely, and his face ravaged with agony. But even as the wounded man fought, he glanced ever and anon at the grinning, evil face of Chu Chul. Chu Chul, by his barbarous cruelty, by his slaying of the one, and Liu Wong, was proving his strength to the Cantonese. Give him six months and he would be able to laugh at the police of New York City.

"He must not! He must not!" Down in Noel's heart the three words kept repeating themselves. Chu Chul must be beaten, forever. If only there were some way . . .

Two men were down, both unconscious . . . one with his head twisted under him at an odd angle. Noel didn't mind killing . . . for this organization, when it was strong, would specialize in murder. Now Chu Chul ordered Sung Liao into the fray. Chu Chul was enjoying himself. Noel knew that he was beaten when Sung Liao took a hand. The chances were all in favor of Sung Liao's knowing *ta cheun*—else Chu Chul would not have brought him from China as bodyguard.

In desperation Noel decided upon a different sort of move. There was no advantage in beating these Cantonese, even if he were able to do it—for Chu Chul probably had a score of others behind half a dozen panels, awaiting his signal to enter. Noel suddenly broke from the fight, hurled himself at Chu Chul. Chu Chul laughed as Noel darted in—laughed and jumped back. But he held the hot tongs in his hand, menacing the face of Noel. Behind, the Cantonese were charging. Sung Liao was now leading them. Noel hesitated. Then he stooped, caught up the *hibachi* of live coals . . . and though the *hibachi* burned his hands to a crisp, he hurled the coals full upon the person of Chu Chul.

Chu Chul's yellow hand released the pronged length of white-hot steel. It fell to the steps of the dais . . . and smoke rose from the rich carpet which covered the steps. Chu Chul screamed and tore at his clothing. Noel grabbed for him, but in the instant his hands would have touched his enemy . . . Chu Chul laughed through the pain he must have been suffering—a laugh filled with menace . . . and promise of revenge—and dropped into his dais, pressed something on an arm of it. Instantly the dais whirled so that Chu Chul's back was to Noel, and shot toward the wall. The wall opened. The "throne" of Chu Chul went through the panel. The panel closed.

Noel whirled back as the Cantonese jumped him, knowing that even though he hadn't captured Chu Chul, he had almost saved himself—for Chu Chul never would have left the scene of a fight so delightful to a man who liked the sort of jests that Chu Chul liked, had it not been that the coals from the *hibachi* had set his clothing afire. His own safety came first, vengeance afterward. What if Noel escape? Chu Chul could always get him back . . . his own life might not be restored to him if he lost it.

So Chu Chul had simply vanished. It was a way he had.

Noel was being borne down by his attackers. But he remembered where the pronged steel had been dropped. He fought with the fury of a wildcat until he drove his enemies back for a moment—not difficult to do now that they were not made desperate by the sight of Chu Chul, who would slay any who failed without compunction—and caught up the steel.

He sprang directly at Sung Liao, the pronged length of steel, now a dull red, held in his left hand. His right hand leaped forward. Sung Liao's mouth was open in amazement, that this man could move so quickly and surprisingly. Noel grabbed at Sung Liao. The forefinger and middle finger of his right hand went into Sung Liao's mouth, while his thumb fastened under the jaw. It was as though he pinched the man's lower jaw with two fingers and thumb.

"Bite down on it, Sung Liao," he said calmly, "and I'll yank the lower jaw out of your head . . . and with this piece of steel I'll do to you what your master would have done to me."

He said it in Tientsinese, in the tone a master uses when he commands a servant . . . and Sung Liao, his face alight with terror, did not even move.

"Now lead me out to The Cricket, Sung Liao," went on Noel. "Or rather, tell me how to lead you. I'll keep this hold until we are back in Mott Street."

The Cantonese charged . . . but he kept them back with the pronged steel.

"The master will slay me," said Sung Liao, moaning, babbling his words crazily around the fingers of Dorus Noel.

"If that were possible," said Noel grimly, "it would save the State of New York the trouble. But you are going to burn, Sung Liao, as proof that even Chu Chul cannot save his minion from justice."

Trembling, Sung Liao pressed something on the wall, and again a panel swung back. Sung Liao nodded. They stepped through into darkness—darkness and the odor of burning clothing and burning flesh—closing the panel in the faces of the charging Cantonese.

With the closing of the panel a light flashed on, to show Chu Chul sitting on his dais, crouched on his "throne," while tendrils of smoke rose from his rigid body. He appeared to be dead.

"Thank God!" said Dorus Noel.

But Chu Chul was not dead. Noel wondered if, after all, there were any power on earth or above it that could destroy the baleful creature known as The Cricket. For, with smoke twisting over his features, with the odor of burning cloth and flesh filling the room, so that it stank in the nostrils and sent Noel into a fit of coughing—The Cricket opened his eyes.

• • •

Noel had never before looked so deeply into eyes that were so utterly malignant and baleful. Chu Chul tried to move his hands. The blackened things tried to form themselves stiffly into fists. The mighty will of Chu Chul was driving its awful power to his hands, trying to make them do his bidding. Noel knew what Chu Chul would have willed: that his hands leap forward and clutch about the throat of Chu Chul's enemy.

But the hands would not be used.

Chu Chul's lips writhed back from blackened teeth. His gums were raw and bleeding slightly. He looked like some beast, snarling in a trap.

By an effort of will which Noel regarded as miraculous, Chu Chul rose to his feet.

He tried to put out his right hand, but it refused his bidding.

"See?" came hoarsely from Chu Chul. "My hand will not obey me, but even in death it will not be thwarted, for you feel it, Dorus Noel, even when your eyes tell you it does not move! You feel it rising to fasten at your throat. To the end of your days you will waken, night after night, obsessed by fear of Chu Chul, even in your sleep and, until you are fully awake, you will fight like a madman against my strangling fingers!"

It was horrible. Dorus Noel could distinctly feel the fingers as Chu Chul had just said. He knew he would always feel them.

Chu Chul did not cry out to his minions who battered at the door through which Noel had just come with Sung Liao. There was pride, majesty, in Chu Chul's bearing. If he were destined to die none would witness his passing. It was awful that the smoke rose about The Cricket's nostrils, yet the man did not cough, his words were clearly, terribly enunciated. Little fires—fires which were too hot for Noel to forge through, even had he been able to release the murderer, Sung Liao, to do so—licked at the flesh of The Cricket, and Chu Chul did not seem to notice. He was mighty in defeat, arousing in Noel greater fear of the man than had ever been Noel's when Chu Chul had had all his faculties.

"Chu Chul is never beaten!" said The Cricket hoarsely. "If the cat has nine lives, Chu Chul has nine times nine . . . and all of them shall be dedicated to the destruction of Dorus Noel and the working out of the mighty schemes of The Cricket.

Noel wished to beat out the flames, but the very eyes of The Cricket seemed to forbid him even a show of sympathy. Really Noel had none, for here stood a monster whose killings would have bathed Mott Street with blood. But Noel could appreciate the satanic greatness of the man.

The Cantonese were still battering at the door as Chu Chul, his eyes set in a fixed stare which never left the white face of Noel, bent in the middle and fell back upon his throne. The flames licked up, and the smoke rose in tendrils . . . and the black eyes of Chu Chul were set in their stare.

The panel cracked. With another charge it would give away and the Cantonese would enter. Noel was satisfied by his reason—though deep inside him there was a doubt, always would be a doubt—that Chu Chul was dead. He was satisfied that the dead man was truly The Cricket, for he saw the distinguishing marks on the man's scarred flesh which were the sign manual of The Cricket and his followers.

A vast relief flooded Noel. But even as he turned away hurriedly, while his enemies began to break through into the chamber where Chu Chul had risen to his most exalted heights of greatness, he could feel those unblinking black eyes, boring into his back. All his life, he felt, he would feel them. They would go with him, watching him, spying upon him, no matter where he went or what he did. He tried to shrug his grim impressions away and partially succeeded. He forced Sung Liao to lead him out of that labyrinth. On Canal Street he delivered Sung Liao to a copper.

"For murder," he said briefly. "Watch him carefully while you call the wagon."

Then he telephoned the Park Avenue number.

"The Cricket is dead," he said flatly, doubting his own words as he heard them. "You will find him in the basement of the shop called Graceful Longevity."

As he clicked up the receiver the sound of heavy traffic came to him from the busy street. The very rule of the whole city, of which this traffic was a part, had just been saved from transfer into awful hands. He grinned as a taxicab rubbed fenders with a truck, and both drivers said, almost at once, the ancient formula:

"Why'n hell don't'cha watch where ya goin'?"

THE WHITE WASP

She tried to warn him from the dead man's hand.

Vengeance Grooms Many Strange Steeds That Murder May Ride; but None as Strange as the One Loosed in Chinatown to Sear the Mark of Bei Tu on the Brain of Dorus Noel.

"I DON'T KNOW," DORUS NOEL spoke softly into the telephone, addressing his police superior out on Park Avenue, the man who had taken on the titanic task of ridding New York's Chinatown of criminals, "whether the death of Chu Chul ends the reign of terror in Chinatown. I hope so. Knowing China and the Chinese, and that Chu Chul had all the nine lives of a cat, I'm inclined to doubt it, despite the urge of reason. I saw Chu Chul, dead, with my own eyes. But I'm not forgetting that I saw him dead once before, sinking in the Pei Ho near Tientsin."

"There is danger for you in Chinatown, Noel?" asked his superior softly.

Dorus Noel, from the depths of his many years of experience with Chinese evildoers, laughed casually.

"In Chinatown, in Timbuctu, in Kamchatka, there is danger for the man who caused the death of Chu Chul," he said. "Chu Chul headed a vast organization. That organization had multitudinous roots. When the head of such an organization is lopped off, a fresh one grows. To destroy such an organization is to harvest the stars with a carving knife."

"Then what is the use?"

"There's always use. We can, you know, keep lopping off heads."

"I leave it to you, Noel," said the unknown.

"Thanks. Then I'll stay in Chinatown, but remember what I said about Chinese organizations. I could tell you many tales of the Society of the White Lily, or the Red Spears and the *Hung Hu Tze*. But never mind. I'll let you know what happens."

Dorus Noel clicked up the receiver. He was calling from a pay phone on Lafayette Street. Now he hurried back to Pell and Mott Streets, near the intersection of which he had a home. It was a strange home. It was like stepping out of New York City into China with a single stride.

There were many clocks in the room, and always they were synchronized.

One had a group of figures inside it which came forth and danced a minuet when the hour struck. Another rolled a gold ball down a flight of steps to count the hours.

There were dragon screens in the corners and paintings on the walls— paintings of dead and gone men and women.

There were feather screens and lacquer screens. The place was China, and to Dorus Noel, China was home. In color he was white; in inclination he was a yellow man, because his many years in the Far East had inoculated him with the virus of the ancient land. So was he fitted for the strange part he was to play in the criminal annals of Chinatown. Sometimes, even, in the solitude of his sleeping room, he dressed in the splendor of China in the days of the Empire, and then even his eyes seemed to take on an almond shape.

He went to his study. Above his head hung a wooden fish, a hollow piece of wood shaped like a fish, and used as a gong. He smote the gong three times with a wooden mallet and his "boy" entered. This was his second boy. The first had died in his service, trying to save his life from the vengeance of Chu Chul, The Cricket. This new one he scarcely knew, but that didn't matter. If he could win the confidence of the boy the latter would be faithful during his lifetime.

"Bring me tea, Wang," he said.

The boy bowed, hands in sleeves, and vanished.

Even as he moved away Dorus Noel was conscious of an irritating buzzing sound in the room. There was something strange about the sound. He had heard it before, at times, but for the moment he could not place it. It merely irritated him. But it chilled him, too, and he shivered.

"Pshaw!" he said to himself. "I'm shivery. Chu Chul hasn't cooled long enough yet on a slab for my nerves to settle."

But what made the buzzing sound? He squinted his eyes and searched the air above him. It wasn't a mosquito's buzzing. It was stronger, harsher, somehow more malevolent. He couldn't rid himself of the idea that there was menace in it.

"Wang!" he yelled, wasting no time on the wooden fish. "Come here!"

Almost instantly, so fast it seemed he could scarcely have left the room, Wang returned.

"Yes, master?"

"There's a bee or something in the room, Wang," said Dorus Noel, "and I can't locate the thing. Bee stings bloat me up all over like a poisoned pup. Find the blasted buzzer."

"Yes, master," said Wang. His yellow face was impassive. He was larger than the usual Cantonese, and Noel suspected that his ancestry might be traced to some place further north. Tientsin or Peking, for example.

Wang was busy searching in dark corners, behind screens, under clocks, putting into his work all that attentive concentration which was the mark of value of the good Chinese servant. From the reception room came a low voice, a feminine voice.

"Is there anyone here?"

Noel knew he had never heard the voice before, even as he asked himself why anyone should enter his house in this fashion. There was an odd quality in the voice. It was rich. The English was excellent and the voice pulled at him. He rose from his place. Wang did not seem to have heard. Dorus Noel, pulling his face into a mask of imperturbability, prepared to suspect anyone and everyone, entered his reception room, where a door gave onto Pell Street.

He gasped at what he saw.

It was a woman, a girl rather. She appeared to be no more than eighteen or nineteen years of age. Her back was toward him. The back was one that would have delighted an artist or a sculptor, or anyone else who enjoyed grace and beauty of line. The fact that the girl wore a coat of white fur which reached to midway between knees and ankles did not rob her symmetry of its beauty. Her dress was light, too.

But there was a quaint touch in her white shoes. They had light red heels. It gave the whole effect a touch of the bizarre.

He could tell by the motion of the girl's shoulders that she was using makeup, holding her compact mirror up even with her shoulders. But that sort of warned him, fanned his suspicions. He was an old-timer in crime and criminals. More than one lady crook had learned how to study prospective enemies in a mirror. But he might be wrong.

Then the girl turned.

Dorus Noel gasped.

He had expected to see an American girl of refinement, a girl of allurement and beauty. What he saw was a Chinese girl, whose face was like peaches and cream. Her eyes were but slightly slanted. Her lips were like cherries, her teeth like little white pearls. And her eyes, so perfectly matching the black hair which peeped from under a tip-tilted toque, were as deep and black and unreadable as the wells of Shallajai.

"I wish to look at some jade," said the girl imperiously.

Dorus Noel understood then. She had mistaken his home for a store. If he told her it was no store, she would merely draw her cloak about her and leave. He couldn't stand that. There was something indefinable about the appeal of this girl, even though down inside him there sounded a tocsin of warning—like a light tapping of a slender wand against the wooden fish. He must hold this girl here, know her better, know more about her. He didn't believe any Chinese girl would enter his home by chance. Chinese girls didn't make mistakes like that.

Dorus Noel, unsmiling, but knowing that his eyes expressed pleasure and surprise, strode up to the girl and bowed, conscious that she stared at him as though he had been her footman.

"Hurry!" she said. "Must Lao Ye be kept waiting?"

In spite of himself Noel started, but suppressed the motion instantly. More than ever he was sure that this was not a visit of chance. "Lao Ye" was no girl's name, that he knew. "Lao Ye" might refer to an Empress, and this girl was too young for that, even if Chinatown went in for Empresses. Usually the two words referred to Buddha. But why?

"Lao Ye?" said Dorus Noel politely. "I do not understand."

Instantly then the girl dropped into swift Mandarin. Noel understood her perfectly, but it was no part of his plan, wholly on guard now, to let her know anything of himself.

"I desire the jade for a god in the Temple down the street," she said. "It is an offering to the household gods for the safety of a departed soul."

"I do not understand," said Noel, though he hadn't missed an intonation of the singsong Mandarin. The girl switched back into English, perfect in enunciation, and repeated her words.

"And who," asked Noel, "is the departed soul?"

"What business is it of yours?" she snapped at him. "Get me the jade?"

"I have," he said, staring her straight in the eyes, "some Chu Chul jade. It is carved in the form of crickets."

But if she understood his allusion to the dead master of crime she gave no hint whatever. Her black eyes were still the wells of Shallajai. Noel was convinced then that his suspicions were groundless.

"I'll get you the jade," he said. "On second thought I'm not sure that the Chu Chul jade would serve."

He turned his back on the girl and again that buzzing sound impinged upon his ears. It was quite close. It made his flesh crawl. The tocsin of warning inside him was sounding loudly, imperiously, as though the wooden fish had been beaten by a hollow piece of heavy, hard bamboo.

But another sound took the buzzing sound out of his mind.

It was a wild, unearthly scream from his study. He knew without thinking that the scream came from Wang, his servant. He was running the instant he left the vicinity of the girl and the buzzing sound died away behind him. He heard the girl gasp and say something in Mandarin that surprised him. It was a Chinese swear word such as he had often heard on the lips of rickshaw coolies, but never from those of a girl like this. He was inclined to believe that he had been mistaken.

He entered his study. Wang, his face a tortured mask, with eyes popping from their sockets, his teeth exposed as though he snarled, was swaying beside the clock upon which were the figures that danced the minuet when the clock struck. Wang was falling, falling toward the clock. Noel prided himself on that clock, so he thought most of it and its imminent destruction when he saw that Wang was falling.

"Look out!" he cried. "Be careful!"

He noticed that the boy held his right hand aloft, tight clenched into a fist, or as though he gripped a dagger in it and aimed a blow at the figures on the clock. Then Wang fell. He fell with a clatter. His body crashed down upon the clock which fell from its pedestal, breaking into a thousand pieces. Bits of spring, tiny wheels, scattered over the floor. Glass splattered over the carpet. The tiny figures rolled and rocked as they broke away and spun from their places, and two of them walked, as though they had lived, a little way together. It was very odd. The two figures almost clasped hands as they walked. Then they angled away from each other and fell on their faces, tiny feet kicking.

In the midst of the wreckage was Wang, stiffening. The cords on his neck stood out. His lips drew further back from his teeth, as though he fought for speech and could not find it.

"Great God!" said Dorus Noel. And again, "Great God! The boy's dead! What in the devil's name killed him?"

In the same instant Dorus Noel knew something else. Another boy had died in his service, saving his life. But how had Wang been killed? Dorus Noel tried to remember what had preceded the falling of Wang, and all he could remember was that strange buzzing sound. Now he listened carefully. One of the springs of the clock was buzzing, but it died as he listened. And the bee-buzzing was finished, too. He wondered whether its cessation had anything to do with . . .

Then he noted that clenched hand again and extended his own hands to grasp at the dead hand of Wang.

"Don't touch it!" said a taut voice behind him. "Don't touch it!"

He whirled, spinning on one knee. The girl who had asked for the jade, the girl in white, stood just behind him. Her hat was off and her wealth of black hair formed a ruff for her shoulders. Her thin, almost white hand, grasped her vanity case. Her eyes told him nothing, save that they were squinted in concentration.

"Don't touch it!" she said. "There's death in the boy's hand!"

"I'll wear gloves," he said. "I've got to know. Why should you warn me?"

"I've seen men die like this before—Dorus Noel!"

"You know my name then?"

"And many other things; and that you understand Mandarin perfectly."

"Who are you?"

"Put me down merely as the girl who didn't run away when death stalked into your home."

And that seemed an odd thing to say.

"I'll get the coroner," he said. "Run and get a doctor."

The girl whirled and was away. Shortly, so shortly she might almost have had a doctor waiting, she returned. Noel's eyes narrowed as he studied the man. It was a Chinese doctor.

He looked a question at the girl.

"No American doctor would know," she said. And to the doctor, "Be careful, my friend, when you examine that clenched hand."

The doctor, his face working strangely, his eyes popping from his head—and such a look of fear on his face that Noel knew the man had seen this death before—reached for the hand of Wang, hesitated, drew back. Then he thrust his hands into his black leather bag and brought out some smooth surgical instruments. Using these as levers, he pried open the hand of Wang. And in the palm reposed a strange, pulpy mass.

The doctor said something in Cantonese, explosively.

The girl said something in Mandarin and Noel knew that she interpreted the words of the doctor.

"*Bei Tu! Bei Tu!*"

It didn't make sense to Noel. Oh, he knew that the words meant "white arsenic," but that didn't make sense, either.

"There are no English words for it," said the girl. "But it means instant death."

"What's that in the hand?" asked Noel in a dead voice. Back across the grave came a warning to the depths of his soul. This death had been meant for him. He was again marked for a horrible passing. But by whom? Chu Chul was dead. Who could so quickly come from nowhere to take the place of the arch fiend?

The doctor bent over the hand. In the midst of what seemed to be a dusting of fine white powder was the pulpy mass, exuding a greenish liquid. Near one end of the area of white and green was a dash of red, a thin crimson smear. It was a tiny drop of blood, and it oozed from the hand of Wang.

But what was the pulpy mass?

"I'll get the coroner," said Noel deadly. "It's murder—police business!"

"And you are in danger?" asked the girl. Noel's heart jumped as he felt the concern in her voice. All his half-formed suspicions about anything and everything Chinese, flew out the window.

He shrugged.

"I don't worry. I've been in danger before," he said. "You'd better go, Miss—"

"Miss—Ghi," she said, oddly hesitant before she pronounced the name, and then she was gone before he could ask where she lived. However, she would be easy to find. She stood out in murky Chinatown like an orchid in a swamp. Everybody in the place would know of her. The doctor, his eyes bulging, stared after the girl. Then he looked back at Dorus Noel. Their eyes locked, and the doctor visibly recoiled, drawing away from Dorus Noel. He even, to Noel's amazement, lifted his hand as though to ward off a blow, or to avert the evil eye.

"What the devil?" began Noel.

"It means death," gasped the doctor. "Death to anyone who aids in any fashion the man or woman upon who is set the mark of the white wasp!"

"The white wasp! What are you talking about?"

"Look!"

The doctor pointed again at the hand of Wang. He prodded at the pulpy mass with a scalpel. Then Dorus Noel saw that part of the mass was a pair of tiny, lacy wings, badly torn.

"The thing was originally a wasp," said the doctor. "It was still a wasp when your boy found it. But its body was covered with that fine white powder which Miss Ghi called *Bei Tu*. Your boy tried to kill the wasp with a sweep of his hand. It stung him. He is dead. It might have been you, or anyone."

Noel bent over Wang, studying those telltale wings. He heard footsteps and whirled. The doctor was departing, running, undignified, fear in the set of his shoulders and the speed of his legs.

And through the mind of Dorus Noel went a singsong of words:

"The white wasp! The white wasp!"

Even as the words ran through his mind he kept seeing Miss Ghi, dressed all in white. The white of her was the white of what? What was its meaning? Chinese girls didn't ordinarily go in for white except as mourning. And her red heels! Why should they make him think of the red spot of blood in the hand of Wang?

Two hours later the body was gone and a charge of murder had been placed against a person or persons unknown. Method, poison. But New York police knew nothing of the white wasp or *Bei Tu*, or how the poison had been administered, or about Miss Ghi. The hand of Wang had been carefully cleansed by Dorus Noel. This was his business, all of it.

Then he went out, seeking Miss Ghi.

For one reason Dorus Noel sighed with relief. There had been blunders made in the attempt to slay him. Chu Chul would never have been so crude. He knew himself better than a match for whoever was trying now to destroy him. Already he felt he could see the end. It came to him as it sometimes comes to men to see the future clearly and certainly. This time he was not destined to die. But someone was. Whom? His heart was saddened as he gave himself the answer. Yet, inexorably, he must be carried on to the final grim denouement.

Every step he took seemed to be charted in advance.

Poor devil, whoever had marked him. That one should have been more careful, more Orientally clever. There was a dash of the Occident in the would-be slayer's clumsiness. He started as the thought came to him, and he remembered the unnatural whiteness of the cheeks of Miss Ghi. She was, he decided, an Eurasian.

A block from his own door a hand touched him on the sleeve. He looked into the face of a Chinese man of around thirty. He studied the yellow face, seeking the marks on it which he had learned to identify as the marks of servitude to Chu Chul, The Cricket.

He didn't find them, but this man might well have been recruited after the death of The Cricket.

"What do you wish?" demanded Noel.

"I have been told that the master requires a new manservant."

"Who told you?" snapped Noel.

"The lady in white!"

"Ah, and which way did she go?"

The man pointed down the street in the opposite direction to that in which Dorus Noel had been traveling. Noel smiled inwardly. The fellow had been coming from the other way. Obviously then he either hadn't been sent by Miss Ghi, or he was lying about the direction she had taken. Either way, the man was suspicious, and suspicious-looking Chinese at this juncture were from the camp of the mysterious enemy.

This man was an emissary from their camp, decided Noel, come to complete the task another had failed at.

Noel always adopted one method in such cases. He went on the assumption that if you shoved your head far enough into a lion's mouth the creature couldn't bite you. This man was an enemy, but in Noel's own house, Noel could watch him. Outside, he might never have known he existed, might have died at his hand without knowing the identity of his slayer.

"What is your name?" he asked abruptly.

The man hesitated, then used the two words Miss Ghi had used.

"Lao Ye."

The man was a coolie, and used the venerable name of the god. Again Dorus Noel smiled inside himself, nodded to the "boy."

"There is my house," he said, pointing. "Go in. I will have Chinese food for dinner. Peking duck, bird's nest soup, rice wine; and it must be served promptly at eight o'clock."

"Yes, master. There is a key to the house?"

"Of what use is a key in Chinatown?" asked Noel. "One cannot close one's house against clever enemies, and others fear to enter. Go on in."

Noel watched until "Lao Ye" had entered his house. He knew that the "boy" would be able to find everything. He looked capable enough. In other circumstances, serving no evil master, he might be an excellent servant. He had even cast down his eyes when he spoke with Noel, the signal of a perfect servant.

Noel, satisfied that the boy was not watching him, continued on down the street. He stared ahead, hard, seeking the girl in white. But the crooked streets were packed with Chinese. They met and passed him, furtive and silent. Their almond eyes stared at him, then were quickly averted as he looked hurriedly into each face. He wondered which were friends, which enemies. There were plenty of honest Chinese who would abhor methods which used murder and theft.

Then he started.

Far ahead, almost at the intersection of the street with the Bowery, he saw a white figure. It came swiftly out of a joss house which he knew, turned toward the Bowery and hurried along. It was the girl.

"Maybe she spoke the truth after all," thought Noel, for the first time in doubt. "She may actually have wanted to say prayers and burn papers for a departed soul. But suppose it were the soul of Chu Chul, The Cricket?"

There came a ghastly scream and a man came dashing into the street from a store. Noel recognized the doctor even before he reached the falling man who had dashed forth. There were the same protruding eyes, the taut muscular rigidity, in the face and neck of the doctor he had seen on the face of Wang. The doctor saw Noel at the same time and called to him.

"I told you . . . white wasp . . ."

By a distinct effort of will Noel kept his eyes on the girl. He must know where she went. But from the tail of his eyes he watched the doctor crash to the pavement. The girl entered a door. Noel marked it in his mind, dropped down beside the doctor.

Chinese came running up excitedly, chattering.

"Keep back," said Noel. "Keep back! There is death and danger."

"It must," came in agonized gasps from the Chinese doctor, "have been under the collar of my coat. I just turned up the collar, intending to come back out on the street—"

Noel carefully turned the dying man on his side . . . and his flesh crawled as he saw the thing. It seemed to be nesting in the hair at the base of the doctor's skull. It was a wasp, whitely powdered. A tiny spot of blood showed on the doctor's neck, just below the hairline.

Police were coming. Whistles sounded. Noel caught the destroyer in his handkerchief. He noted that one of its wings was broken off. Confinement under the collar had done that. Then he remembered that second buzzing sound, when first he had turned his back on Miss Ghi. And he knew that if Wang hadn't screamed and sent him, Noel, racing away, he might himself have been dead at this moment.

But why hadn't it stung the girl?

The answer was simple. She knew it was there and could avoid it. Noel hadn't known, exactly.

He raced down the street and stopped before the door by which she had vanished. He entered. A Chinese, bland of face, met him.

"I wish to see Miss Ghi," said Noel.

As he put the request, knowing it would not be granted, he looked around. The place was Chinese enough, except for a French telephone on a small stand. He bent his neck, reading the number on the card, memorizing it.

"Don't know any Miss Ghi," said the Chinese sullenly.

"The girl in white then."

"No girl in white."

"The white wasp?"

There was a brief hesitation. He wasn't looking at the man, but he could sense a quick tension, a deadly danger. There was a quick intake of breath.

"Don't understand," said the Chinese, but Noel knew he did. There must be some other way to go about this.

Noel stepped outside, beckoned a copper.

"Watch this place for a girl in white," he said quickly. "Police business.

If she comes out, tail her. I'll be responsible."

Before the man could frame an answer Noel was gone, grimly chuckling. He had no authority to issue such an order, and he daren't stop to explain. If he were known, his usefulness would be at an end. But he knew the copper, out of sheer curiosity, would keep his eyes glued to the store called Beautiful Fragrance.

Noel returned to his home at exactly eight. Lao Ye bowed to him. He was dressed in careful Chinese livery, the perfect servant.

"Supper leady," he said softly. "Bird's nest soup."

Noel washed and entered his dining room, wondering exactly how the next attempt would be made. He loved bird's nest soup. He dipped his spoon into it and the spoon touched something, something small and round and hard. There should be nothing small and round and hard in bird's nest soup. He bent forward, smelling the steam from the soup. It had an oddly vinegary smell, as though the soup were ever so slightly sour. Had he not been suspicious he never would have noticed it, so slight was the odor.

"I never heard of 'em using a dash of vinegar in bird's nest soup," he thought.

He was still holding his spoon in the bottom of the soup bowl, and his flesh tingled as he felt something strange happening, down there through the gray green of the soup, which was too thick to see deeply into. Those little hard round things in the soup were bumping against his spoon, darting back, bumping in again. Noel whirled.

"Lao Ye! Come here!"

The boy came quietly.

"Take a spoonful of this soup and drink it!" commanded Noel.

With no expression of surprise the boy brought a spoon, dipped it full of soup, drained it—audibly, as Chinese coolies did, with great gusto.

"It's gleat soup," said Lao Ye, backing away.

Noel, watching the boy, who appeared totally unconcerned, was puzzled deeply. The boy stood there, eyes lowered, and nothing happened. Yet Noel felt sure of something. There was death in that bowl of soup. But if there were, why wasn't Lao Ye writhing on the floor?

Noel almost persuaded himself, as seconds passed and Lao Ye suffered no ill effects, that he was being overly suspicious. Yet he couldn't get over the belief that if he drank that soup he would die, almost instantly.

Well, he would take no chances.

He rose, stepped to the telephone, called a number. He saw the Chinese boy jerk a little as he called that number. Someone answered it, in Chinese.

"I wish to speak to the white wasp," said Noel in English.

"Not here!"

"Tell her Beautiful Fragrance is surrounded by police, that even a beautiful woman may be compelled to sit in the electric chair for double murder! Tell her to come immediately to the house of Dorus Noel, where proper explanations may save her from execution! I give her ten minutes to reach me."

He clicked up the receiver, looked at Lao Ye and found that the ghost of a smile twisted the boy's yellow lips. But he may have been wrong, for when he looked again there was no smile.

Eight minutes later by his wrist-watch, the girl in white, her face whiter still, entered his place. His heart was heavy as he noted the proud lift of her head, the squareness of her shoulders, the gallant beauty of her.

"Sit down," he told her softly. "I am sorry to be so brutal, but two men have died. It would be well for you to tell the truth."

"I am here," she said.

There was drama, stark, terrible, Oriental, in it.

"What relation were you to Chu Chul, The Cricket?" asked Noel.

She hesitated. Her chin lifted.

"His daughter," she said at last, "by a French wife. Yes, I'm responsible for what happened today. I meant to punish you for slaying my father. Whatever he was to the world, he was my father. He loved me. No one else ever has, except in an evil way, if I would let them. Yes, I brought the wasps, in my vanity case. My powder was not powder, but *Bei Tu*. . . ."

"But since you warned me not to touch Wang's hand, I don't understand," said Noel.

She looked straight into his eyes.

He shifted, uncomfortably. She could do things with those eyes. She could melt a man. It would be so easy to give way to her, to love her, to go to the ends of the world for her.

"I found I couldn't," she said.

But she had sent a servant to him, Noel told himself fiercely, trying to hate her, knowing she was playing, using all her woman's wiles, to keep him from turning her over to the police. She even was capable of pretending a sudden love for him.

"It would be ghastly," he told her, "to send one so beautiful to prison, or to the electric chair."

"Must you?"

"If only I were sure—" he began. Was Lao Ye her minion?

"Who is, or was, Lao Ye?" he asked abruptly.

"My father's name, to his people, and to me," she said in a dead voice.

Noel whirled to stare at his new "boy," but the boy kept his eyes cast down. There still was a test, despite her almost-confession. He suddenly pushed the rapidly cooling bird's nest soup toward her.

"Won't you try it?" he asked. "It's very good."

Grimly he watched her. Would she know of the little bean-like things in the soup, which, acted upon by vinegar, moved in the soup as though alive? Her black eyes met his. Her hand went out, touched the spoon. Distinctly Noel heard the invisible things in the bowl, beating against the spoon.

Her lips moved, then there came audible words in Mandarin:

"*Du mo tzu!*"

And before he could stop her she had seized the bowl and drained it, risen from the table, swaying.

"Lao Ye!" he called.

The boy darted forward, gathered her in his arms.

"I didn't really drink," said the boy. "But the soup does contain the little poison beans called *du mo tzu*, from the Province of Szechuan. She will die. Let her die among her own. Do not keep me. I'll come to you when it is finished."

Lao Ye vanished through a side door, into darkness. Noel sighed. It was better this way. It would have been hell to send one so beautiful to the chair. After all, he hadn't tried to make her drink the poison. He tilted the bowl, poured off soup until he could see the little poison beans on the bottom. They required vinegar to make them active. A little had been poured in his soup. Surely fate had been kind to give him an acute sense of smell. But his heart was heavy.

The girl was so gorgeously beautiful.

Now he would wait for news. Would the American press chronicle the passing of a Chinese beauty? Perhaps not, but the Chinese bulletin boards would show it.

But ten days passed and he received no word. He was beginning to suspect that he had been fooled, outwitted. But the girl must be dead, for there had been no word from her, no sign of sinister activity.

Then, literally out of a clear sky, he received a wireless from a vessel at sea, somewhere in the Pacific.

"*Du mo tzu* by itself is deadly poison," said the wireless. "But it is an antidote for many other poisons, notably the slow poison called *tu yao*. Lao Ye knew he would be asked to drink of the soup, so he first took a dose of *tu yao*. I took *tu yao* also, before entering your house. So when I drained the bowl, *du mo tzu* did not slay me, but prevented my dying slowly from the effects of *tu yao*. I shall not trouble you again my friend because, perhaps, a little of what my eyes must have told you was true."

The radiogram was not signed. No signature was needed. Somehow Dorus Noel, in spite of two dead men, was glad.

He crumpled the radiogram in his hand and stared for a long time at the wall of his study.

BELLS OF

PELL STREET

*Noel's pistol bore full on the forehead of
Chu Chul. He pressed the trigger.*

**A Weird Melody Those Tinkling Brasses Toned Out as
Life Itself Hung by the Balance of a Chime When Dorus
Noel and Chu Chul Matched Cunning in the Grottos of
Chinatown.**

"WELL, I'M DAMNED," SAID DORUS NOEL, "if this isn't the queerest day I ever
spent! Three hours on Park Avenue, at a tea given by the elite to a Chinese
actor. And China's best though he is, is still an actor, than which profession
there is none lower in China. He was made over by all the society folks as
though he had been a king or something."

As Dorus Noel spoke, ostensibly to his Chinese "boy," his hands absent-
mindedly fingered the strange gifts which had come to him during his absence
at the tea. He scarcely saw the ancient musical instruments, much as he liked
such things, for a moment or two, because he was thinking of Mei Ying, the
actor. From the second he had clasped hands with the actor—doing it with

his tongue in his cheek because his society hosts expected it of him—he had had a feeling of repulsion. There had been something unclean about Mei Ying. He had felt sure, too, that he had seen something akin to hatred in the eyes of the gorgeously, Orientally gowned actor.

He shrugged his shoulders, though, and gave closer attention to the three-barred frame, shaped oddly like an "H" with an extra bar across its middle and one across the top, containing the nine bells, three bells to each bar.

Those bells were the Chinese musical scale and were sounded by a little wooden mallet which was part of the gift.

The other instrument was the oldest known to the Chinese. It looked like a teapot and one played it by blowing into the spout. Where the lid should have been were twenty-four resonance tubes, with holes in the sides. One played them by fast manipulation of the fingers, and one had almost to inherit the art of playing them.

How was Dorus Noel to guess that both the instrument of the nine bells and that of the twenty-four resonance tubes were really weapons of murder—and the strangest and most horrible that had ever come to Chinatown?

Dorus Noel was undercover man for the police in Chinatown, chosen for the job because he had lived years in China. His task was to see that the Chinese kept the peace.

He gave the nine bells a caressing tap of the mallet before he bade his boy good night. Then he turned in and was instantly asleep. He was dreaming of Mei Ying, the actor, and seeing him as a bird of prey with long talons, when he snapped awake as though someone had slapped his face. For a moment he thought what he heard had been part of his nightmare. But that it had been very real was proved by the fact that his whole body was bathed in perspiration.

"Hold onto yourself," he whispered softly, his heart pounding with excitement. "Maybe a cat went sleepwalking on the frame."

The sound which had wakened him had been the rhythmic chiming of the nine bells! No cat could have caused their chiming like that. The bells had been played by human hands—talented hands—Chinese hands. Yet how? Why? He had taken all the usual precautions that even the bravest man of good sense takes when he lives in the land of his enemies—barring his doors and windows, affixing to them noise-making devices of his own. Nobody could have entered without making a noise, and he had been alone in the house on retiring, Sang Chiu having gone back to some hovel near the Bowery. The boy wouldn't return until morning.

Even as he listened, his eyes narrowed in the darkness and he felt his hackles rising like a fighting dog's; for the bells had started ringing again, and this could not possibly be a dream! The gifts of musical instruments which, according to Sang Chiu had been delivered as coming from "a friend of your Peking days," were tied up with some new horror in Chinatown, for Chinese are not given to practical joking. Who could it be? Chu Chul, The Cricket? He was dead. The White Wasp? She had left the country between sunset and dawn on the heels of a murder charge. Dorus Noel had brought about both happy events. Who, then? Friends of either Chu Chul or The White Wasp?

Noel, grasping his automatic in his right hand, left his bed without sound and strode on tiptoe to the door which gave onto the room of his Chinese relics. At the door he did a strange thing. He stooped, his torso straight forward from his waist, and covered his throat with his forearm.

"Who's there?" his voice cracked like the lash of a whip.

There was no answer. But a breath of wind fanned his cheek and something smacked into the wall of his bedroom, many feet behind him. He sucked in his breath. He knew the feel in passing, and the sound in striking, of a thrown knife. No ghost threw knives. Had he stood erect the knife would have got him. His hand went to the light switch inside the door.

His bedroom was flooded with light. So, too, in a second, was the room of the bells. Both rooms were empty of human occupancy, save for himself. He strode into the room of relics and held his ear close to the nine-bell frame. The bells were still vibrating. The player had vanished in split seconds, as though the light which had vanquished the darkness had erased the player. It was uncanny, but Dorus Noel was accustomed to Oriental eeriness.

He whirled back into his bedroom. His face was grim and hard as he stared at the knife which had been driven a good two inches into the wall. The blade was of slender, tempered steel, razor sharp. The haft was a golden dragon with beady eyes of polished red coral, gruesomely and marvelously carved. The tongue of the dragon, red as blood, licked out at him as though it were alive. Noting the color scheme of the knife Noel knew one thing at once; it had come from some treasure house of imperial relics. Whence? Peking? Jehol? The Mukden Palaces?

When he answered that he would know why this attempt was being made upon him. Why hadn't he been stabbed in his sleep? That question must wait, too. Chinese were not prone to direct action. What did all this queer stuff presage? His excitement mounted to fever pitch. This sort of thing was his element, the reason of his appointment to Chinatown. He lifted his hand to the knife, thought better of it, dropped his hand without touching the weapon. One never could tell about Chinese weapons.

He went to the front door of his dwelling and found his alarm-giving instruments intact. No windows had been forced, doors were still locked. How had the would-be slayer, and the bell ringer, entered and escaped?

He opened the front door. Outside on Mott Street a meager after-midnight crowd, mostly Chinese, walked along the sidewalk. They all seemed furtive, withdrawing their eyes from him as he stared. He stepped into his bedroom and dressed. Fifteen minutes later he was in a telephone booth on Lafayette Street, calling a number on Park Avenue—that of a police official, the one who had secretly commissioned him to work in Chinatown. A sleepy voice answered.

"Noel. What did you expect to develop in Chinatown that you didn't tell me?"

"What do you mean?" There was excitement in the voice.

Noel guardedly, in a low voice, related what had happened.

"Ah," said the voice on Park Avenue, "we've been expecting something— nobody guessed what. Those musical instruments, Noel. Have you any idea who might have sent them? And tell me this: are they decorated in any way?"

"Yes," he said, "the frame of the nine bells is hung with faded yellow tassels. I should have known the whole shipment belonged to some collection. But I won't be able to ask Sang Chiu until morning. But what does it mean?"

"Any idea how much duty would have to be paid on even a small portion of the imperial treasure from Peking, Jehol, or the Mukden Palaces?"

Noel whistled.

"I only know that an American millionaire once offered four million dollars for the relics belonging to Ch'ien Lung—most colorful Manchu Emperor. There were nine Manchu emperors. They had treasure in all three places. If some huge smuggling syndicate . . ."

"Exactly. And millions in duty would be saved if some way were found . . ."

"I get it. Weighing human life against millions makes human life damn' cheap. I'll be getting back."

"Need help?"

"No. This is my job. I know Chinks better than most. Any help would merely hinder. But if I'm not heard from in thirty-six hours . . ."

"The police will turn Chinatown upside down! Good night."

"Good night!"

Noel clicked up the receiver. Racing back toward his house, just off the dogleg where Mott and Pell Streets cross, he came up standing when a wild scream rang through all Chinatown. It came from his house. Passing Chinese paused, looking affrightedly over their shoulders, then hurried on about their nocturnal business without looking back.

"They know!" said Noel to himself. "They *know!*"

He dashed into his house. The lights were still on. His heavy footfalls sagged the floor as he ran, shaking the bells in the room of the frame. The bells jangled musically. He did not pause. He entered the bedroom.

Sprawling on the floor beside his bed was a Chinese. It was Sang Chiu, his servant. His face was a twisted mask. His right hand clasped the haft of the knife Noel had left sticking in the wall. There was blood on the ball of his right thumb. The ruby tongue of the dragonhaft was moist with that blood.

"There, but for more luck than brains," thought Noel, "lies Dorus Noel."

He looked about him. The receiver of his telephone was down. He placed it to his ear. The operator was saying exasperatedly:

"Number please! Number please!"

Noel barked into the transmitter.

"What number was called from here just now?"

"You called . . ."

She repeated a number. It was that of a house on the Bowery, in which Sang Chiu had his lodgings. Somebody, in Noel's absence, had called Sang Chiu back to the house to be slain. Why?

"Who called?" snapped Noel.

"Didn't you? The voice sounded the same."

Noel, swearing, clicked up the receiver. Somebody had spoken with his voice so well that even cunning Sang had been fooled—to his death. Who could possibly do that? The Cricket? He was dead. Or was he? That touch of the bells was so like Chu Chul, The Cricket.

Noel closed the outer door and sat down in the bedroom, near the body of Sang Chiu, to think it out. Somewhere in his brain, which could think in the Oriental fashion from long practice, he must find the answer, else he would be joining Sang Chiu.

Who had called Sang Chiu? How had the unknown known what number to call? Noel himself had not called it three times since Sang had been his servitor. Sang had seemed as faithful as only Chinese can be faithful. That face told the story, Oriental poison. The kind didn't matter. There were many, all terrible. Noel lifted his eyes and stiffened.

The light in the room of the bells had gone out. Pitch darkness had taken its place. Anything or anybody could be out there now, looking in at him without fear of detection. A knife man could slay him in a second. But for a second he did not move. How could he? The bells were chiming—again— those nine bells of the scale!

And a new sound was added to the chiming of the bells, the low, muted, sighing sound of music on the twenty-four resonance tubes. The playing was expert, though Noel knew that probably not two persons in Chinatown could play the difficult instrument shaped like a teapot.

With a savage oath Noel dashed to the door again, taking a chance on a second knife. This stuff was irritating. While his fingers searched for the light button outside the door, his eyes tried to accustom themselves to the darkness in the room of the bells. Maybe his eyes played tricks on him, but he could have sworn he saw two white ghostly figures, there by the frame of the bells. Even as he watched, the chiming of the bells began to die, the muted sighs of the tubes to diminish. The two white figures began to fold in upon themselves, growing smaller. When the light went on, the room was empty. The table was between Noel and the bells. The "teapot" was on the table.

It was warm to Noel's touch. Other hands had just relinquished it. He studied the table, the floor about it. There was a carpet runner, a thick one, on which the table sat. The runner extended several feet beyond either end of the table. It was drawn taut and held solidly in place by the table's ponderous legs.

"Hell!" he said. "I wonder . . . lots of things . . . and why has nobody investigated the scream Sang Chiu gave when he died? It's because the Chinese *know*. They're in league, or scared stiff of whatever is behind all this hocus-pocus."

What was something or somebody trying to do to him, or get from him? His life had twice been spared, and that might have been design. If so, why? For what purpose was he being saved?

Four hours remained of the night. He decided he would know the answer before morning. He'd find it if he had to tear his own house down. But he could use help. Should he use police? That would attract too much attention. They couldn't go anywhere without a wailing of sirens, and they tried to run things, and knew little or nothing about Chinese. He was out on the street, intent upon calling his superior again, when he came to a decision. He turned back. He hadn't been out of the house five minutes.

But Sang Chiu's body had vanished!

"What the hell?" he asked himself. "Is someone reading my mind? Does someone watch every move I make, even anticipate it? They, or he, or it, waited for me to go out and moved the body. If I don't find it I can't enter a murder charge against anybody, even though I find out who did it. Now, here we are: bells ring, I appear, they stop . . . and there's nobody around. Crazy! Nobody enters or leaves the house by the usual way; yet somebody must have entered to ring the bells and play the resonance tubes—two somebodys, since they were played at the same time, an obvious impossibility for one person. Everything took place right here in this room."

Anything might happen in the Chinese room, where Noel kept all his relics of the Orient. His own collection, on which he had paid full duty, was worth many thousands of dollars. The addition of the musical instruments had made it almost priceless. One relic was a clock which sounded the hour by dropping a gold ball down a staircase which circled the works of the high clock. This phenomenon could be seen because the clock was encased in glass. Now, as Noel looked at the clock, the gold ball came forth from a hole and rolled down the steps, making a thumping, musical sound. It was three in the morning.

Noel swore softly.

The secret, he felt, was in the room. Where should he begin? He remembered the two white, ghostly figures, how they had seemed to melt away and vanish. The table must figure in it somewhere. Aiding his search with a flashlight, whose beam he played over the floor, he examined every inch of the space about the table. On the shadowed side, opposite the frame of the nine bells, he found a tiny red spot, moist to his questing finger.

"Sang Chiu went out this way. How? Was he really dead?"

Dorus Noel grasped the table and yanked it toward him. It came easily, sliding along the floor. It shook slightly and the bells set up a soft tinkling. The "teapot" fell to the floor, breaking two of the resonance tubes, thus reducing the value of the ancient instrument by hundreds of dollars. Noel swore.

The thick runner under the table had parted, separating into three pieces. It had been one piece when he had bought it, weeks before; now it was in three. The two ends were twisted up under the legs of the table, where they had been dragged askew. The central piece, covering the area under the table, remained in place. The points of separation were sharply defined, as though the runner had been cut with a razor.

Noel whistled softly. His eyes were bright as coals. His nostrils quivered like those of an eager hunting dog.

He thrust an automatic into his belt, dropped extra flashlight batteries into his pocket, stood for a long moment looking down at the central piece of runner. He dropped to his knees and grasped the piece. It was solidly affixed to the floor! He thrust the flashlight into his pocket, freeing both hands, tugged at the carpet. The floor shook as he tugged. The bells tinkled. The piece of runner was rising as he tugged, bringing with it a section of his floor!

"The unmitigated gall of the dogs!" he muttered.

When he had lifted the runner as far as possible, he thrust the leg of the table over the black gaping hole which was thus exposed, to hold the trapdoor up. A flight of stairs led down into abysmal darkness. Up came a musty odor, mingled with that of fresh earth. Some of the black cavern was old, some of it new. It probably hid many secrets. It hid, he was sure, the secret of the two white figures and the playing of the bells. What else?

At the last moment he decided against leaving the trapdoor open. He wasn't one to back out of anything he had started. Leaving a way of exit seemed to indicate he expected defeat at the hands of the unknown. He'd never admit that.

He lowered the door, sat for a moment in darkness at the head of the stairs. Then he started moving down the steps, inching his way, feeling with his feet, automatic in one hand, flashlight in the other. Lifted elbows told him a dirt wall was close on either side. He went down what he judged to be about thirty feet—and as he went he thought how simple it had been for his baiters to spend, literally, hours at the head of those steps, trapdoor raised a fraction of an inch, so they could listen to every sound. He encountered hardpacked earth and the end of the stairs.

Fingers on the nib of the flashlight, he stood erect—and out of the darkness came flailing arms to fasten themselves about his neck. A heavy body fell against him. His finger closed over the trigger of his automatic, but he did not pull it, for instantly realization had come to him. There was no life in those flailing arms. The hands against his face were cold.

He knew he had walked straight into Sang Chiu, who, for some diabolical reason, had been placed in his pathway, suspended in such fashion, probably by a cord which exactly held the dead man's weight, that it would fall when he walked into it. Simple and horrible and rather like a game!

Like a game!

Noel gasped as the three words kept playing through his mind. Could it be possible that—but no, it couldn't be what he had suddenly begun to suspect. It was too fantastic.

He had dropped his flashlight. He felt around for it with his foot. He found it, snicked it on, turned the beam on the face of the dead man. Yes, it was Sang Chiu, the twisted expression which had been on his face when he died, still there but slowly fading as such expressions do when the body cools.

There was no sound in the place. The strange odor still persisted, now with a new, pungent odor added, the odor of opium. And it came to him he had smelled that odor earlier today. It was not new to him—nor to anyone who knew China. Noel's lips twisted. His eyes were large in the darkness, gleaming behind the flash.

He raised his left hand, to bore the light of the flash into the blackness ahead. Instantly his hand went numb and the light flicked out. It came on the heels of a whistling sound from directly ahead—and he knew that a deadly knife had been flung with unerring accuracy. His thumb, thus jarred, had snicked out the light when the knife struck it.

Out of the darkness ahead came a burst of rollicking laughter which brought an amazed oath from the lips of Dorus Noel. He had expected to hear, or experience anything, but never to hear laughter from beyond the grave—the laughter of Chu Chul, The Cricket! His power for evil had extended throughout the world, until Noel had caused his death. But The Cricket still lived. This laughter proved it. The power of Chu Chul seemed greater even than that of the grave, for the laughter proved that he had come back, even from there, to play again with death and match wits with Dorus Noel, his arch-enemy. There were scars on the body of Noel to prove that he had not always won in past encounters. And now . . .

"Dorus Noel!" said a lilting voice, interrupting the laughter. "Dorus Noel! Dorus Noel! How have you been doing?"

Explosively Noel spat out the name:

"Chu Chul! I saw you die!"

"You should have embalmed the body, Dorus Noel," came the answer. "Only so would The Cricket have been denied resurrection."

"What do you want of me? What is the meaning of this stage-acting?"

"Stage-acting? This is very real, Dorus Noel. Have you ever known The Cricket to play at life and death?"

"No, but there is always the first time. What do you want of me?"

"You will know presently. You stand well with police officials. You can do anything with them. You can approach any of them, and all have their price if properly approached. With you to act for me I can manage everything and still save millions, even though we make some of the highest officials rich."

"Bribery?" Noel spat the word as though it were alum in his mouth.

Again a burst of pagan laughter.

"What difference does it make? Money spells success."

"Why did you use the bells as a means of contact?"

"Rather intriguing, weren't they? I knew your love for old Chinese things. I could not very well have approached you openly. You might have been frightened, thinking me a ghost. . . ."

"And wanting you for murder!" snapped Noel, trying to peer into the darkness, striving to make out the form of the speaker. He sensed that the speaker was not alone, that the whole darkness ahead was filled with menacing forms.

"Precisely!" The unseen one's English was perfect, without a trace of accent. But The Cricket spoke many languages. Now he confounded Noel by a brazen piece of mimicry:

"Hello! Hello! Is this Worth 2-1474? I wish to speak to Sang Chiu."

Noel did not speak, but that voice was his own—and it came from the blackness ahead—followed by a chuckle which broke into the pagan laughter of The Cricket.

"You've been keeping close tabs on me, Chu Chul," said Noel, edging forward in the darkness. "There's another murder to be chalked up against you. Why didn't that knife hit me in the beginning?"

"It was not so intended. I knew by the height whence your voice came that you were stooped over. My knife man could have got you if I had wished."

"And the poison on the haft?"

"I knew you too well to think you would touch the knife. I wanted someone else to die by that poison, to prove to you that The Cricket still has power."

"What do you propose?"

"A partnership. It is worth millions of dollars to you and you can have it in your hands in ten days."

"How?"

For a moment there was no answer. Then blinding light flashed in the face of Noel. It showed him Sang Chiu, at his feet. It also showed him a huge room, packed and crammed with treasures in aged bronze, porcelain, cloisonné and jade, especially jade, all of it of the deepest, flawless green. There were ancient brocades in piles on priceless Ming tables. There were screens of lacquer, paintings by ancient and brilliant artists. There were yellow robes worth fortunes in themselves because they had been worn by emperors. There were ancient weapons studded with gems. Thousands of dollars could not have purchased the least of them. From somewhere among the rabbit warrens of Chinatown all this smuggled wealth had been transported to the vast storehouse under Dorus Noel's dwelling place because Chu Chul had been sure that even Noel had his price.

"Your proposal?" Noel's voice was strange and harsh, scarcely his own. That treasure, so utterly priceless, had gripped his throat and his imagination.

"That you fix things with customs officials and with the police, using money without stint, that you contact men with millions enough to buy these things. I know you can, for you are as much at home on Park Avenue as Chinatown. When all have been sold there are still other ways of making money."

"Yes?" Noel's blood was boiling. That such gorgeous things should be used for such base purposes made him cold with abysmal fury. "How?"

"We can force yet other millions from purchasers for silence as to the circumstances of purchase . . . after which we can cause the things to be confiscated by the customs officials and turned back to us. The possibilities are endless."

"The answer," said Dorus Noel, "is no. What are you going to do about it?"

Chu Chul laughed.

"Kill you, if you don't change your mind. Someone else will be found who will help us. It's merely a matter of time, and selection. Perhaps the man whose number is"—here Chu Chul spoke the number of Noel's superior on Park Avenue—"would listen to a proposal, provided he believed that by so doing he could secure the return, unharmed, of Dorus Noel! He'd have to trust my emissaries. He wouldn't know until too late that you were dead. Then he would not dare speak because he would be too deeply involved."

"The answer is still no!" said Noel harshly. "Let's get on with the business, whatever it is."

His automatic lifted, spouting flame and bullets toward the spot whence the voice of The Cricket had come. He heard bullets slam into bronze vases, giving off golden chimes, oddly like the ringing of the nine bells. He heard pieces of porcelain smash to the floor as the light which had shown him the wealth of the world went out. Then a high wind of hurricane strength seemed to possess this underground treasure vault—and Dorus Noel knew that the minions of Chu Chul were being vomited forth from every secret door and panel, charging in to destroy him.

Now his life *was* forfeit, but he laughed aloud as he waited, loving a fight for its own sake. Bodies crashed against him with a shock. He pressed the muzzle of his automatic against them and pulled the trigger. The odor of blood and burned flesh was in his nostrils. He pulled trigger, released it, pulled again—and again—and yet again.

Blows rained upon his head. He used the muzzle of his automatic when bullets failed him, striking savage, bitter blows designed to rip through scalp and skull. His left hand wielded his flashlight. It became bent and broken in his hand.

"Why don't you mix in, Chu Chul?" he shouted. "I would give my life to have my hands at your throat when I died!"

Came the laughter of Chu Chul, ahead in the darkness—and the laughter was filled with glee. Chu Chul also liked a fight, as long as he personally were not in it. Noel was borne deeper into the vault by sheer press of numbers. His feet, as hands grabbed at him, lifted him, swung him about, collided with precious vases which rolled to the floor, breaking with musical explosions.

The stinking Chinese were all over him. He could feel the queues on their heads, coiled like serpents. He could smell their sour sweat, feel the grease on their oily bodies, proof that they were *ta chuen* men, trained fighters. The odds against him were heavy. But he knew something of *ta chuen*, Chinese *jujitsu*, himself. He fought like a tiger, glad that the press of bodies was too heavy for the enemy to use knives with success.

He did a strange thing. He saved one bullet and it wasn't for himself. He knew who it was for, and he prayed a little as he fought. He had a use for that last bullet, if ever a chance were given him. Even death should not cheat him. If it did . . . then New York City would be in the hands of a smuggling ring, whose machinations would shake the very foundations of the land. Its tentacles would reach into the homes of the rich and from them into Wall Street, into rich banks, into every home where there was money. It would be a sweeping, catastrophic thing.

"Give me a chance, Chu Chul," said Dorus Noel, shouting, his voice panting, spent. "There are so many against me. Let me have light by which to fight."

Out of the darkness came the laughter of Chu Chul, then swift commands in Cantonese, which were answered by the coolies who were fighting Dorus Noel.

Said Chu Chul: "Are you strong enough to handle this foolish American? He asks for lights."

"Give him lights," said a coolie hoarsely. "We too need them, for he is hard as nails, and slippery, and we hamper one another in the darkness."

The lights snapped on. Noel paused in the fight for a brief second to stare at the figure, standing apart and some distance away, alone. Chu Chul, in the robes of an emperor; Chu Chul with the two parallel bars on his forehead, crossed by a transversal which was the Chinese character for "wong," meaning "ruler." The egotism of the man!

A heavy blow smashed against the back of Noel's head. He felt himself falling. He fought to keep his right hand clasped about the butt of his automatic. He slid down among the close-pressing bodies, strength pouring out of him. But his eyes never left the face of Chu Chul, who, grinning with delight, was advancing toward the heart of the conflict.

Noel was down, and heavy feet were trampling him.

"Secure him!" snapped The Cricket.

For a second the coolies, huge North Chinese, held their hands, stepping back, looking down, deciding how to obey the order. Noel rolled to his stomach. His eyes were on that birthmark on the head of Chu Chul. His right hand swung into position as Chu Chul, noting how he had been trapped, uttered a thin cry. All eyes turned toward the master at the cry—just in time to see a black hole appear in the very center of that birthmark, as Noel's automatic barked savagely.

Screaming once, tottering, fighting to remain erect, but with eyes already glassy, dead even as he stood, Chu Chul sagged at the knees and fell forward on his face.

"How," said Noel hoarsely, as the coolies stood, stunned, "can you keep out of the hands of police when you no longer have the brains of the master to instruct you?"

He spoke to them in the dialect of Tientsin . . . and cries of fear broke from the leaderless coolies. The lights went out . . . and there was the pattering sound of racing feet as the erstwhile minions of Chu Chul ran for safety, driven by fear of consequences, now without a leader who had brains.

Dorus Noel staggered to his feet. He felt in his pocket for matches as he moved through the darkness toward the sprawled body of Chu Chul. He lighted a match and looked down into the face. It was an expressive face. In its time it had expressed many things, including the emotions of others.

"I saw Chu Chul die," said Noel hoarsely, looking at the dead. "I was sure he was dead. I was just as sure that he had many lieutenants who were not dead, who would try to take his place. I scarcely expected that the next move would be made on Park Avenue. It was a tough break that I was invited this afternoon—or rather yesterday afternoon. You were a good actor, Mei Ying! You'd have made your millions honestly if you had wanted to . . . all society was at your feet. Yes, you should have stuck to acting, for you were good . . . even the voice of Chu Chul was perfect . . . but you should have made yourself a birthmark that wouldn't smear!"

The words had hardly left his mouth when the crackling of weird laughter filled the tunnel. Again and again it came like a wave receding and breaking in on the shore.

It was the voice of the real Chu Chul!

"A wise man, my dear Noel, has servants to act in his place, if he would live long." Again a crescendo of laughter filled the tunnel.

"We shall meet again. I shall send you more presents. Until then . . ."

The laughter and all sound died out, leaving Noel standing there in black silence.

RED TASSELS

Machine guns stopped the funeral parade.

Though Chinatown Defied Its Gods to Escape Terror Coiled in the Tassels, the Menace Spawned and Dorus Noel Had to Plunge Into the Secret Bed of Death Itself.

AS DORUS NOEL, SECRET AGENT PAR EXCELLENCE in New York City's Chinatown, entered his house on Pell Street, he smiled with satisfaction. It was always great to be home, no matter if he had been gone but an hour. For his home was a different sort of home, a home where two worlds mixed. There he lived in China—which for so many years had known him—or in the United States, merely by passing from one room to another.

It was China which greeted him as he entered the door, for from his room of curios came the many-toned bonging of his fourteen clocks. In the matter of clocks he seemed to be rather Chinese, for the Chinese went in for clocks. However there was a difference. Chinese liked many clocks because they liked the varied noises they made and delighted in variation of design.

Dorus Noel was somewhat of a collector. In his mind's-eye, as he crossed the threshold, he was seeing the interior of the curio room, whence at this moment came the many-throated noises of the clocks, striking noon. That noise would have pleased a Chinese beyond measure. But a Chinese would have had no two clocks set at exactly the same time. Chinese, liking to hear clocks make all the noise possible when striking, usually saw to it that periods of from one to fifteen minutes separated the time on each clock.

Noel's clocks were always synchronized to the second, set exactly with his high-priced wrist-watch. He glanced at that watch now. Minute and hour hand masked each other exactly at the hour of twelve. As usual, all his clocks were synchronized.

Chung Liao, his Chinese boy, came from his bedroom, grinning widely.

"Everything ready, master. Tea an' cakes."

"Good! Anything new?"

"There was a visitor."

"Chinese or American?"

"Chinese. But whether American or Chinese citizen, do not know. I never saw him before."

"What did he wish?"

"Merely to see the master and—so he say—to bring a warning."

"A warning?"

Dorus Noel's brow wrinkled in a frown. For three weeks nothing had happened to disturb the even tenor of his way. He had almost forgotten that he had been sent undercover into Chinatown to see that the section's denizens kept the peace. In the past when there had been trouble, all his efforts to remain undercover had been in vain. All Chinatown, in spite of the best precautions, knew of his retention by the police. But Chinatown kept its secrets. No other "foreigner" would have had a chance to penetrate them. Other foreigners, undercover or not, would have been ignored by the Chinese, no matter what nefarious schemes they might have afoot. But they knew that Dorus Noel was always a factor with which to be reckoned.

"In just what words was the warning conveyed?" Noel asked. Chung Liao, stalwart North Chinese—in contradistinction to most American-Chinese who were Cantonese, of whose dialect Noel had but the slightest smattering—wrinkled his brow in his turn, trying to recall. Then, to make it easier for himself, he began to speak in Mandarin, a dialect which Noel understood perfectly. It was China's official language, or had been during the Empire.

"He said his name was Pan K'u," replied Chung Liao, "and that it would be advisable for Dorus Noel to absent himself from Chinatown before the funeral of Liang Tzo, who died three days ago. Liang Tzo, as the master knows, was a great man among his people and his funeral celebration will be a thing of great grandeur."

Noel's eyes narrowed ominously.

"And did he say what the alternative would be?"

"He said that he knew very well that the master had strong friends among the police; that if Dorus Noel were slain, many in Chinatown would die at the hands of police. Therefore he did not threaten the life of the master—which means nothing, my master, since you would be slain in any case if it pleased your enemies. But he said that if Dorus Noel persisted in remaining in Chinatown during the funeral, or came back to it within ten days of interment of Liang Tzo, many people, some of them foreigners, would surely die."

"Did he give a hint of the manner of death?"

"Yes, my master, but your humble servant did not understand his meaning. He said that many people, perhaps innocent ones, would die by the 'kiss of the Red Tassel'!"

"Never heard of it. Must be something new. And he said his name was Pan K'u? How silly. According to Chinese legendary history, Pan K'u was the first man, and therefore the father of the Chinese race. Obviously it was not his name."

Chung Liao said nothing. He merely waited, interpreting the frown on Noel's brow as concentration in thought which he did not interrupt.

"Did he say anything further?"

"Only that there was vast power behind his words . . . proof of which would be given you hourly after this message had been delivered to you."

"Which means," Noel said grimly, "that even these words are heard and that the organization—if there is an organization, which is a foregone conclusion when Chinese voice threats—knows every move we make. Chung Liao, there have been warnings like this before—and threats. These threats have cost me the lives of several of your predecessors. Do you wish to resign from my service until this matter has been adjusted?"

Chung Liao's yellow face showed much concern, but he straightened his shoulders and answered without hesitation.

"Where my master is, there shall I be. The life of a truly good servant belongs to his master."

Dorus Noel raised his voice a trifle, speaking each word distinctly in English.

"I ask you but one favor, you unseen ones who listen," he said. "I ask that you note the loyalty of my servant Chung Liao and spare him in your attacks on me."

He wasn't speaking to Chung Liao. It was rather eerie, to thus apostrophize the empty air. It showed Noel's respect for the powers of his unseen enemies, that he thus spoke to them when he could not see or hear them. It proved he knew himself under the closest surveillance.

He pushed past Chung Liao into his dining room, where the boy had placed the tea service on a taboret beside an easy chair. From the next room came the ticking of the many clocks . . . the clock on whose top danced several tiny figures in the minuet when the hour was struck . . . the clock which rolled a gold ball down a flight of steps to count the hours . . . the clock which called the hours in grains of yellow sand which had once been spread along the highway traversed by a great empress dowager of China—an adaptation of the hour-glass principle . . . the clock that was like a beetle with wings folded . . . clocks that were small as dimes . . . clocks that were tall as men . . . clocks of all shapes, sizes and of various and eye-filling beauty . . . priceless clocks.

Even the noise of the clocks would not have kept the keen ears of Dorus Noel from hearing had there been anyone moving about in the room of the clocks. As far as he could hear or see he was alone, save for Chung Liao, in the house on Pell Street.

At one o'clock, if the warning had been bona-fide—and Chinese were not given to empty threats—there would be a demonstration. He could enjoy his tea, if anticipation did not dampen his enjoyment, until one o'clock. Containing himself in patience, but with his stomach as taut with nervousness as though it awaited the caress of a knife, Dorus Noel sat down to the tea. Leisurely he drank of the tea, ate of the cakes, while the minutes sped on winged feet. Each minute, each second even, brought him closer and closer to an impending grim activity in Chinatown.

Men—and women, too, perhaps—would die unless he could prevent it. And he already knew he had no intention of quitting Chinatown. If he were driven out by threats his usefulness would be at an end. And Chinatown being such a ferment of lawlessness at times, even the threatened slaying of innocents would be better than giving lawless ones free rein.

At one minute of one, Dorus Noel sat back from his tea. As an added precaution, so that all the room with its two doors should come under his scrutiny, he placed his chair so that his back was hard against a thick wall, through which even a sharp hatchet, thrown from somewhere outside, could not have reached him with fatal results.

He kept his eyes glued to his watch.

The hour hand masked the figure one.

The minute hand masked the figure twelve.

And from the room of the clocks came the first manifestation of the power of Noel's enemies.

He heard a single clock strike the hour. It was the clock on which five tiny figures came forth from inside the clock and danced the minuet. That clock had come from France in the long ago to become one of Tzu Hsi's most prized possessions. Tzu Hsi had been China's greatest female ruler. Now Noel owned the clock. Noel, sweat bursting forth on his forehead at the significance of what was happening, listened. Distinctly he heard the tiny dancing feet of the figures on the clock—which had once been broken in a sinister engagement in Chinatown, and repaired by a master of clocks—move through the figures of a minuet.

But only one clock struck! There should have been fourteen!

He waited a full minute, as though glued to his chair. A second clock struck the hour. It was the clock of the gold ball. The ball came forth and rolled down a single step, striking the hour of one in the afternoon. Now Noel, with an oath, dashed from his chair, at full run from the start, and entered the room of the clocks. Something had happened which had never happened before. No two clocks struck the hour together. His eyes flashed over them.

No two clocks showed the same time. Seconds, sometimes minutes, separated them. Sometime, somehow, during the last hour in which he had never quitted his chair, when he should have heard everything that transpired in his house, the clocks had been changed. It was uncanny, impossible. Somebody had set each clock at a different time; somebody had actually touched hands to those fourteen clocks, and neither Dorus Noel nor Chung Liao—and Chung Liao had ears that could almost catch the footfalls of a house fly—had heard or seen a thing.

Noel's face was white, not with fear, but with determination. He had never underestimated the skill and cleverness of any Chinese or Chinese organization in which he had come in contact. He couldn't do it now. This warning was proof that Pan K'u would do exactly what he had promised to do. People would die if Dorus Noel failed to heed the grim warning and leave Chinatown.

Just how close to himself were his enemies?

To make sure of this he went to his telephone and called the jeweler from whom, just before twelve, he had secured the exact time for his wrist-watch.

"Listen," he said tensely, "I want the exact time, to the second."

The jeweler told him, and Dorus Noel gasped in amazement.

His own watch was five minutes wrong!

Which meant not only that all his fourteen clocks were wrong, but that his enemies had played a grim jest upon him by synchronizing his watch with the clock of the tiny figures. And his watch had been on his wrist every second of the time. Had some invisible enemy pressed against him and twisted the stem of his watch? Absurd! Impossible!! Yet impossible as it seemed, there was proof.

Dorus Noel stood for a moment in the room of the clocks. His eyes searched the room for a sign. Into this room someone had penetrated. There might be hostile eyes on him at this very moment. There must be a way of entry to his place. There had been, in the past, but he had taken care to have all of them sealed against further use. As far as he knew no one now lived who knew that secret ways of exit and entrance had ever existed. Noel himself used but two doors, the front and the rear.

But there was no sign. Only silence, broken by the ticking of the clocks which seemed a part of the silence. Then his eye caught a sudden movement, a flash of scarlet in one corner of the room. Chung Liao caught it at the same time and hurled himself forward. But Dorus Noel went forward with him, clutching him by the arm.

"Don't! My last boy was slain by a thing that moved."

Now the two moved forward, master and servant, eyes fixed on the splotch of scarlet on the floor no bigger than a dime. They bent over it. At a signal from Noel, Chung Liao snicked on the electric lights so that both could see better. The splotch on the floor, they now saw, might have been the rosette from the dancing shoe of a female midget.

"Red tassel!" gasped Chung Liao. "Oh, my master, it is the sign. It means death."

"Not yet. When is the funeral of Liang Tzo?"

"Three days hence."

"Then we have that time to live, and it is not I whom they would slay. You had better heed my warning and quit my service."

White of lips, trembling a little, his arm held by Dorus Noel's hand in a viselike grip, Chung Liao spoke.

"Never this side of Purgatory, my master!" he said. "Let me procure the thing for examination."

"No! Note the color. The thing is red, with the brilliant red of that paint known as Chinese Red."

"A tassel that moves!" ejaculated Chung Liao.

For the little red tassel, there on the floor as though it had fallen from someone's hand or been thrown, was moving erratically toward the wall nearest to it. It moved, hesitated, moved again.

"My shoes are thick of sole," said Chung Liao. "If I were to step upon the thing . . ."

Chung Liao, suiting the action to the words, sprang forward again, pulling himself free of Noel's restraining hand.

Instantly the red tassel dashed toward the wall—*and vanished into it!* When the two dropped to their knees on the floor and examined the place where the moving tassel had disappeared, there was no sign of a hole in the wall. Noel stared into the black eyes of Chung Liao, who stared back, his olive cheeks dewed with perspiration. Noel gingerly ran his fingers over the spot. The wall seemed unbroken.

"The thing had intelligence," said Noel.

"Or was controlled," replied Chung Liao.

"It *was* controlled, Chung," said Dorus Noel. "But how?"

"One confesses that one does not know. But what is the next move?"

"Remain here, if you insist on remaining with me, or go to some far place. I have work to do."

Dorus Noel, immaculately dressed, even to spats and a cane, strolled from his house with a nonchalance which he was far from feeling. He headed for Canal Street, down which he turned left to Lafayette, where from a cigar store on a corner he telephoned his superior out on Park Avenue, the unknown boss he had never seen, whom he did not know save by vocal intonations.

"This is Noel," he said. "Something will happen in Chinatown during the funeral of Liang Tzo. There are threats of death. Prepare quietly to fill Chinatown with secret agents at my request. But do not have them in evidence unless I signal. If I do not signal—and my signal shall be three rings on your telephone, when I will hang up without speaking if you answer—then you will act when the first death occurs."

"Right, Noel, any help I can give you. But what is the idea?"

"I don't know. I intend to find out. I have been warned out of Chinatown, which probably means that some tremendous coup is being planned—criminal of course. Chinese . . . it may portend anything."

Noel clicked up the receiver.

He quitted the cigar store, turned back into Canal Street. He noted, on the corner, a Chinese in Occidental dress, who seemed to be lost in thought as he stared blankly at passing traffic. The man was a stranger. He did not seem to be watching Noel, but Noel's eyes narrowed as he saw the man. And there was reason.

The fellow held a red stick of some kind, on the end of which was a tiny red tassel, or "tickler." Idly the man waved it to and fro. Noel looked back over his shoulder, just as the Chinese seemed to lose control of the stick. This happened as another man, a "foreigner," stopped on the curb beside the Chinese. The newcomer did the natural thing as the tassel fell from the hand of the yellow man. He shot forth his hand to grab it.

Instantly Noel whirled back. The Chinese now noted him, and flung himself forward into the thick of traffic. He had jerked the stick and tassel from the hand of the man who had grasped it. The man had held it for a moment by gripping the tassel end. Now Noel noticed, as he started to follow the retreating Chinese through the maze of traffic, that the white man stood on the curb as one transfixed.

Noel dared not wait to see what happened.

The Chinese must not escape.

Even as horns screamed warnings to Dorus Noel, weaving in and out, dodging charging fenders, escaping death by the proverbial eyelash under the wheels of speeding cars, a wild scream rose from the curb he had quitted. He made the opposite side of Canal Street, turned for a snap-glance over his shoulder. The man who had grabbed the red tassel was down and people were racing from all directions, with the swift curiosity of crowds. Noel knew that the man would not be moved until the ambulance arrived. He dashed on after the Chinese.

The man fled southward, turned left at the first intersection, where a run of a block would bring him back to the edge of Chinatown. Noel raised his voice in a shout:

"Stop him! Stop that Chinese! He's a murderer!"

But it was Noel himself who was stopped. As he passed a doorway, half a dozen Chinese came boiling forth, apparently in the throes of a free-for-all fight. They were chattering shrilly, brandishing fists, yelling. They were clawing and spitting at one another like so many cats. They didn't even seem to see Dorus Noel. But the center of their fight engulfed him and the very weight of their numbers bore him to the sidewalk. He fought out savagely. He struck with fists, kicked with feet. But many hands, their activities hidden by the bodies above them, held him hard against the concrete pavement.

His heart was heavy with disappointment. He knew that by now a crowd like that surrounding the still figure on the sidewalk on Canal Street would be all around him. Somehow he fought his way to his feet. Crouching, he shot out savage rights and lefts. The Chinese, while seeming to fight one another, still managed to keep him from leaving the place. He knew that the man he had pursued had easily reached Chinatown, where a needle in a haystack would have been easy to find by comparison.

A siren screamed. The Chinese vanished as by magic, into the door which had vomited them forth. With clothing torn, cheeks scratched and bleeding, Dorus Noel swayed on the sidewalk. Then he lifted his eyes to the windows which rose, tier on tier, above the street. A face at a third-story window darted back.

It was a dark yellow face, set in a mask of utter malignancy, and across the right cheek was a livid red scar. All this he saw in the brief glance. People were pressing him with curious questions. He evaded them all, using his elbows freely to escape from the press about him. In five minutes he was back on Canal Street.

• • •

An ambulance was drawing up to the spot where a still bundle—a man with his knees drawn up into his stomach as though he suffered with the cramps—rested half in and half out of the gutter. Noel pushed his way through unnoticed. He knew it wouldn't be long, for the crowd who had seen his fight with the Chinese was on his trail. Seeing him there, and here, they would put two and two together and make sure that the events were related. And there would be questions. He took time only for a quick glance at the dead man.

The fellow was obviously a drifter. His face now was set in a bloated mask of surprise, pain, horror. He had died with his mouth open. His body was rigid, twisted all out of shape. The fingers of his hands were stiff and straight, his hands themselves so puffed that his fingers were all straightly separated from one another. The ambulance interne made a mark in his book which Noel saw: "DOA," which meant "dead on arrival," and the body was carted away.

In the receiving hospital, Dorus Noel knew, the man would be found to have died of poison.

Noel, as questioning eyes were turned on him and whispers were starting from many moving, taut lips, broke through the crowd and was away again, doubling back on his tracks. He went into a door, cut through a building, went out another door, and slipped into Chinatown, reached his Pell Street house without mishap. Chung Liao met him at the door. His face was suddenly all concern.

"Chinatown is a-murmur, and afraid, master," said Chung Liao.

"And they might well be," Noel said grimly. "Tell me, Chung, what did this Pan K'u look like?"

"Darker than most Chinese, with a red scar . . ."

"That's enough. I've seen him. There has been a mute declaration of war. It may be death, Chung, but will you do additional work for me, at excellent wage?"

"Of course, master."

"Then go out and find out what Chinatown whispers!"

Chung Liao did not hesitate. He was out and away without waiting to don a hat. Dorus Noel went into the room of the clocks, now all synchronized again and ticking away merrily. They said two o'clock. Perhaps five minutes after. Hourly, the warning had said, there would be manifestations. The first had been the clocks, the second the horrible death of the drifter. The "red tassel" had struck . . . and its striking was murder. Now it must be war to the death against "Pan K'u." Noel sat down for a moment to collect his thoughts, to make plans, and try to anticipate the next move of the "red tassel." To anticipate the movements of Chinese, he knew to be almost a hopeless task. But he had a better chance than anyone else he knew.

Though no foreigner would have noticed, Chinatown was as noisy—with a silent undercurrent of noise audible only to the ears of the initiate—as a swarm of invisible bees. That Pan K'u had struck fear into the hearts of all Chinese who were not in his organization was certain. There would be plenty of trouble, which might cause the death of more "foreigners." The death of the drifter had been accidental, as far as the drifter himself was concerned. He had happened merely to be in the wrong place at the wrong time. He had paid with his life. Others might pay, because Dorus Noel would not leave Chinatown at the mercy of Pan K'u. But he would never leave.

His wrist-watch showed that approximately fifteen minutes had passed since the death of the drifter. At three o'clock there would be another manifestation. Nobody could even guess—nobody who did not actually know—what the next move of Pan K'u would be. Nor did Noel have the slightest idea how big his organization was, or who belonged to it. Chung Liao himself might belong! Any or all of the Chinese he met on the streets might belong, and carry in their clothing hatchets or knives sharpened for the life of Dorus Noel—or for the innocent ones who would die during the funeral of Liang Tzo if he did not leave Chinatown.

"When the funeral procession starts," he told himself finally, "I shall signal to my boss. From every window in Chinatown we can reach we will cover the procession with guns. We'll hold it tightly without moving, and search every person in it . . . to find the agency or agencies with which they expect to do their killings."

The boss could be called from any telephone, though Noel usually used the cigar store phone from which he had just contacted his superior. There were plenty of telephones in Chinatown. But could the boss hide the number of men in Chinatown which would be required to hold the funeral procession in check? The boss himself would have to figure that out.

At exactly three o'clock a terrific hubbub rose in Pell Street, outside his door. It seemed to be caused chiefly by one man gone berserk. His door banged open and a man came staggering in. His eyes were wild. There was a touch of froth at the corner of his lips. He stared unseeingly at Dorus Noel, who hurled himself forward to block the further advance of the stranger. He was another drifter by the look of him, and one driven mad by bad liquor— or something else. Noel knew it was not liquor. The man seemed to be held in the power of some queer hypnosis.

"Where," came stiffly through the fellow's lips, "are those clocks?"

He brushed past Noel. Noel tried to stop him, to find him easily the strongest man he had ever encountered. Noel persisted, and the man rained blows into his face, savage, bitter blows. Noel grabbed at him, clung, like a tackler to a runner packing a football. But he couldn't stop the maniac. The fellow reached the room of the clocks, caught up a chair which Noel himself—always in the best of physical condition, and as strong as a bull—could not have lifted, and began a crazy weird attack on the clocks.

He smashed the clock of the tiny figures with his first blow with the chair. The clock was broken into many fragments. The legs of the chair were snapped off. The man struck again, and golden sand spilled crazily over the floor as though scattered by the high wind of a hurricane. Noel clung to the man and the man didn't seem to notice. Short of a bullet, Noel knew, he could not stop the fellow.

Nor did he stop him, though when the wreckage was complete, and the fourteen clocks were utterly silent save for broken, clattering works that seemed to have gone mad, Noel was again bleeding from many wounds and his clothing all but torn from his body. The intruder then hurled the heavy chair through a red lacquered screen—the precious screen decorated with gorgeous white feathers, the acme in Chinese artistry and attention to detail—and whirled so suddenly that Noel lost his grip.

The intruder, with Noel at his heels, reaching out to clutch at him again, gained the open door and plunged straight into the thick of the crowd there. They parted to allow him to pass. He got through, to fall in a heap in the gutter, screaming his life away. A Chinese broke from the crowd, waving a red stick with a tassel on the end of it, and laughing. It was strange for a Chinese to laugh aloud, and this laughter was sinister and terrible beyond belief. The man was the same one who had slain the drifter on the Lafayette and Canal Street intersection.

The crowd impeded Noel, intentionally or otherwise, until the man had again escaped. Noel turned back as he saw Chung Liao dashing up the street as though the devil were at his heels.

The boy came in, panting.

"Chinatown is indeed afraid," he said. "Pan K'u has delivered an ultimatum. They must obey it, yet they dare not disobey their *feng shui* . . ."

Chung Liao spoke in Mandarin. *Feng Shui* were wind-and-water spirits, and no funeral ever took place that their rules were not obeyed. It was almost a science of life with the Chinese. Good luck days were invariably chosen—by masters of *feng shui*—for the burial of Chinese. Then it was decided exactly who would attend the funeral and where each would appear in every part of the ceremony.

"Pan K'u is so eager for the master to leave," panted Chung Liao, "that he has ordered the Chinese to hold the funeral this very night. They have agreed, but since they thus disobey the spirits of *feng shui*, they must treat with the spirits . . . and every last person supposed to attend the funeral must do so. It will be a time of lamentation, and already the people know of the two dead foreigners."

"But only one had died when you heard the whispers!"

"They knew the second was marked. All Chinatown knew, which is why there was so much furor in front of your house just now."

At loss just how to proceed for a moment, Dorus Noel re-entered the room of the clocks, with Chung Liao at his heels. Chung gasped when he saw the wreckage of the clocks.

"Get Lun Feng, the clockmaker, at once, Chung!" he said. "He must put these clocks to rights—at his own price."

"I saw him just now, master, and he sent a message . . . that he could under no circumstances repair any clocks for you, or show you any favors, because he has been forbidden by Pan K'u."

"Then he must have known the clocks were to be broken!"

"All Chinatown knew!"

"And that means?"

"That dire trouble is as inevitable as the ultimate coming of death!"

"We'll be ready for it."

Now, wishing to check up on several points, because they might give him some further inkling of the methods of Pan K'u, Dorus Noel called his jeweler again.

"Was there a Chinese visitor to your place of business just before I telephoned a couple of hours ago?"

"Yes. I meant to call you back, but got no answer. It was a swart man with a scar on his cheek. I meant to call you back because I discovered, after you called, that my clock had been tampered with. I had to go into a back room while the man with the scar was here . . . ."

"Thanks," said Noel, with a sigh of relief, clicking up the receiver. This proved, at least, that no one had actually tampered with the watch while it was on his wrist. The jeweler, unsuspecting, had given him the wrong time, and had discovered it later. Naturally, Pan K'u had not waited long enough for the jeweler to discover his mistake.

That left the mystery of the tassel that had moved of its own accord to be unraveled. Dorus Noel, grimly deciding that a bit more wreckage could make no difference now, caught up a heavy leg of the broken chair the maniac had used, and savagely attacked the wall into which the moving tassel had vanished. After a savage rain of blows, which brought the sweat forth anew on the face of Noel, the wall gave inward. It was hollow. He got a flashlight, peered down into a black pit out of which came cold air, and saw the platform.

Chinatown—lawless Chinatown—had contacted his room through its own underground warrens, in spite of the fact that he had caused previous entrances to his place to be sealed. A small aperture had been cut in the wall. It could be instantly closed, so tightly that not even the breaks could be found—an easy matter for a Chinese craftsman of even minor skill—and out of this had come the moving tassel. But why the erratic course it had taken, up to the time Chung Liao had hurled himself forward to step on the thing?

"There was an invisible thread or wire attached to it," decided Noel. "But such a thing could not be pushed to make the tassel enter the room. Therefore the tassel must have moved of its own power—an obvious absurdity."

The crazy behavior of the clocks remained unexplained, too.

But if the Chinese enemies could contact his curio room through the wall, they had probably been able to enter it in some analogous manner. The way must be found. That Chinese could move almost without sound he knew very well. He grimly resolved to tear his house entirely apart to discover the secret, then to rebuild it on a concrete foundation mixed with steel which even acetylene torches could not penetrate.

At four o'clock Chinatown was a sinister, grim place. A policeman died on the corner where one of the north-south streets intersected with Canal. When Noel, pushing his way into the crowd, managed to go through the pocket of the man's uniform—the pocket into which one of the copper's hands was stiffly thrust—he found a little red tassel. The touch of it sent a chill of horror along his spine. But the tassel was—just a tassel, whose center was a small piece of bright red thread, slightly unraveled. Noel studied it for all of a minute. The thread seemed not to be holding the tassel together, but merely to be wrapped around and around the tassel's center—with one end swinging free. Noel's eyes narrowed.

"But for the grace of God," he told himself, "I'd have died as the copper died. That tassel . . . well, Pan K'u isn't leaving any clues behind him."

A sergeant of police was asking questions of a crowd. One man, while Noel listened, described a Chinese he had seen near the scene—and Noel knew that the fellow who had slain two drifters had struck again.

Chung Liao came bursting through the crowd. Noel saw him. He frowned at Chung to be quiet, not to shout his name, then followed the boy out of the crowd.

"The funeral procession starts, master," said Chung Liao, "from the joss house just off the Bowery. It comes this way. And master . . ."

"Yes?"

"All the mourners dress in white, as is the custom, but they wear conical hats which are topped by little red tassels. The whispers are that Pan K'u ordered them worn, though red is the color of marriage . . . and men-children."

Noel swore softly.

He dashed down the street toward the head of the procession which, to the tune of much banging of cymbals, the screeching of Chinese flutes, the shrill noises of many dialects, was coming up toward Canal. It would parade through the main streets of Chinatown. Noel raced to within a block of it . . . and noticed in the vanguard a man who removed his strange cap and flicked with it at the face of a passerby. The passerby dodged instinctively, and Noel knew that the dodging had saved the stranger's life. Noel dashed into the nearest store, raced to a telephone without permission, took down the receiver.

The line was dead!

Madly he came out . . . fought his way with brutal savagery, his play backed by Chung Liao, through a group of Chinese who tried to hold him, and entered another store. Again the line was dead. He knew then that he had been balked, that there was no use trying further to contact his superior out on Park Avenue. He would have wagered all the money he possessed that there wasn't a usable telephone in all Chinatown. There was an alternative: when someone died as a result of close contact with the funeral cortege of Liang Tzo, the boss would act . . .

Dorus Noel, beside himself with rage and disappointment, hurried toward the procession. Again a man removed one of those queer hats from his head, brushing his partially shaven poll as though the heat bothered him—though the heat should have bothered no one—and extended the hand which held the hat toward a passerby . . . playing the tassel across his face. The man screamed and started running. Noel hurled himself at the man with the tassel. The man who had been touched by it—a Chinese—plunged face downward in the gutter in midstride, his knees already drawn up against his abdomen. Noel knew he was dead. Now was the time for the boss to act in accordance with the request he had made to the boss.

But nothing happened. Now half a dozen men were doffing their hats. Several were edging toward Dorus Noel through the procession, in the heart of which was a casket. Their faces were impassable, but their eyes spoke murder. A minute passed, or maybe it was a second, a heartbeat. From far out on Canal Street sounded the screaming of police sirens. Noel's heart jumped.

The boss was on the job, but coppers were of little use.

Stay, however!

Suddenly a siren blared from a house directly ahead of the procession. It was followed by the voice of authority, grim and purposeful.

"Stand where you are, all of you, or lead will fly. If bullets happen to go into the casket of your great man, Liang Tzo . . ."

Every Chinese realized what such sacrilege might mean to the spirits of *feng shui*. But Noel did not believe that was the only reason why the procession froze to immobility. One of the tasseled men broke away, started to run. The others stood immobile. A machine gun spoke spitefully, a single burst. The running man fell, his back a red froth from the bullets. Noel dashed forward, fighting off men who would have grabbed up the tasseled hat the dead man had worn. He caught it by the brim, as far as possible from the tassel, and held it in his left hand while he fought off his attackers with his right.

"Stand back!" came that voice again. "Or we'll shoot into the thick of you, even though we kill the tall foreigner!"

Noel knew that he himself was the "tall foreigner."

He yelled.

"Send me half a dozen coppers!"

They came dashing almost instantly out of the house whence the machine gun bullets had come, raced to his side.

"Get as many of those hats as you can, but don't touch the tassels as you value your lives!"

Now the procession was indeed turned to stone. It was as though the fatalism of the East held them all in check now. They were caught and must take whatever came. The coppers procured seven hats. Men who tried to discard the hats with quick thrusts of the hands, were knocked flat. One man clutched at the tassel of his hat, and had his wrist broken by a policeman's billy. Noel spoke to the stolid Chinese of the broken wrist.

"You do not escape the electric chair by suicide, my man," he said grimly. The Chinese said nothing, his face impassive. Even the pain of a broken wrist seemed not to trouble him. Noel looked around him. The coppers were carrying the hats gingerly by the brims . . . the tassels swinging free.

Noel suddenly strode to the coffin of Liang Tzo.

"Open it up!" he commanded abruptly.

Instantly a great wail of lamentation rose from the throats of the Chinese. They started moving, a surge toward Dorus Noel. Noel, his lips set grimly, lifted his face to the window of the gun—which so emphasized the difference between the East and the West. Again the authority of a police sergeant's voice broke the spell.

"Interfere and we turn the gun on the lot of you!"

Noel lifted the lid of the casket, stared at the man inside it . . . a man who was very much alive, whose eyes were wells of malignant hatred.

"Well, Pan K'u," Noel said. "Maybe you'll explain your racket?"

The coppers, pressing close about the "corpse," stared dumbfounded at a man very much alive . . . a man with a livid scar on his cheek.

Pan K'u snarled.

"Chinatown is rich," he said. "Tong leaders and merchants would have paid much money for the passing of the curse. But they had to be shown. They didn't care as long as only foreigners were slain. I had to show them they too could be killed. After the 'funeral' I could have levied on all the coffers of Chinatown in return for my promise to allow Chinese to go in peace—until I should need money again!"

"I thought so," said Dorus Noel grimly. "You foul beast, to prey on your own kind. If they had come to me . . ."

"They would have," said Pan K'u, sitting up in his casket—no one noting the weirdness of the corpse thus miraculously brought to life, "which was why I would have driven you away. But only as a last resort, which this was intended to be!"

"About the clocks . . ." began Noel.

"Up through your floor, in utter silence. The man who killed the white drifter on Canal Street did it," said Pan K'u, his voice harsh with pride. "You will find the trapdoor behind the feather screen. The crazy man was partially hypnotized and doped with raw opium . . ."

In the midst of his talk Pan K'u made a sudden movement. He grabbed at the nearest red tassel. Noel yelled too late. Pan K'u succeeded in grasping the tassel. He screamed . . . and died in his casket, his knees drawn grotesquely up.

Now Noel took a pencil from his pocket, signaled the nearest copper to hold out a hat . . . and spread the tassel of it wide. Held in the tassel's heart, with a red string tightly wound about its body, was a red spider, mad with his imprisonment. He was smaller than a dime. The copper dropped the hat as though it were hot.

"It comes from the caves behind Shanhaikwan," said Noel softly. "Its bite means almost instant death . . . in terrible agony. Now, get the other hats. Chinatown can be depended on to find the rest of the spiders."

"But how," asked the man on Park Avenue, when Dorus Noel finally got him on the telephone, "did you know your man was inside the casket?"

"He had to be somewhere, conducting operations," said Noel patiently. "It had to be the casket, because it was the last place one would think of looking."

"Sounds reasonable, but why should you believe that the casket contained anything but the body of Liang Tzo?"

"Easy enough. Liang Tzo was to be buried three days hence. That date was set weeks ago and might not be changed on pain of offending all the wind-and-water spirits of China. So I knew Liang Tzo wouldn't be in the casket. It had to be empty . . . or hold Pan K'u . . ."

Noel clicked up the receiver. Outside a hundred coppers marched, in close guard of the strangest, most ghastly funeral procession Chinatown had ever seen. They were making sure that not one of the "mourners" had a chance to escape . . . for they were so obviously the minions of Pan K'u.

"You are guilty," he said. "You managed it in some devilish fashion."

THE GOLDEN COCOON

His Soul's Blackness Hid His Conscience Until the Eerie Voice of Chinatown Vengeance Gnawed Into His Memory—and Dorus Noel Raised the Curtain of the Stranger's Past.

DORUS NOEL SAT AT THE WINDOW OF HIS HOUSE on Pell Street and gazed musingly out at the blistered pavements. His shirt was open at the throat and little beads of perspiration ran down the bronzed V at his throat. His eyes were wide open, apparently engaged in watching the passing of Chinatown's people. As a matter of fact he scarcely saw them, for his mind traveled backward—back to the time when he had lived in China. This was so much like it, despite its real lack of resemblance.

The passing Chinese were garbed in Occidental dress, with their hats pulled low over their ears. Only the women affected the garb of the land that most of them had never seen. Their gowns were bright splotches of color against the unlovely houses. He knew that the gowns were thick and heavy and just to look at them made him perspire more freely.

It was so easy to sit there and visualize. Before his mind's-eye the unlovely houses vanished, giving way to burnished pagodas and watch-towers from which came the odor of incense and the chiming of many-toned bells. He saw the bare Western Hills, beyond Peking, and coolies, their chests worn raw from the flat piece of board across it, to each end of which was fastened part of the splayed rope they used to drag unwieldy barges along the green-scummed canal. He saw squatting farmers at work in a thousand fields where flowers nodded; and the farmers themselves, seen at a distance, were oddly like flowers because of their huge, spread-rimmed hats of rice straw.

And this heat, too . . . it reminded him of the heat of a North Chinese summer; the blasting, searing heat of the first of the *fus*, that heat period in which life came to a standstill to gasp and pant, and the sun was a blazing ball in the sky. The roofs of houses became furnaces, rooms were like ovens, birds perspired like men, and only hardened coolies labored along the scorching pavements, and became beasts of burden because ponies and oxen could not stand the heat.

He wiped his forehead again, ran his silk handkerchief down over the exposed part of his chest. He muttered something in Chinese and looked around as though expecting a Number One Boy to come with a cooling cocktail or with cold juicy fruits in a big glass bowl. But he was alone in the silent, baking house.

"I'd give my soul for all the pumelos I could eat," he said to himself. "Thank the Lord that the heat is too intense for criminals to work at their trades, for if I had to do anything now I wouldn't be able to stand it."

Then he leaned forward, his sandaled feet striking the tile floor with an audible thud. He saw something out there on the street that seemed somehow alien to Chinatown—a Western Union messenger. Probably they came, often, but however often they came they would still be alien to the place. People were like figures on a frieze. The scuffling messenger boy was a visitant from another world entirely.

• • •

Dorus Noel knew, with a sinking feeling about the heart, that the messenger boy came for him. Thinking back swiftly, he remembered that none had ever come to him since he had been transplanted from China to Chinatown.

The boy turned in at his door. Through the house, whose interior was completely Chinese, sounded the summons of Noel's bell. It was a Chinese temple bell, its sound melodious, out of place in America. It was as though one of the temples of his recent musings had become real and were sending some ceremonial summons across a blasted, alien, Chinese countryside.

He strode to the door, opened it. The messenger boy had no illusions, no sense of strangeness. His cap was cocked on one side of his head. He leaned against the door jamb, panting. He did not look up. He took a pencil out of his pocket.

"Noel?" he said.

"Yes."

"Sign here."

Noel signed, gave the boy a quarter. The message was brief. It carried Noel's own address and the message contained exactly one word.

"*Telephone.*"

It was unsigned, but that made no difference to Noel. That the message was urgent he knew instantly. It didn't need the word "rush" on it to emphasize that fact. He went back to his study, filled with bronze trays, porcelain figurkins, rugs from Chinese Turkestan, *tung hsis*, gongs, everything one could hope to find in the home of a man who loved, almost worshipped, Chinese relics. He donned his shoes regretfully. Sandals were more appropriate for the season.

Ten minutes later Dorus Noel, in a cigar store on the corner of Canal and Lafayette Streets, was telephoning his superior. He had never seen this man, whose influence with the police had placed Noel in Chinatown as a peace arbiter among the tongs and between Orientals and Occidentals.

"This is Noel," he said, when he heard the familiar voice.

"There's something queer going on in Chinatown," said the voice. "It's beyond the police department. They've quit without even investigating, recognizing the strangeness of whatever it is."

"Something criminal?"

"We don't know. But it has to do with Purnell Theleen."

"You mean that queer old codger who came to Chinatown three weeks ago after years in China?"

"Yes. Only he's not queer. He isn't old. And he's very wealthy. And wealth always attracts the avarice of thieves, who are potential murderers. It's—"

"I know the place. I'll look into it."

Purnell Theleen lived in a house off Mott Street. Noel knew something of the man's history, at least by rumor. His Chinese background was somewhat blurred. That he feared things out of his past was generally believed. That he was a recluse who all but feared his own shadow was an established fact. No one knew exactly of what his wealth consisted or where it could be found.

But the fact that he had established himself in Chinatown spoke of love for Chinese things that should make him a boon companion of Dorus Noel. The whole picture seemed to promise interest, and not too much activity—and activity at this time of the year Dorus Noel dreaded. He wondered how Theleen had contacted the police. It must be desperate to make him take the step. Rumor had it that he was exceedingly self-sufficient.

Dorus Noel rang the bell of the house on Mott Street. He was a trifle surprised at the man—obviously Theleen himself—who answered his ring. Under fifty, straight and slim as an arrow, impeccably dressed, Theleen was a striking figure. He wore a spade beard and slender mustache; his beard and hair were tinged with gray. His eyes were of that blueness which is difficult to plumb. Noel caught a flash in the eyes, either of fear or resentment—he couldn't be sure which—after which the face of Theleen became bland, expressionless. Foreigners of long residence in China were likely to acquire that manner of expression.

"I'm Dorus Noel," he said. "The police . . ."

Theleen lifted his right hand. The expression on his face now was one of relief, with the fear still in evidence.

"Come in!" snapped Theleen. His voice was like the crack of a whiplash, with a queer break in it at the end. Noel gathered that Theleen controlled himself with an effort, but didn't trust himself to speak too many words in succession.

He followed Theleen into the house, whose coolness was a welcome relief from the pavements. Noel noted with appreciation everything in the succession of rooms through which his host led him. His own rooms held rugs of priceless value; so did Theleen's. There were jade ornaments, scrolls on the wall which must have dated back for centuries. There were paintings by great Chinese artists who had been dead for half a thousand years. There were bells, bronzes, porcelain.

They entered the study, a huge roomy place, cooler than any room yet encountered. Here, with the door shut, the world outside was shut off. Host and visitor were in the heart of China, in the study of a *taotai's yamen*, where neither beloved first concubine nor favored son might intrude. Theleen waved his guest to a chair, took one himself. He panted a little. His blue eyes bored into the black ones of Dorus Noel.

"You handled the Chu Chul and the White Wasp matters, didn't you?" demanded Theleen. "Also the affair of the Pell Street bells and the murders associated with red tassels?"

He put his words in the form of questions, but they were statements, really. Theleen knew.

Dorus Noel waited. Finally he said:

"There is something that troubles you? Something strange? You fear for your life perhaps?"

Purnell Theleen shifted uncomfortably in his seat. Finally he jumped to his feet.

"I thought I'd got away from it," he said, his voice breaking on the edge of hysteria. "I thought I'd run away from it! But there's something about the Orient that puts its mark on you, once you've been really touched by it. If this keeps on . . .

"My God, and I don't know where to turn! I can't escape it, even in my sleep. It's always here, in this room, my prize room, which I love beyond any I have ever occupied. Whether it goes with me into other rooms, or even to other places, I do not know. Maybe it's my own imagination. But if something doesn't happen to break the spell . . ."

"If you'll be more coherent," interrupted Dorus Noel, "and give me some idea of what you're talking about. Have you been threatened? Is there anything in your past life which somebody known to you might wish to avenge? I've got to know everything if I'm to do anything."

"Maybe it's imagination," said Theleen, more subdued. "Let's wait and see. I haven't asked another living soul, but I know you're to be trusted. Just sit, shut out the world, even myself, close your eyes to concentrate if you will . . . and listen."

Certainly it was a strange request. Theleen himself leaned back in his chair, his eyes closed, but he didn't relax. He was taut as a bowstring, tense, rigid. There was no semblance of peace about him. Noel could feel the tension, absorbed it himself. His only escape from it was to do as Theleen had bidden him: close his eyes and relax, though why he did it he hadn't the slightest idea. There seemed no sense in it. Theleen was overwrought, might attack Noel while his eyes were closed. But no, he wasn't insane, whatever his obsession might be. Noel relaxed, waited, not even guessing for what he waited.

Minutes passed. Dead silence held sway in the study of Purnell Theleen. Not even the breathing of the harassed man could be heard. A fly buzzed against the windowpane, then alighted and went silent himself, as though even it were affected by the strange tension.

Dorus Noel tensed a little as the first faint thread of sound—vague, indistinct, somehow stirring, as muted, far whispers are stirrings—touched upon his sensitive eardrums. The sound, if it could be called a sound at all, was more felt than heard. "A vague stirring," described it. It ran along one's nerves like the touch of silk against fevered cheeks. It was like a cobweb dragged over the back of the hand. Yet it was sound and not feeling.

As Noel listened the sound increased, grew in volume. It became louder. He tried to read meaning into it, tried to find words to describe its impression upon him. Several came to mind: "voracious," "greedy," "gluttonous," and then "cannibalistic." They all seemed to fit, yet none did. He could not sense danger in the sound, yet knew it must be there, if only in the danger to Theleen's nerves. He lifted his lids slightly, to peer through the slits at Purnell Theleen.

Theleen's eyes were wide-open, staring at Dorus Noel with fierce, fixed intensity. His whole heart was in his eyes, showing a strange, terrified sort of hunger. His hands were so tightly clasped across his middle that the knuckles were dead white with the strain. Noel knew that at any moment Theleen might break into a scream and start breaking things, or dash from his house like a madman flagellated by the figments of his nightmares. The sounds continued, continued and grew.

Theleen leaned forward. Then he whispered.

"Hear it! If you don't hear it . . ."

But with his whispers the sound receded, died away. Noel snapped his eyes open.

"Shut up!" he said. "Of course I hear it. It's nothing, really. You know what it is as well as I do. But I want to be sure of things, of direction, feasibility, everything. And you interrupt like a hysterical woman!"

Great beads of sweat had broken out on the face of Purnell Theleen. His clothing was soaked with perspiration. But there was relief in his face now, and Dorus Noel knew why. He's been hearing the sound, yet hadn't been sure that anyone else could hear it. Purnell Theleen had feared for his sanity. Now he was relieved, Dorus Noel guessed, because Noel had also heard the sound.

He leaned back, closed his eyes again. Noel did likewise. The sound, after what seemed an age, began again. It seemed to be everywhere: in the air above their heads, underfoot, on all sides, coming in equal volume from every direction. Noel listened for all of ten minutes, as long as he felt he dared trifle with the frayed nerves of Purnell Theleen. If he went on there would be a nervous explosion; and there was too much heat for emotional strain. On days like this, dogs went mad and bit people.

"Well," said Dorus Noel at last, opening his eyes, speaking conversationally, as though nothing untoward had happened, "what's the answer?"

He was conscious that he himself was bathed in perspiration, and wondered why that should be. The sound was simple, easy to explain. But it was impossible that the sound should come from this house, or any other house in Chinatown! It wasn't possible, even though two men had heard it. Noel leaned toward Theleen.

"There's something you haven't told me," he said. "I've got to know, or I've got to investigate. You're going to die, either by your own hand, through fear; or, if you weather this storm, at the hands of an enemy. You know who that enemy is. Name him—or her! Is it Chu Chul? The White Wasp?"

Theleen shook his head.

"None of those. Nobody you ever heard of. I can't tell you."

"Then I can do nothing."

Noel rose to his feet, started for the door. Theleen jumped at him, grabbed his hand, even dropped to one knee. His face was dead white, horrible.

"You can't leave me!" Theleen's voice rose to a high shriek, then broke badly. "I've got to have help. I need pity."

"Pity?" repeated Noel. "Pity? And did *you* have pity?"

Noel had no sooner asked the question than he wondered what in God's name had made him put it into words. It had no meaning. Or had it?

"No," Theleen was saying, "perhaps I didn't. But Davedova . . ."

Then Theleen shut his lips hard against his teeth, his face whiter still. He cried out again.

"I won't tell. It means . . . it means . . ."

"I know. You deserve to die. You know it. You've run away from it, and you know you can run no longer, no further. You have to face it. You're yellow, yellow as hell. But you're human, I guess, and I have to help you. But Davedova—it's a name, isn't it? And it isn't Chinese. It's . . ."

"Please!" said Theleen. "Don't say it! I'm as much afraid of it as I am of the sound. It's part of my dreams, waking and sleeping. It pursues me along the streets. I fight out at it as I walk, sometimes, until people stop and stare at me, wondering what invisible phantoms attack me."

Noel's lips pursed with contempt.

"Horrible!" he said. "But I'm wondering if, bad as you've probably been, the punishment isn't too drastic for the crime. And it's fitting, I imagine, or it wouldn't affect you so. What do *you* think it is?"

Theleen mumbled.

"I don't know, for sure. I think of many things: of ants gnawing at woodwork, of worms eating into trees, of scabrous bugs chewing at the bark of bamboo . . ."

"That's it!" said Dorus Noel. "That's it—the word I was seeking. *Gnawing!* It fits exactly."

"What are you saying?"

"The word I wanted to find that fitted the sound I heard, that both of us heard. It's gnawing!"

"God almighty!" said Theleen.

Noel pushed him back into his chair contemptuously and said:

"Better get out of here, go uptown, downtown, stay on the streets, or you'll be cutting your own throat."

"No! No! Outside there are so many doors from which knives could be thrown, so many places from which death could strike! In here is only the gnawing sound."

"Well," said Noel impatiently, "if you won't tell me I'll have to go it blind, but Davedova means more than you think. Maybe I can discover something. Say, let me have some of your clothes, and the use of your bathroom for twenty minutes!"

Twenty minutes later a man with gray hair, a wisp of a mustache and a spade beard stepped from the house on Mott Street. The man looked like Purnell Theleen, aped his nervous gestures, his every characteristic. But it was Dorus Noel. He hesitated, with a queer tightening of the nerves, as though donning Theleen's clothes had actually endowed him with Theleen's mental and physical turmoil. Nothing happened.

His eyes searched the baking streets, almost empty of people. He stepped to the curb, stood for a moment. Under him was a grating. His eyes played over it, then widened into a fixed stare. At the edge of the grating, just starting to crawl into it, was a white worm. There was nothing strange about worms, if one hadn't heard the sound in Theleen's place, hadn't just come from there in Theleen's clothes, hadn't guessed at many unspoken things. As it was now, that worm, which disappeared into the hole in the grating, had a sinister significance. But what, exactly?

Dorus Noel shrugged, started down Mott street. As he passed the third house from Theleen's, a woman wearing a white veil stepped out of a door and walked ahead of Noel with a lithe, sinuous motion, oddly serpentine in its grace. A tall, slender woman of regal carriage, she thrilled one merely to see her. Noel gulped. He'd seen women like her. He knew that her face would be almost dead white, save for carmine lips, and that her skin would be soft as silk to the touch—though a man might get a knife in his throat if he dared to touch her.

As though part of the sound he had just heard, Dorus Noel was conscious of a name. It hung in the air, one with the gnawing sound.

"Purnell!"

It was Theleen's first name, and he'd have sworn it came from the lips of the veiled woman. His heart quickened its beat. He knew he played with dynamite. He knew that his resemblance to Theleen, which was as nearly perfect as one man could resemble another and not be that other, had caused the speaking of the name.

"Yes, what is it?"

He tried his level best to make his voice sound like that of Theleen, even with the queer breaks of fear in it. The woman, walking on ahead, did not turn, did not show that she had heard, if she did. Dorus Noel decided on action.

He stepped up behind her swiftly, touched her on the arm.

"Davedova . . ."

He was trying the name as an experiment. It might or might not mean anything. He went on.

"I can't stand any more of it."

The woman stopped, turned with a slow turning, as though she were a puppet moved by strings in the hands of an invisible prompter. He could feel her eyes, hard on him through the thick veil.

"Sir!" there was a harsh quality in her strangely accented use of the word. He could feel her drawing away, drawing into herself, oddly like a serpent coiling to strike. "How dare you touch me?"

There was grimness in her voice, the grimness of cold anger. The voice was a woman's voice, but a voice without kindness or feeling in it.

"I've got to know," said Noel with the voice of Purnell Theleen.

But she would not listen. She turned back the way she had come and strode past him, drawing aside as though she feared contamination. Noel, having committed himself to this task, was not the kind that drew back. With his lips pursed he turned and followed her, to the very door of the house from which she had stepped as he passed.

Noel looked up and down the street. Few people were on it, and none of these seemed to be paying either of the two any heed. Noel closed the gap between himself and the woman and when she had entered the door, he put his foot in the opening to keep her from closing it.

She went on, apparently not noticing. Noel pushed his way in, closing the door behind him. The woman turned now, staring at him.

"You are persistent, Dorus Noel!" she said.

He started.

"Oh, I knew the moment you spoke that . . . well, Noel is well known in Chinatown."

"Who are you?" asked Noel. "And why did you speak a certain name? And why did you manage to step out onto the street just ahead of me?"

"Fool!" came the cold reply. "It may be possible for you to outwit Chinese, to make fools of criminals, but now you deal with something else—and with a mind better than your own. I will not stand for meddling, Dorus Noel!"

"And I," said Noel grimly, "will not stand for murder!"

"You speak in parables. I am just a woman whom you followed from the street, forcing your way in. Even your own police would stand by me if I called for help."

"Try it!"

"They are stupid. I handle my own affairs, in my own way. I have told you I will not stand for meddling. *Li la!*"

Dorus Noel tensed. The two words were Mandarin, meaning something like, "come to me at once!" So highborn Chinese called their servants. Doors opened without sound on two sides of the big, almost bare room in which Noel had intruded. They were big men, men who wore queues. And their eyes, as they gazed at the woman, were filled with adoration, like dogs' eyes. That they would die for the veiled woman, Dorus Noel instantly knew. And they would slay for her.

"Do you think I would go as far as I have to be balked, Dorus Noel?" asked the woman. "You know too much! Dispose of this offal!"

They were quite calm about it, those servants of the veiled woman. Their right hands came forth from their sleeves, holding knives. Noel started when he saw the shape of the hafts of those knives. Without a single exception the hafts were of white jade, and the jade was carved in the shape of white moths. That made things tie together, somehow, and lent something real to the fear which obsessed Purnell Theleen. Dorus Noel spoke quietly while he waited for the Chinese to charge.

"Murder means the chair, lady," he said, "even for a beautiful woman."

"I do not care," she said, "as long as payment is made . . . in full. And your laws are cruel and unjust if they send *anyone* to the chair for performing an act of simple justice."

"If you killed a mass murderer it would still be murder!" snapped Noel. "I'm here to prevent it. There is always recourse in a court of law."

"For Davedova . . ." began the woman.

Then she stopped and he knew that she bit her lips with vexation at herself for having mentioned a name, the same name he had mentioned. He did not know what it meant. She did. She probably thought he knew more than he said. She wondered, perhaps, how much Purnell Theleen had told him, how much he in turn had passed on to the police. On his part, Noel wondered how long she had been in Chinatown without his knowledge. That the Chinese were her allies was proved by the fact that he had known of her existence only when she was ready to disclose it.

"Yes, Davedova," said Noel, his heart racing. "She has a debt to pay."

"And she will pay it!" her voice was fierce, as cold as ice.

"Would she show me how to reach a certain house—the house of the gnawings—without going out onto the street?"

The woman stiffened.

"You *do* know too much," she said. "Obey me!"

The last two words were snapped at her servants, six in number. Now they hurled themselves at Dorus Noel, moving without sound. The woman sat down in a chair to watch, taking a cigarette from some receptacle in her clothing, lighting it without a tremor of her fingers. Her nails were long and tapering. She had to lift her veil slightly to smoke. He had been right. Her lips were the color of blood—rich, healthful blood—but the color had come out of bottles or jars. Probably, naturally, her lips were as pale as he was sure her cheeks would be.

This Noel glimpsed as he leaped back, until he was against the wall. His attitude of a man unsure of himself, nervous, afraid, dropped from him like a garment. Though he still was disguised as Purnell Theleen—and feeling a bit ludicrous about it since she had penetrated his disguise so easily—he little resembled his erstwhile host. His hands came up as the moth-hafted knives reached for him. The Chinese came on in a sort of semicircle. They had a plan of attack. They had been used for this sort of thing before.

One reached for him with licking blade. His left hand shot out, thrusting the blade aside. Then he stepped in and his right fist, packing all the power of his mighty body, the coordination of eyes and muscles, went straight to the Chinese's jaw. The man fell like a shot deer and scarcely moved after he had hit the floor. Noel could not have rendered him more surely or quickly *hors de combat* if he had used his automatic, now at home, utterly useless to him.

There still were five. As he fought he was conscious of the woman's voice, softly modulated, seductive, but cold still, as wind over a glacier. "Perhaps, Noel, if you knew all the facts you would help rather than hinder me. He deserves death."

"Then the law should decide."

"But the newspapers would tell the whole story, blacken many names, search out scandal in high places . . ."

"Only if the scandal deserved to be searched out," he panted.

A second Chinese fell, and the others hurled themselves at him in a body. He fought like a fiend. His fists lashed out, left right, right left, with all the power of his body. The heat was beginning to tell on him. In his nostrils was the odor of unwashed bodies, the odor of the Chinese coolies, not one of whom had spoken a word.

Knives ripped his clothing from his torso, tore at his flesh. Blood dripped down on his trousers, his own blood. As he fought, whirling like a dervish dancer to save his life, so that none could send a blow directly to a fatal spot, he saw the woman blow a smoke ring at the ceiling. She was so terribly, fatally, cool while he fought like a madman for his life. It was diabolical. It wasn't Chinese, yet it was. This woman was no Chinese, but she used all the weapons of China.

"Your servants will slay me," he panted, "but let me see your face!"

Maybe it was a strange request in the circumstances, but the woman hesitated for only a moment, then tossed her veil back over her toque. Her face was gorgeous; but it was like alabaster, like the white jade of the knife handles. The skin looked as though it would break under a hard-pressed thumb, and there were little blue veins making delicate tracery just underneath. Noel gasped—and a knife blade bit into his shoulder.

"You can't do it!" he said. "I won't let you. A woman like you . . ."

"Has nothing for a man like you!" she snapped. "Nor for any man, thanks to that—that . . ."

He knew she meant Purnell Theleen, but she steadfastly refused to mention the name, as though to do so were a species of confession.

The Chinese were pressing him more closely. Now the woman rose. It was all he could do, statuesque and strange as she was, to keep his mind on the most important fact at the moment—that he was fighting for his life. Another Chinese fell. The three who remained were fighting in grim, terrible silence. They would not be denied. The woman moved toward one of the doors. If Dorus Noel raced after her he would expose his back to knife thrusts, which he dared not do. He redoubled his efforts. His breath came in panting gasps, rasping his throat. He tasted his own blood, salt on his lips. His whole body was bathed in perspiration.

The woman spoke again.

"Know, when the knives reach you," said the woman, "that you have looked at Davedova, whom others . . . and the one . . . long ago, knew simply as Anna."

It was cryptic, senseless, and he almost cried out his exasperation. The woman went on.

"I'll stand inside the door. One of the remaining three will slay you. I shall slay whoever is left, so that all lips be closed. No human being in Chinatown was close enough to recognize me, no one that would tell—even if anyone knew. You see, Dorus Noel, my work is finished. I go through this door and vanish."

And she went through the door.

A knife came at Dorus Noel. He grasped the wrist. A thin cry of pain burst from his lips. The blade apparently had been driven to the hilt in his heart. He sank against the knife wielder, dropped to the floor. The man who had stabbed him was almost dragged down with him. Then a weapon barked from the thin crack of the door through which the woman had gone. The Chinese dropped, a bullet in the back of his head. He dropped across the body of Dorus Noel. Noel heard the door close.

Instantly he slid from under the dead Chinese. Noel hurled himself at the door. It burst from its hinges under the drive of his weight, the impetus of his savage charge.

He was through, in another room.

• • •

He came up short in surprise. The woman was there, and she had tossed aside her veil and toque. Her dead white face was a snowy mask as she whirled on him. She had thought him dead, had thought she had plenty of time to escape. She hadn't hurried. She moved as one dead.

She turned her silver-mounted automatic, a small weapon that looked like a toy, on Dorus Noel. He didn't hesitate. She did . . . between firing and turning the weapon on herself. But he caught her hand before she could pull the trigger.

"Let me finish it myself," she said hoarsely. "I thought, when I did my work, that I could go on to something else. It's been two years. I find my desire for revenge has kept me alive. Now that it is sated there is nothing left, nowhere for me to go."

"Yes," said Noel, fighting off the overwhelming desire to pity her, "there is something left to live for—to enjoy the fight you will have to make to beat the chair."

"And when I've done that?"

"God knows. But there is always something, even for those who find life empty of hope. Now, come with me."

And he led her out, his hand fast about her wrist, onto the sidewalk and so to the house of Purnell Theleen. He rang the bell and there was no answer.

"I told you there had been an end made of things," she said. "He won't answer. He can't. Purnell Theleen is dead."

Noel, his heart a dead thing in his breast—because he pitied this woman in spite of all he could do—kicked in the door of Purnell Theleen's house, and led the woman across the threshold. They went to the room where they had heard the sounds, and encountered only silence.

"He was a coward," she said. "Try the bathroom."

They pushed open another door and found Theleen. He was quite dead. His right hand gripped the handle of a small revolver. There was a hole in his temple.

"He did it himself," said Noel, "but you are responsible. I know you managed it in a devilish fashion. You see, I knew what the gnawing sounds were, but not how they were possible, where they were heard. There is one chance for you. You killed a Chinese. I saw you. But a jury might not electrocute a white woman for killing a yellow man, especially when he was armed with a knife and trying to slay another white man. You could say that the white man was trying to protect you."

He sat down opposite her.

"Before I call the police," he said, "I want to know something. I know what made the sounds, for I have heard silkworms at their labors. But whence come the sounds?"

"There is a way here from my home," she said in a dead voice. "It was easy for my servants, who helped me with silkworms in China, after the horror at Vladivostok."

"I know, you are Russian, a Russian refugee . . . what is called a White Russian. I know the plight of their women in China. You might be a countess, a princess perhaps. You meant that when you spoke of scandal in high places."

She nodded, and spoke herself.

"He, Theleen, was a high official with the Chinese army. I accepted his protection in preference to degradation at the hands of the Reds. But he was a beast. Few of us ever broke away from our bondage in China. You know what that bondage was . . . is? Well, I intended to break away. I made friends with other foreigners, tried to hold up my head. I had a gift for many things.

"I found out about silkworms, their culture, how they are fed. I vanished from the life of Purnell Theleen, even took a new name. I would make such silk, I promised myself, as the world had never seen, even out of China. Once in so often there are worms which produce yellow silk, rare, almost priceless. By experimenting over a long period I found I could produce worms which spun only the yellow silk. It would have meant a fortune, my rehabilitation. I felt secure, had almost forgotten the horror."

She hesitated, showing her first signs of agitation, as though she could not go on. Dorus Noel helped her by breaking in.

"I've marveled at the silkworms," he said. "They live on mulberry leaves. Hundreds, thousands of them, all in one place, eating of the leaves. Voracious as army ants, they make a strange, endless noise. They eat, then they spin their cocoons. The cocoons are boiled and the larva destroyed. But if allowed to live out its cycle, the worm is finally ready to break forth from its silken cocoon to begin the cycle again. It is in the shape of a white moth, which becomes a worm, which spins, comes forth again from the cocoon."

"And my cocoons were golden," murmured the woman. "But Purnell Theleen found me. I had made many friends, foreigners, Chinese, high diplomatic officials. I must come back to him, he said, or he would tell of my past. I refused. He told, after I had refused to make him a partner in my business as an alternative. My only recourse afterward was . . . ."

"I know," said Dorus Noel, "you went back to the old bondage. Brutal men like beasts . . . horror . . . degradation. The rotten beast!"

"My friends all turned against me. It meant ruin."

"But why," said Noel, "this?"

He waved his hand vaguely at the room.

"When I could, I let him know I intended to seek payment," she explained.

"I knew he was a coward. Only a coward would treat a woman as he treated me. He knew the sounds silkworms make, eating of the mulberry leaves. That sound would remind him of me. I traced him to America. He loved China. Sooner or later he would come to Chinatown.

"I had a house ready. I saw that a newspaper, carrying an advertisement of this house reached him. *His* paper was the only one which carried that ad! He took the place, and I waited.

"My Chinese friends—whom I will never name; but you know how Chinese feel about such things—helped me with the walls of this house. They are honeycombed. The spaces are filled with boxes, like boxes which hold jasmine tea. In each box, supplied with mulberry leaves enough to last the life cycle of the worms, is a silkworm."

Noel rose at last, quitted the house. When, two days later, the police searched for Purnell Theleen and found two dead people in his house—one a woman who sat in a chair and smiled—it was a mystery which promised never to be solved. Noel's superior out on Park Avenue was a discreet man who never asked questions, or told things that should not be told.

Noel had one thing left to do. When the house of Theleen burned in a fire of mysterious origin, the police charged it off to a firebug—while Dorus Noel sat in his house on Pell Street with a queer look in his face . . . wondering what poison Anna Davedova had used which could leave her face looking so peaceful.

CLOISONNÉ

"I shall save you," Noel panted—
"for the electric chair."

**In the Chinatown House of the Soul-Slayer Appeared the
Sinister Room. And When Dorus Noel Defied the Gods
to Enter, He Found Only the Hands Which Had Put the
Mark of the Beast on a Girl.**

WHEN DORUS NOEL, SECRET AGENT OF THE POLICE in New York City's Chinatown, took down the receiver of his French telephone he had a feeling that the communication he would receive would be startling. People seldom telephoned him and but two men knew his secret number. They were the commissioner of police and his superior who lived on Park Avenue. Noel had never seen the latter, though his voice was as familiar to Noel as Noel's own. Noel had been selected for his strange post because of his wide knowledge of Chinese, born of many years of experience in China.

"Yes?" he said, giving the speaker no encouragement beyond the single word, and taking care to make his voice sound natural. If the caller were someone who should know Noel, he would recognize Noel's voice.

"You know me, Noel?" came the voice.

Noel stiffened. The voice was that of his Park Avenue superior, and it was the first time that one had ever communicated with Noel of his own accord. Usually, which meant at least once a day, at varying intervals, Dorus Noel called his superior. Now . . .

"Yes, chief?" said Noel.

"I understand, Noel," said his superior, "that the queer house on Mott Street has been completed."

Noel licked his lips. No need to mention what house was referred to, for the "queer" house was one of Chinatown's mysteries. The laborers on it were all Chinese workmen, men who came of generations of builders. They could neither read nor write, but artistry was in their souls and in their fingertips, so that they performed miracles with lacquer, bronze, cloisonné and Chinese pigments.

No one knew to whom the house belonged, but that there was something strange about it one knew merely by watching the Chinese who passed the place, day or night. They would glance aside, avert their gazes quickly, and hurry on. Dorus Noel knew, when the first Chinese workman appeared on the scene and began to work, that some time in the future he would have more than a passing interest in the place. But even then he had not thought it would be a matter which would cause his chief to violate all precedent and call him direct by telephone.

"Yes, chief," said Noel.

"Its owner moved in last night," said the chief, "and he telephoned the chief of police around midnight!"

Noel gasped.

"Why?" he said.

"Nobody knows. He's scared to death, or was. There's something strange about the call. He wanted the police to know that something queer was going on, but he didn't wish them to make an actual investigation, except through someone not connected with the police."

"All Chinatown knows I am connected with the police."

"Yes, but Chinatown trusts you . . . and it is not unusual for you to visit anyone in the section on a purely social call."

"Which means that I am to call on the new owner of the house known here as 'Delicate Fragrance'?"

"Yes. After that it will be in your hands. It may be anything from opium and hashish to . . . well, you know the Chinese. Boreo knows the Chinese and wouldn't be afraid of ordinary things."

"Boreo?"

"Yes. The owner of Delicate Fragrance."

"What's his nationality? The name sounds peculiar."

"His nationality, nobody really knows. His features have a Mongoloid cast. Goodbye."

As Dorus Noel clicked up the receiver, his mind was harking back to something, something out of the China of his own memory, in which the name of Boreo figured. What was Boreo? Who was he? Somehow his name recalled tales Dorus Noel had heard of fabulous riches . . . tales of Chinese women, of queer rites, of a certain forbidden marriage. Noel's face was covered with perspiration, for the tales he had heard recalled certain strange disappearances of women . . . and an investigation into murder.

He knew where the house on Mott Street was located. He'd passed it at least four times a week for several months. Now he dressed with meticulous care, strode from his own house near the dogleg where Pell and Mott Streets intersect, snapped a few words at his Chinese "boy" regarding *tiffin*, or lunch, and stepped onto the street.

As he reached the sidewalk he lifted his eyes, gazing down the street toward the house he intended to visit. It stood out from the other houses of Chinatown like a burnished Oriental temple from among the homes of coolies. Noel shivered a little, thinking of other temples in a far country. He reached the door of the house, which was reached by the traditional nine steps which are part of every Chinese temple. He ascended the steps, paused again.

The knocker on the door was shaped like one of the "lions of Fo," which the uninitiate call "dogs." The creature seemed to glare at Noel with its agate eyes, as though it warned him away. Noel thrust out his hand gingerly, as though he expected the fangs of the thing to snap into his flesh.

The knocker was warm, as though it had long been cupped in someone's hot hand. He lifted the knocker, but did not drop it, for with the lifting a peal of musical bells sounded within the house. He lowered the knocker carefully, raised it again. Again the peal rang through the house.

For a long moment there was no response. Then a voice seemed to speak in Noel's ears.

"You come as a friend, Dorus Noel? Or as an enemy?"

Noel did not make the mistake of looking around for the orifice whence issued the voice. He must seem to take the strange question, and its origin, for granted.

"I come with an open mind, Boreo *hsien sheng*," he replied quickly.

Instantly the door swung back. A yellow face peered out. Noel passed through the door, followed the soundless-slippered boy down a long hall covered by a thick runner, to a far inner door opening on the hall, at which the boy knocked discreetly.

"Enter, Dorus Noel!" commanded the voice he had just heard.

The door swung open. Noel entered. The door swung shut behind him without sound. Noel stood just inside, staring at a man who sat on a teakwood chair under a window whose panes were painted with delicate tracery of Chinese whites and brilliant reds. The man was white, but he dressed as a Chinese. His brows angled away from his nose, and his eyes were catlike, horizontally. His countenance had a distinct Mongoloid cast.

"You are Leed Boreo?" said Noel.

The man bowed, removed the stem of a water pipe from his mouth. Noel's eyes went to a taboret beside the teakwood chair, on which rested a long-stemmed bamboo pipe with a small bowl. Beside the pipe was a peanut oil lamp and a *yen hok*—a piece of wire which resembled a hatpin without a head.

Noel's eyes narrowed. He had seen many opium layouts. The eyes of Boreo seemed hard, black, and deep as the wells of Shallajai. But Noel, knowing men—especially men with the mark of the East on them—could see the fear his host tried so hard to hide.

Boreo spoke softly.

"Bring tea and cakes," he said.

It didn't surprise Noel, this casual command to an unseen servitor. Many "foreigners" went in for Eastern mysteries, like talking devices which might be expected to mystify the uninitiate. Noel knew that somewhere in the walls of the place were dictaphones.

"Be seated, Dorus Noel," said Boreo.

Noel seated himself on one of half a dozen chairs which faced Boreo in a sort of semi-circle, as though others sat there on occasion, when Boreo held court. The chair was warm under Noel. He knew that someone had just quitted it. Carelessly he dropped a hand on the seat of the two chairs to his right and left. They too were warm.

"Yes, Noel," said Boreo, "I have had visitors. They just left me . . . after an ultimatum!"

"Pardon," said Noel, flushing. "I'm crude, perhaps."

"There is no need," said Boreo. "I will tell you anything you wish to know."

As Noel leaned back in the chair faint, delightful music broke in the room. It seemed to come from everywhere, alow, aloft, on all sides. It had a tinkling, Chinese quality. Noel's eyebrows lifted. Then he leaned forward in his chair and the music ceased instantly. Boreo did not seem to consider the music worth explanation.

Thus he paid Noel the compliment of showing his belief that Noel knew Chinese fashions enough to know whence the music came . . . from the six chairs which faced Leed Boreo. The chairs were musical chairs, which played when pressure was brought to bear on their backs. But the effect, with the sunlight trying to get through the painted windows, and drawing strange designs on the parquet floor, was eerie, even to one as accustomed to the Orient as Noel.

"The mark is on you," Noel said suddenly. "The mark of the East!"

The effect of his words on Boreo was strange indeed. The man shot forward in his chair, his face purple, convulsed.

"What's that?" he snapped. "What's that you say?"

Noel was surprised. The fear in Boreo was somehow communicated for a moment to himself.

"I merely meant," said Noel, "that once a foreigner has eaten of the lotus of the Orient he must always have something about him to make him recall it. These chairs, for example, the *yen hok*, the water pipe . . . those windows, the lacquer screens, the feather panels . . ."

Boreo, without apology, drew a handkerchief from his voluminous sleeve and mopped his suddenly perspiring brow.

"Of course," he said, "of course. For a moment I thought . . ."

Noel leaned forward.

"You thought it was part of the threat against you, eh? Tell me about it. The six who came to see you . . . what did they say?"

"They said that if I left my new home without permission I would die horribly on the street. They said that within a week I should die here, unless . . ."

Boreo paused, gulped convulsively.

"Well," said Noel, "unless?"

"How much do you know of me?" asked Boreo.

"I've been trying to recall," said Noel. "Enough, I think. You're a swine for money. You have millions. It is bathed in the blood of men, haunted by the souls of women, delicate, gorgeous women. You have been a man of taste, in women.

"There was a story of a *taotai's* daughter. She was fragile as a willow branch, beautiful as lotus on the surface of the Jade Fountain. Her father was richer even than yourself, and could not be tempted with money. He was a mandarin of the old school. He refused you his daughter.

"Soon thereafter you left China. The daughter had vanished . . . and the *taotai* was a pauper. Prior to that, for three weeks, he had been missing from his home, and strange *chits*, or memoranda, went to his many banks. When the *taotai* returned home he was a haunted man, a skeleton. He had been through Purgatory.

"Shall I go on? This is supposition, understand? The *taotai* was worth forty millions of *taels*. When you left China it was whispered that your wealth, in the last month of your sojourn, had increased by forty millions of *taels*."

Boreo nodded, even smiled a little. Noel hated him then. His hands itched to fasten themselves in the throat of the grim Boreo. But all this had happened in China, beyond any jurisdiction of New York's courts. Here Boreo, an American citizen, could command the protection of the police—and Noel was of the police.

"And what," said Noel abruptly, "of Lan Fei, the *taotai's* daughter?"

"It required us twenty-one days to cross the Pacific," said Boreo unctuously, "and it is a marvelous woman indeed who can interest Boreo for more than that length of time. Besides, she could not enter, and this country has laws against people who smuggle . . ."

"And she was tiny," said Noel grimly, "no larger than a porthole . . ."

"It was far beyond the three-mile limit," said Boreo, "and the vessel was Japanese!"

Noel shrugged.

"I despise you," he said. "I hope I fail to protect you, though I will do everything in my power. What do you fear?"

"The *taotai's* vengeance. And there is a room, a room of cloisonné, fit for a *taotai's* daughter. It was built into this house without my knowledge. It is a secret room . . . and out of that room will come my death if you cannot help me!"

"Let me see it," said Noel.

Boreo rose and passed close beside Noel, going toward the door. Noel drew back as from contamination. Boreo noticed, his lips twisted into a grim smile of amusement. Boreo turned aside before reaching the door, pressed a button near a corner.

A panel slid back, disclosing a room out of which came the odor of sandalwood, of "Buddha's hands," of faint wisps of incense. Noel strode to the threshold, peered in, gasped. No more gorgeous room had he ever seen, even in the aged palaces of Peking, Jehol or Mukden.

The floor seemed to be of cloisonné, polished like a mirror. At the far side of the room was a *kong*, or bed, also of cloisonné. Delicate vases stood on fragile stands in the corners, and out of each protruded the stems and the blooms of rare flowers. Old brocades, rich beyond the dreams of avarice, hung on the walls. The coverlets on the bed were of the finest Chinese embroidery.

"How would you feel," said Boreo, "to come to a house which was born of your dreams, and have a room shown you like this one? A room you never expected to see, hadn't ordered built?"

"It would depend," said Noel, "on the state of my conscience. How does this room strike you?"

"Have you noticed the characters on the vases, on the embroidered pillow of the *kong*?"

Noel now noticed the Chinese ideographs for the first time. His lips shaped their sounds:

"Lan Fei!"

"Exactly," said Boreo. "This is Lan Fei's wedding chamber. And this is the ultimatum delivered me by the six relatives of the *taotai*: that if within a week I do not install Lan Fei in this chamber as my wife, the chamber will slay me."

"And Lan Fei?"

"I told you. You described it yourself. She was tiny, the porthole small."

"God," said Noel, "I wish I dared throttle you myself!"

"But you will help me instead. You will remain with me until the danger has passed. You will live in this room, guard its door and see that I never, no matter what strange things may happen, cross the threshold!"

"If I sleep?"

"That means my death," said Boreo coldly, "and what can your laws do to the dead? You will die!"

"You never give even your allies an even break, do you?" asked Noel.

"Why should I? Did you not just say that you would throttle me yourself?"

"I did. I can guess now why you are here. There are beautiful women in Chinatown."

"They do not interest me . . . though after the time stipulated in the ultimatum it may be different."

"I have no choice," said Noel. "I'll stay here."

"I sleep in the room across from this one," said Boreo, indicating another door. "You will be between me and death, always. If you fail . . ."

Noel, in the depth of his contempt and disgust, slapped Boreo resoundingly across the face. Instantly the room was filled with coolies with lowering brows. Boreo motioned them back with a gesture. His black eyes were wells of malevolence. He rubbed his burning cheek with his left hand.

"Here is an ultimatum, too, Dorus Noel," he said. "You die one day after my enemies say I must pass. And you die whether I live or die! Leed Boreo will not be thus insulted."

Noel's lips pursed. He slapped Boreo again.

"Some day," he said, "I shall kill you!"

There was a tense pause. The coolies, poised for the attack, their black eyes burning into Dorus Noel; Leed Boreo, his face a mask of convulsed hatred; Dorus Noel hating his job as he had never hated anything in this world . . . and beyond them the fatal wedding chamber, to be occupied by a bride who was dead.

It made Noel shiver, as though the chamber were already haunted by the ghost of Lan Fei. In his mind's-eye he could see her, dressed in, say, a gorgeous Ming costume, floating in the black depths of the Pacific, her ebony hair the plaything of the currents of the deep. So must Boreo often see her, hardened though he must be, in his waking hours and in his dreams.

But Boreo was hard, merciless. He could banish such a picture by etching another in its place, even more tragic and horrible. His life had been filled with such pictures.

"I'll stay, of course," said Noel, "but if you come near me in this room I shall knock your head off your shoulders!"

Boreo half smiled, a wolfish smile, and entered the other room. The coolies followed him, bearing the teakwood chair. The door closed behind them. Dorus Noel began his strange vigil. Knowing the Orient, he knew that the *taotai's* friends had made no idle boast. But they must believe that somewhere Lan Fei still lived, else Leed Boreo would have been slain before now, in some horrible manner.

At meal times Noel's food was served him in the room where he had met Boreo, by a boy who did not lift eyes to him, who did not speak. The food was Chinese, and of the very best. There were cigarettes and cigars. Noel, knowing Chinese, did not believe that any attack of any sort would be made during daylight. He granted himself two hours of sleep, stretching himself on a rug before the secret panel. Anyone, to enter there, must step over him.

When he wakened it was dark.

He sat in a chair, then, facing the secret panel. Darkness came swiftly. Faint light came through the painted window. The house seemed utterly silent. Noel could picture Boreo in some part of it, cowering in fear, waiting for something to come to him from the wedding chamber of Lan Fei.

Dorus Noel was calm. He sat quietly, waiting, wondering just how the relatives of the *taotai* would go about forcing the issue with Leed Boreo, behind whom, ironically enough, was the might of New York's police. They would find a way, he thought, in spite of Noel's best efforts, if they could, and educated Chinese were resourceful.

He stiffened. A sound!

Nobody sat with him, but one of the musical chairs gave off a slight tinkling sound, as though a phantom hand had touched its back, while through the secret panel came a *rustling* sound, as though—Noel thought—heavy embroidery, a woman's gown, perhaps, were being dragged across lacquer or cloisonné . . . and a voice whispered in Noel's ears.

"It is no affair of yours, Dorus Noel, and we will not be balked! Sleep and forget! Sleep and forget!"

There was an odor in his nostrils, too, the odor of incense. In a few minutes, he knew, that odor would overpower him, drug him, and then . . . He rose to his feet, raced for the window, tried to lift it. It was fastened solidly down, as though whoever had created it had foreseen that some enemy would try to open it. He struck his fist against the glass and it did not break.

"Bulletproof!" he ejaculated.

Invisible walls were closing on Leed Boreo, whom Noel was honor bound to protect. Noel raced to Boreo's door. It would open, but he didn't open it. The hall door was closed, locked. It was of heavy wood. Hours would be required to batter it down. Noel fumbled for the button of the secret panel, paused with his hand hovering over it.

What would he see in the wedding chamber when the door swung back? That voice still came to him, softly, insistently, bidding him sleep. It was a woman's voice, soft, gentle, alluring. Out of the secret room, through the thin panel, came other sounds now. The sounds were growing. Noel shivered anew as he tried to compare those sounds to others he had heard.

They reminded him of the gentle swell of waves across the shingle of a quiet beach. He thought of Lan Fei, lying on that beach, just beyond the reach of the tide, her long black hair washed by the sea, mingled with the sand. His body went cold.

There was something in that room! It must have been there when Noel had last—and first—seen it, for none could enter that room save past Noel, and even had they tried it while he slept, he would have wakened. He had so trained himself that none could enter a room where he slept that he did not waken. And yet . . . well, it was his duty to investigate. His finger pressed the button.

The secret panel slid back with a whispering sound, and out to Noel's nostrils came the odor of incense, more overpowering than before. He looked into the wedding chamber, which was lighted by shafts of electric light that came through high windows. And his heart almost stopped beating as his eyes fell on the *kong*.

Despite the fact he knew nobody could possibly have passed him, despite the fact that what he saw was impossible, the *kong* was occupied by a woman, a Chinese girl, dressed in an ancient Ming costume. Her hair was flung wild across her face. She rested on her right elbow, her right cheek cupped in her hand, and mysterious eyes stared at Dorus Noel. In the girl's left hand she held a comb, with which she constantly combed her hair.

Noel thought of *"Die Lorelei"* who combed their golden hair as they lured sailors to their doom on the rocks. For there was lure in the eyes of the woman. And the *kong* on which she rested rose and fell gently, as though it had been a small boat on the bosom of a gentle ocean.

". . . her body was tiny . . . to fit a porthole . . ."

His own words came back to him freighted with meaning. Of course the figure there could not be that of Lan Fei, and yet . . . what else could it be? And there were rustling sounds in the room, though Noel could see nothing that lived or moved save the figure on the *kong*. But it was as though the whole room were filled with invisible figures—of girls perhaps—who dragged their gorgeously embroidered gowns across the floor of this menacing bridal chamber.

"Who are you?" asked Noel, scarcely above a whisper.

The girl's expression did not change. The bed rose and fell, rocking slightly on waves Noel could not see. Her left hand still played through her hair. Now Noel, watching closely, choking a little because of the fumes of incense, noticed something significant: the girl's every motion was repeated endless times.

She stared at him without blinking; her left hand made the same motions through her hair. Her bed rose and fell with each movement exactly like the last. Noel's eyes narrowed, turned toward the window of the chamber. He glanced behind him, at the door of Boreo's room. It was closed. There was no sound in the room behind Noel, only the faint, wispy sounds from the room directly ahead.

Noel stared down at the cloisonné floor. It seemed to be undulating. It made him think of a floor of writhing serpents. The whole thing was mad. But ahead of him the girl continued to go through those same motions with monotonous regularity. Noel could imagine what effect those movements might have on a mind whose conscience was heavy with murder. A light began to dawn on him.

He stepped into the room, and horror seized him.

The floor of the room was in motion! Not erratic, terrible motion, but the soft gentle motion of a ship's deck in a slight sea.

". . . tiny body . . . porthole . . ."

The whole symbolism was there. Noel fought to keep his nerves under control. He mustn't lose confidence in himself. That would be fatal, not only to Leed Boreo, who didn't matter, but to Dorus Noel. He ran across the room, with a jerky, uncertain series of strides which nauseated him, and examined the high windows, while the floor of the room seemed to move away under him, carrying him past the window, so that he had to keep moving backward to stand before the window.

His eyes, while he panted to maintain his position, searched the window, found nothing. But across the street was a Chinese restaurant, with an electric, moving sign. It seemed to leer at him. There was something about its monotonous, shaky movement. Noel's body partly blocked out the light of it as it came through the window. He turned with his back to the window, looking at the *kong* again. Part of the woman had vanished?

Her bed still rocked and undulated. Her left hand still combed at her hair. This much Dorus knew, though the hair was invisible, and the beautiful face blotted out. He stepped aside . . . and there was the woman again, looking at the door where he had stood, rising and falling and rocking on her bed.

Noel laughed, a bit shakily, started back for the door. As he started it came to him with a rush of certainty that he must reach the door in a hurry, that to delay another minute meant his own death. He sensed fingers reaching for his throat from behind. The shadow figure on the bed had become a thing of horrible menace. He hurried. He used long strides, making for the door.

But something had happened to the floor of the bridal chamber.

It had turned soft with an awful, quicksand-like softness. It sucked at his feet, pulling him down. It dragged at him. And the secret panel went shut. His eyes stared at the panel, as he fought to keep his feet under him. He felt the slimy, soft substance of the floor clutch at his ankles, reach for his knees.

He cried out, or started to—but clicked off the cry. Leed Boreo would give him no help, this much he knew. Besides, probably the sound would not penetrate that secret panel. But no, the sounds in here had gone through the panel before he had ever swung it open.

With the strength of despairing resignation, he hurled himself at the panel, wondering if there were a button on the inside coinciding with that on the outside, to swing back the door. His whole body was bathed in perspiration. He felt vast abysses under him, wondering what in God's name caused the sensation as of quicksand, or as of a ship going down under his feet. His hands found the panel, played over it with clawing fingers, feeling for the button. If there were no button he was lost.

And then . . . all at once the floor was stationary. The light which had come through the window vanished. There was a sound as of a shutter falling into place . . . and the room was in total darkness. Noel whirled, and heavy bodies hurled themselves at him out of the darkness. He faced them, back against the panel. He could tell by the odor that Chinese coolies attacked him. Here was something that he could understand, something that didn't smack of the unknown, something . . . well, the chance to exchange blows with tangible people. And the voice was in his ears again.

"We are sorry, Dorus Noel, but we warned you. Nothing in life can thwart the vengeance of the *taotai!*"

But Noel was of the police and his first loyalty, no matter what might be behind the whole horror, was to Leed Boreo, whom he himself would gladly have slain with a clear conscience. His left hand crashed into a soft face. His right followed. He heard a man go down with an agonized scream. Others flung themselves upon him, fighting without sound. Knives seared his flesh, ripped the clothing from his torso.

He bowed his back, hurling his attackers from him, fought like a crazy man, but sending every blow to what he guessed to be a vital spot. He heard men fall, grunting. Knives, thrown knives, clattered against the panel at his back, missing him by fractions of inches. He panted with the exertion, wondering all the time what horror this room personified. Vengeance? Of course, but something more, something eerie and terrible, something Oriental beyond his previous experiences.

There was a lull in the attack . . . and his right hand shot out again, seeking the button which would free him, if there were a button. And all at once the panel behind him was gone, and he fell backward out of the room, his legs lifting to his stomach. He heard the panel slide shut. Rough hands dragged him to his feet.

The voice of Leed Boreo was in his ears.

"What's in there, Noel?"

"Death!" The word came from Noel's lips as though torn from them against his will. "Inside there, an enemy of . . . the *taotai* must die . . ."

"The lights!" snapped Leed Boreo.

The lights were snapped on. Nothing came out of the bridal chamber but silence, the silence as of menacing forces lying in wait. Boreo stared at Noel, noting the perspiration on his face . . . and Noel spoke to Boreo.

"Lan Fei!" he said. "In there, on the *kong!*"

The face of Boreo went pasty white. His lips twitched. His eyes were wild. Noel meant to explain the eerie trick of the electric sign outside the window, to advance his theory of how the shape on the sign was thrown onto the bed, but Leed Boreo gave him no chance. Boreo stared at one of his servitors, several of whom were in the room.

"You, Chang Tzo!" he snapped. "Don this gown!"

He spoke in the Peking dialect, which is Mandarin. The Chinese to whom he spoke paled, met the eyes of his master, and the fatalism of the Orient stared out of his eyes. He was doomed and knew it, knew there was no way out. If he refused obedience he died instantly. That was manifest in the knives which suddenly appeared in the hands of his compatriots, the other coolies, whose sharp points were pressed against his back and sides. He sighed a little as Boreo removed his own gown and slipped it onto Chang Tzo.

"Now, extinguish the lights!"

Again the words were barked in Mandarin. The lights went out obediently.

"Now, Noel, the panel," said Boreo.

"No!" This was murder! But the coolies moved. They obeyed the inflexible will of Leed Boreo. Noel's hands were pinioned at his sides, so firmly held that even his great strength availed him nothing against his captors. The lights went out. The panel whispered as it opened. Chang Tzo was literally hurled into the bridal chamber. The panel was shut instantly, before anyone who might be inside could be sure that the one who had entered was not Leed Boreo. Noel noted that it was the hands of Boreo himself which had hurled Chang Tzo into the bridal chamber.

"Now, the lights again." Boreo's voice was very low. The lights went on for a second, were snapped off. Boreo was just making sure that he had thrown the man of his selection to the *taotai's* vengeance. Then darkness again.

And for a long moment there was silence.

The silence was broken by a ghastly shriek, followed by others and yet others. The sound as of water over a shingle came again, now with a new sound intermingled with them, the sound as of small cakes of ice rubbing together in a troubled pond. The shrieks of the luckless coolie seemed to be moving away. Then was added another sound . . . horrible, crunching sounds, as of flesh and bones being destroyed by the fangs of some unimaginable predatory beast. The voice that Noel remembered came out of the air.

"It did not trick us, Leed Boreo," it said. "What is the life of one coolie more or less, since his death will prove to you that our words have meaning?"

An oath came from the lips of Leed Boreo as all sound ceased inside the room of Lan Fei. The lights went on again at Boreo's command. Two white men and five yellow men stared at one another with dilated eyes filled with horror.

"The panel!" said Boreo. "You will look inside, Noel."

This time willing hands held the panel back as Noel stepped across the threshold. The secret mechanism had lifted the shutter again, and the bridal chamber was filled with a subdued light. But the *kong* across the room was vacant, save for the richly embroidered pillows, the brocade coverlet.

Noel knew that the sign across the street, by which, through some strange necromancy which would be scientifically explained at the proper time, "Lan

Fei" had been brought to the *kong* intended to be her bridal couch, had been extinguished. He stared at the floor under his feet. It was utterly solid. A gasp came from his lips.

There was a pool of crimson on the floor near the side of the *kong* . . . and protruding from under the bed, which appeared to be of solid cloisonné, was a hand, visible almost to the wrist, with the fingers outspread as though in agony! There, Noel knew, was all that was left of Chang Tzo.

"Bring implements," said Noel hoarsely, "and we'll take the bed apart. The secret of it is here . . . and the secret of the moving floor."

"You will not have the secret, Dorus Noel, nor you, Leed Boreo!" came the voice out of the air. "Look at the panel!"

Noel whirled.

Boreo, intent on Noel's actions, and his coolies, had stepped into the room. The panel had closed behind them. With a cry Boreo hurled himself at the panel. It opened as all of them hurled themselves at it . . . and all piled pell-mell back into the room where Noel had first met Leed Boreo. Boreo's breath came in panting gasps. His eyes were wild. The lights were on again.

The voice came again out of the air, as Boreo's enemies made use of his own dictaphones, or some of their own installing.

"There is no need of waiting, Boreo," said the voice, "for now it is known that Lan Fei will never come to her bridal chamber. Your words were heard. But we keep our promises. You have, Leed Boreo, exactly ten minutes of life, ten minutes in which to think of your sins. . . ."

Boreo turned to Dorus Noel.

"You have to save me, Noel," he shrieked. "I take back what I said about slaying you. I forgive the slap on the face. I shall give you money. I shall make you a millionaire."

"Why do you not offer *me* millions, Boreo?" came out of the air.

"Those forty millions," answered Boreo, "are yours. You shall have them back when the banks open in the morning."

A brittle laugh was Boreo's answer.

"Not forty times forty millions, Boreo!" came again. "For not all the wealth of the world can return an old man's daughter to life . . . a daughter whom he loved beyond all loving because she was beautiful, and good and sweet, beyond all saying. And she died with the mark of the beast on her, and she was tiny . . . small enough for a porthole . . ."

Boreo went mad. He attacked the panel with his hands, beating against it until his fists bled. Noel broke from his captors, tried to drag the man back from the panel, and the voice sounded again.

"Do not molest him, Dorus Noel. The punishment meted out to him is so little with what he deserves. He cannot woo death, however, before ten minutes have passed."

They passed in madness and horror, with Boreo fighting at the door, struggling to break through the panel to meet his tormentor.

"I shall save you, Boreo," said Noel grimly, fighting at the struggling man. "For you must pay in the electric chair for the murder of Chang Tzo. It was your hands which sent him to death in your place."

Boreo did not seem to hear. Blood from his broken knuckles dyed the secret panel. The ten minutes passed. Silence held away again as the panel swung back and Boreo fell into the bridal chamber,

The "girl" was back on the *kong*, upraised on her right elbow, her left hand combing her hair. Drooling words came from the lips of Boreo.

"Lan Fei! Lan Fei! I have wished for you back every waking second since that night in the stateroom!"

Dorus Noel hurled himself at Boreo, grabbed at his heels, while the floor rocked and rolled under him. Now one thing was plain. The whole floor, undulating, as though the segmented blocks of cloisonné were moving over a rough, uneven surface, was moving straight toward the side of the *kong*. The pool of crimson had vanished, as had the dead hand of Chang Tzo. Noel thought he had the answer now, shrieked it aloud.

"The floor is built like an endless belt, a conveyor belt, Boreo!" he shouted. "It is worked by someone who watches every move. The *kong* is heavy. When you reach it, it will lift, and lower again, and you will go out as Chang Tzo went!"

But Boreo was beyond hearing. Noel turned to yell at the coolies for help. They had vanished. He knew that by now they had left the house entirely, fleeing in dread from the horror of Lan Fei's bridal chamber. It was up to Dorus Noel. He dragged Boreo back in spite of his struggles. He fought back two feet, losing one foot with each two negotiated. He stopped, long enough to fumble at his pockets, drag forth a police whistle.

Through all the queer house rang the strident summons of the whistle. A long moment passed. The two struggling figures had moved so close now to the *kong* that the figure of "Lan Fei" was blurred by their perspective. Noel saw the edge of the *kong* start to lift, as though the *kong* and the floor were a pair of jaws, opening slowly to swallow a victim.

By a superhuman effort, perspiring, almost sobbing with his struggles, Dorus Noel fought back from the jaws of death . . . death for Leed Boreo, death perhaps for himself. His ears caught a far sound . . . the answer, picked up and repeated in several places in Chinatown, to his own whistle.

He gained the door, fighting at the clinging stuff, dragged Boreo through. He panted. Boreo fought him. He smashed Boreo on the jaw with all the power of his right hand. Boreo sighed, relaxed. Noel turned back, looked into the bridal chamber. It was as he had first seen it. He lifted Boreo to his shoulders, started from the house with him.

He found the door, went down the nine steps, stood on the sidewalk with his burden on his back, waiting. His mind was busy with the secrets of that room of the *taotai's* vengeance. He could see it all . . . the pieces of cloisonné, solidly fastened together when the room was not "in use," capable of segmental separation when the *taotai*—whose minions had, he could now see, constructed the whole building, contracting to do it for the sole purpose of building in the secret room—wished to work out the details of his vengeance. Then it was as though the floor of jelly—as though its solid supports had given away to foundations of mesh wire—as invisible machinery did the bidding of the *taotai*.

The wagon came, and the coppers. Boreo moved, sighed, wakened, and Dorus Noel set him down.

"Take him in," said Noel briefly. "The charge is murder!"

Boreo was instantly the Boreo whose reputation Noel so well remembered. His eyes stared at the manacles one of the coppers extended toward him. Then he stared at Noel. He licked his lips with a dry tongue.

When the manacles were fast on his wrists, Dorus Noel's work was ended. He had saved Boreo—for the electric chair. From here on it was up to the uniformed minions of the law. But Boreo was not yet finished.

With a shriek he whirled back to his door.

"I'd rather it be the bridal chamber!" he shouted. "I can't stand waiting for the chair!"

The coppers hampered Noel when they bunched to pursue Leed Boreo. Boreo gained the door, opened it, slammed it. Precious seconds were wasted while the coppers fought to get it open. Sick at heart, Noel led the way to the room where he had first met Boreo. The coppers were at his heels. No sound came to them from anywhere in the house.

Gingerly Noel opened the door to the room off the hallway. As the coppers crowded in he glanced at the secret panel which he would never forget. For a moment he could see nothing. He fumbled for light switches . . . and even the bridal chamber sprang into a blaze of light. Still nothing untoward could be seen . . . by anyone but Dorus Noel. But he knew exactly where to look.

Then a copper gasped, pointed.

"Yes," said Noel softly. "I know. He had it coming, and more."

Two hands, the wrists held close together by glistening manacles, protruded from under the bottom of the empty *kong*, which everywhere rested flush against the solid floor.

SPHERES OF CATHAY

"Don't touch that ball," Noel said, and tensed himself for the expected shot.

Dorus Noel Had to Enter That Chinaman's Den, Though He Knew What Waited for Him, Because the Lives of Millionaires' Sons Were Spotted for the Black Pocket.

DORUS NOEL, FRETTING A LITTLE because for three weeks there had been little activity in his strange field of criminology, walked slowly along Pell Street. The laziness of Chinatown was not natural, he thought. He had the feeling that he skirted a crater filled with powder in which at almost any time some fool might drop a lighted match. Many Chinese who met him smiled a little, and their smiles seemed secretive, as though they knew something he did not know, something he should know.

He had a distinct feeling that he walked with danger such as he had never before experienced. It was in the air, a menace of some sort that was as intangible as he felt it to be real. He wondered if he should not telephone his unknown superior out on Park Avenue to ask if he had heard anything which would seem to indicate that Noel should be on his guard. But he shrugged his shoulders, decided against it . . . at least until he had made several calls he had in mind, two especially.

There had been building activity in Chinatown during the past month, rumors of which had interested him. One place of amusement seemed oddly out of place. He wondered about it tremendously. A Chinese, a graduate of a great American university who, with all his education, had returned to his own. There were stories of some social scandal linking the name of the Chinese, Chung Hua, with a "foreign" woman, which hadn't harmed the prestige of the Chinese, but had set tongues to wagging about the woman. Chung was opening a pool and billiard parlor. The man had made no call on Noel, which wasn't a slight exactly, but which puzzled Noel no little because the educated ones usually sought him out . . . unless there was something secretive about their presence in Chinatown. He wanted to look at Chung Hua.

He whistled with surprise just as he would have turned into the ornately decorated door of the new amusement place.

"Funny I didn't know of this," he told himself.

He read the characters over the door. The place was a carver's establishment, and Noel, remembering all his experience during his many years in China, could vision squint-eyed coolies, squatting on their heels through endless hours, doing miracles in wood, ivory and coral. Chinese delighted in doing mystifying things with their carvings. Before he had been an undercover man, Dorus Noel had been a passionate collector. Things truly Chinese always delighted him and untied his purse-strings.

He could delay his visit to Chung Hua for a few minutes. He walked down the five steps which led to a darkened basement. Chinese artisans were all alike. They worked in subdued lights. A man shuffled forward. He was old and bent. Noel pursed his lips in a soundless whistle. The man wore the beard of venerable wisdom, the traditional beard of five strands—which in the old days had been reserved for scholars alone.

The beard was little known to the west. The strands hung down, each about two inches long, two from the sides of the upper lip, two from below the ears, and one from the chin. Noel closed his lips on the whistle of surprise, and his eyes narrowed a little.

"I did not know a carver had come to Chinatown," he said in English.

"No savvy!"

Noel repeated his statement in Mandarin.

"No savvy."

Noel had no Cantonese, and it didn't matter. This man, he would have sworn, was a North Chinese, probably a Peipingese in spite of his refusal to be drawn into conversation. As well try to lead a balky mule as to make a Chinese talk when he didn't wish to, as this man so plainly did not. But why? Noel might be a prospective customer. Surely the man must talk to his customers.

Noel shrugged and turned away. His lack of insistence would probably puzzle the old man, but that's what he wanted. The feeling which already possessed him, of something wrong in Chinatown, of danger to himself, grew and was stronger than ever.

He reached the top of the steps and fell face forward. Darkness blotted out the world. There had been an explosion in his skull before oblivion . . . then nothingness. A man scurried forward out of nowhere, then vanished again . . . and a crowd began to gather about the prone figure of the unconscious Noel.

Noel wakened in a hospital, where he was informed that he had been rendered unconscious by a blow on the back of the head which should have slain him, and was told that he wouldn't be released from observation unless a relative called for him, within ten days. He fought against the ultimatum until the doctors threatened to put him in a straight-jacket, and finally compromised on being allowed to use the telephone. He called his superior on Park Avenue.

"Good Lord," said that worthy, "we've been scouting the whole city for you. Something has happened."

"Yes? What?"

"Morton Breese is dead!"

"The wealthy polo player?"

"Right . . . and it's in your line. He attended the opening of a pool room in Chinatown . . . and died within an hour of his arrival home. Doctors are mystified. It looks like heart failure . . . but the family physician says it's ridiculous. . . ."

"Get me out of here at once and I'll look into it."

In answer to a question, Noel's superior informed him that it was eleven o'clock at night of the day following that on which Dorus Noel had walked down Pell Street to make his two calls. He had been unconscious around thirty-six hours.

It required exactly fifteen minutes to effect his release, to the tune of profuse apologies on the part of those who had held him. He took a fast taxi to Chinatown, stopped in front of the pool room he had not yet visited, entered the place, asked for Chung Hua. A neatly dressed—in the Occidental fashion—Chinese came out of an office to meet him. The yellow man smoked—incongruous touch—a long cigar. His eyes glittered like obsidian. They stared unblinkingly into those of Dorus Noel.

Noel ignored him long enough to look around the pool room for a few moments. The interior of the place had been decorated to represent the Temple of Heaven at Peking. Huge columns held up the roof. The walls were covered with decorations of every kind imaginable. They seemed to be of some sort of lattice work, and every square inch of them were worked with painted little Chinese figures out of the legendary of the Middle Kingdom. Shepherds herded their flocks . . . and angels waited upon the shepherds. Gods and goddesses disported themselves in fields of blue or light yellow grasses which could only have been born in the fertile brains of Chinese painters who went in for imagery rather than realism. The floor was of teak or an excellent imitation thereof.

A faint odor of incense hung over the place.

The roof was no higher than the average, perhaps twelve feet, but so skillfully had it been painted, it looked as though the huge columns reached up and up to a high temple dome, trickery with the lights helping to create the illusion of immense height. This place, without a doubt, would attract "class" and wealth. It had been created for that.

"Well, Dorus Noel?" said Chung Hua.

Noel expressed no surprise that Chung Hua knew him. There were no secrets in China, why should there be any in Chinatown?

"Quite well, Chung," said Noel quietly, deliberately misinterpreting the man's question. "Thought I'd like to see your place. Mind?"

"Honored by the presence of Chinatown's keeper of the covenants," said Chung Hua blandly, a delicate hint of sarcasm underlying his words. "But first you might tell me exactly what you are after. Dorus Noel does not make aimless visits."

"Morton Breese is dead."

Chung Hua exhibited no surprise.

"All men die," he stated. His eyes roved over his place of business. There were pool tables and billiard tables, all well patronized. The clicking and clacking of balls broke through their words, so that they had to lift their voices to make themselves heard. "But why do you tell me?"

"He died an hour after visiting your place of business. He was rich, in good health. It seemed odd. Isn't that Barry Hymer there? The son of George Hymer, the fifteen-cent-store millionaire?"

He pointed to a young man, flushed of face, loudly talking, who showed signs of having imbibed perhaps a bit too freely, who played pool with three friends. Even as Noel looked at the young man, he picked up the cue ball and turned to an attendant with it. He had just "broken" the racked balls with the white sphere. His voice rose over the hum of conversation and clacking balls in the place.

"What's wrong with this ball?" he demanded. "It's underweight."

The attendant, a Chinese in Oriental garb—which Noel had seen so often in China in gambling establishments—took the ball, hefted it, turned about to study it closer to the nearest light, handed it back, answered in perfect English.

"I think you must be mistaken. It seems all right to me."

Young Hymer took back the ball, hefted it, said, "Damn funny!" And demanded that the balls be racked again, broke them and ran down a round dozen. . . .

"Yes, I said that was Hymer."

Chung Hua's voice came through Noel's abstraction, reminding him of the presence of the Chinese owner of the place. Noel nodded. He started walking, with Chung Hua at his side, down one side of the place. As he neared the table where young Hymer played, the latter spoke abruptly.

"Think I'll beat it, you guys. How much do you owe me?"

Noel stopped in amazement when he heard the amounts mentioned. Hymer had been gambling on his game . . . and the answers of his friends told Noel that he had won four thousand dollars—which those same friends now paid over to him in cash! Chung Hua strode up to the group after Hymer had thrust his winnings into his pockets.

"Gentlemen! Gentlemen!" said Chung Hua. "Do you not see the signs which forbid gambling?"

"Gambling? Who's gambling?" said young Hymer. "We're settling last night's bridge scores."

Contempt—the contempt of the average Occidental for a Chinese—twisted the face of young Hymer as he strode past Chung Hua. Noel excused himself and hurried after Hymer, caught him by the arm as he reached the street.

"Come with me to the nearest hospital, Hymer," snapped Noel. "It's a matter of life and death. We'll take a taxi. I may be wrong. I don't wish to frighten you, but . . ."

Hymer, opening his mouth to protest, went glassy-eyed and offered no objection when Noel signaled a taxi, helped him in, followed him, and yelled at the driver to make plenty of speed. He didn't waste time in talk. In front of the hospital—wondering even as he stepped from the cab how he could gain admittance without the assistance of a doctor to make a commitment—he grasped Hymer by the shoulder.

"Make it snappy!" he said. "There may not be much time."

Hymer's answer was queer, to say the least. He simply said nothing at all. He fell forward, crumpling in the tonneau of the cab. Noel's hand slid instantly under Hymer's coat to feel his heart. It had stopped. Hymer was extremely dead. He took him over his shoulder, carried him inside, deposited him beside a desk, snapped identification of Hymer at a gawping interne, turned and raced from the place—to discover that the taxicab driver had left without waiting for him, or for his fare.

He paused on the curb, undecided. That taxicab driver must have seen that Hymer was dead and had skipped to avoid any possible questioning by the police. Noel scarcely blamed him. Noel's face was bleak. His eyes were narrowed grimly. His jaw muscles were sharp ridges against his face. He knew now what he was up against, knew that but for the merest chance he would have missed it . . . and all Hell would have broken lose in Chinatown. Hell which would have cost the lives perhaps of many of New York City's millionaires.

He knew that the medical diagnosis of whatever had slain Breese and Hymer would be correct, and would end in the doctor's statement that both had died of natural causes—unless Noel did his work thoroughly. And he knew it was cut out for him. Not for nothing had he been placed in his peculiar post in Chinatown. His knowledge of China and of things Chinese had saved lives ere now . . . and had cost others. But the others were lives which were better spared for the general good of humanity.

He alighted before the door of Chung Hua's establishment. A careful observer might have seen the slight bulge of his coat under his arm, where now he carried a snub-nosed automatic. He'd stopped at his own house on Pell Street just long enough to get it. He glanced at the door of the carver's place as he passed it, but it was dark. No, it wasn't utterly dark, but very nearly.

Far back, almost beyond his vision, there was a dim spot of light. The old carver, like a gnome in a cavern, or like a witch preparing her hell's brew, was back there among his shadows and whatever images his aged imagination might create in the semi-darkness, sitting alone, smoking perhaps of the poppy weed, or merely thinking . . . or even, merely sitting, as aged Chinese so often did, comforted by their ages-old philosophy. There was something eerie about that glow of light, but Noel had no time for it now. There was bigger game ahead of him.

He strode into the place which was still running full blast. He wended his way among the many players, cues in hand, who stood about the tables. There was high-pitched laughter, much bawdy language, and Noel was sure that Chung Hua's establishment supplied other things than merely games. He thought he detected the odor of rice wine and wondered how consumers and seller had managed to get together so soon, with no police interference. He strode to the table at which young Hymer had been playing.

Four men played there now. Without so much as an apology Dorus Noel interrupted the play, scooped up the cue ball, stared at it long and intently, turning it over and over in his hands. The fact that he wore gloves may or may not have been noticed. Perhaps it was a concession to the place somehow, for the Chinese attendants, immaculate in their Oriental garb, all wore white cotton gloves . . . as though they hated to contaminate themselves by touching anything touched first by "foreigners."

"What the bloody hell are you trying to do, fella?" demanded one of the players.

"Lay off me!" snapped Noel, not even looking up.

"Then don't interfere with this game, or I'll bend this cue over your head!"

Noel ignored the man and his threat. He was circling the table, shouldering aside players who had bellied up against it. He was running his gloved right hand along under the bottom edges of the cushions, where lint usually gathered on tables which had been used for any length of time. When he had completed his circuit of the table he paused for a moment in thought, shook his head dubiously . . . then crossed the room to a row of telephone-booths, looked up two numbers in the book and dialed the first one: that of Morton Breese.

A woman's voice answered. Noel wasted no time in preliminaries.

"Did Morton Breese have any money on him when he came home?"

"No . . . I . . . who's calling? Who's calling?"

But Dorus Noel had already clicked up the receiver, rang again and spoke to his superior out on Park Avenue, asked exactly the same question. His superior answered.

"It's been kept quiet. Not even his family knows that Morton Breese was mixed up with several shady things, not because he needed money, but because he needed action and excitement. We have it from a close associate of his—information furnished confidentially—that he carried over twenty thousand dollars on his person, to be paid over to two men the night of his death. It appears that he spoke about it several times during the course of a convivial evening which came to a close at that pool hall. This associate informs us that the twenty thousand was never paid to the two men. They themselves made the claim."

Noel knew too much about "putting wires in the bag" and "putting birdies on the line" to ask how his superior had gained such information. Telephone wires had been tapped the very moment Noel's superior had suspected foul play . . . which he had done solely and only because Breese had visited Chinatown just before his death. Chinatown, where so many strange things might be expected to happen to rich men. Noel clicked up the receiver.

He started to dial the second number he had looked up, hesitated, dialed another—the hospital at which he had deposited the body of young Hymer.

"Was there any money on the body of Barry Hymer, just left there?"

"His pockets contained nothing. . . . Who the hell . . ."

He clicked up the receiver without waiting for the rest of it. His head swam with thoughts of the new development. Hymer, to his knowledge, had tucked four thousand dollars into his pocket before leaving Chung Hua's. He hadn't been out of Noel's sight—except perhaps for brief intervals while en route to the door, when he had wended his way through the other players—until Noel had left him at the hospital. Yet somewhere along the way, either before or after the death of Hymer, the money had vanished from his pockets.

Noel stepped from the booth, shut the door behind him, stood with his back against it, surveying the room. His eyes picked out a door slightly ajar, which he was sure led to the private office of Chung Hua. He felt eyes on him from the open crack of the door. They seemed to be malevolent eyes. He shivered a little, unaccountably. His eyes played over the others in the place. Nobody was looking at him.

The Americans seemed intent on their games. The Chinese attendants, two to each table, seemed to be watching their guests. They had their heads lowered after the manner of good servants, but Noel had the distinct impression that every one of them was watching him from the tails of their eyes. He stared further, picking out each table in turn.

He watched a man take his cue ball to the end of the table opposite where the fifteen numbered balls were racked in the shape of a many-colored V. The man placed the ball, stooped, adjusting his cue, preparatory to "breaking." In the midst of it he hesitated, looked strangely at his fellow players, and extended his hand for the cue ball. As he did so the attendant stepped forward, apparently to caution the player to move the ball closer to himself, and covered the ball for a moment with his hand. Then he stepped back.

The player stared at the Chinese belligerently, took the ball in his own hand and placed it back where he had previously planked it down. Then he stared at it in surprise, shook his head, turned to his friends before making the play. His words came distinctly to Dorus Noel.

"Must have been drinking too much. Thought there was something screwy about the cue ball. But it's all right, I guess. And you—you damn'

Chink, keep your nose out of the game unless you're asked to butt in!"

The attendant appeared not even to have heard. Noel felt the sweat starting from his forehead. Things must come to a head soon, he knew, else there would be other deaths. That young man was Carter Hammond, young playboy son of one of New York's richest merchants. How could he bring matters to a head? He decided on a sudden course of action. There seemed little sense in it, but he often played his hunches, especially when it didn't seem that they could do any harm. He raised his voice in a harsh command.

"Don't any of you people—those of you who have large sums of money on your persons—touch your cue balls! Make the attendants handle them!"

Silence settled over the room like a blight. Someone uttered a raucous sound with his lips, deriding this strange man who stood apart, patently drunk. Noel realized that the men must think him either drunk or crazy or both. But he wasn't wasting time now, for he sensed a change in the atmosphere. The two attendants at each table had imperceptibly moved closer together, two by two. They didn't look at him, but their behavior proved to him that his hunch had been a good one.

Now he turned deliberately, momentarily expecting a bullet in the chest, and stood straight toward the door which stood ajar. Once his hand flicked past his lapel, making sure of the snub-nosed automatic which nestled under his arm. He reached the door and nothing happened. He pushed the door open, stepped in.

Chung Hua, smoking a fresh cigar, seemed deeply immersed in a pile of papers on his desk. He didn't even look up. Dorus Noel found a chair which he pulled forward. He sat down, pulled a cigar from his own pocket, lighted it. The sound of the dragging chair caused Chung Hua to hear him, and the Chinese looked up.

"You back again?" he said. "Who's dead now?"

"Barry Hymer."

The Chinese's eyebrows lifted, his slitted orbs widened. That was the only sign of interest he vouchsafed.

"Well?" he said, finally.

"Get your attendants in here, Chung!" snapped Noel.

"My attendants? Have you gone crazy?"

"Maybe. If you're on the up and up it can't do you any harm. If you're not . . ."

He left it there, for Chung Hua to make of it whatever he cared to.

"If I refuse?" said Chung.

"You won't," said Noel quietly. Chung Hua's eyes lowered to the weapon which lay in the palm of Noel's hand on his knee. Noel allowed him a glimpse, then covered the hand with his left palm. Chung Hua shrugged, pressed a button. No sooner had he pressed the button than Noel was out of his chair, with his back against a wall, where he could face both the desk of Chung Hua and the door. He thought he could make out the outlines of a second door, behind and to the right of Chung Hua as the Chinese sat at his desk, but he commanded that, too.

His one concern was the fact that his automatic held but seven shots, that he had but two extra clips, neither of which he might have time to insert in the weapon . . . even if he ever had a chance to fire the seven which nestled under the weapon's hammer.

The door which gave in from the billiard and pool room opened and yellow men, whose faces were grim and hard now, whose eyes were not cast down at all, whose attitudes were those of arrogant self-assurance, entered. Their black eyes went at once to the form of Dorus Noel standing against the wall. Chung Hua barked a command at his men—all of them table attendants . . . and they lined up against the walls not used by Noel. The hands of most of them were inside their gowns, over the breasts . . . and their left hands, still gloved, held their right-hand gloves! Their bare hands were hidden . . . and Noel was sure that in their gown they grasped the butts of weapons of murder. He let out his breath slowly, awaiting developments.

Chung Hua, all trace of friendliness gone from his face—if ever his face could have been said to have shown friendliness at all—looked up at Dorus Noel.

"Well, fool?" he barked.

"Make them show their right hands," said Noel.

Chung Hua stared at Noel for a moment, his lips twisted in a snarl. Then he turned to his men, his eyes following their ranks around. He snapped out a single word in Cantonese. One of the Chinese moved. His hand came forth from his sleeve with the speed of a serpent striking. At exactly the same moment Noel's right hand lifted a little . . . and his automatic flamed. The Chinese who had made the movement plunged face forward to the floor . . . a small hole squarely in the center of his forehead.

"In murder cases, Chung Hua," said Noel quietly. "One cannot always take time to analyze every movement of the enemy. Too bad if I had made a mistake and his hand hadn't held a knife, eh?"

A knife quivered in the floor at Noel's feet. Only the forward plunge of the Chinese had deranged his lightning swift aim so that his cast was too low for the knife to bury itself in some vital spot in the body of the undercover man. Chung Hua let out his breath with a queer sibilance. His eyes were very round, but even as Noel noticed this, they narrowed again. The face of the Chinese did not change in the slightest. If he looked again at the dead man Noel did not catch him at it. His voice did not change as he spoke again.

"You are careful of your safety, Dorus Noel."

"Naturally, since on my safety depends the safety of so many of New York's rich men's sons."

"I am afraid you know too much, Dorus Noel, however much of it may be guesswork. You are a dangerous man."

"Thanks. Do you care to tell me what the big idea is, before whatever happens between us that is due to happen. I wish—"

The automatic flamed again as an attendant made an almost imperceptible movement of his right hand. The bullet pinned the man's hand to his left breast for a moment. His knees gave away. He toppled forward. His hand came forth, with blood dripping along the backs of the fingers . . . and a second knife clattered to the floor as the fellow sprawled his length, coughing slightly. The bullet had gone through his hand, into his heart. It had probably mushroomed, blasting its way through the man's chest, placing him beyond all possibility of saving by even New York's greatest physician. He died with the breath wheezing from his paralyzed chest.

"—that you would be a good guy," went on Noel imperturbably, "and give me the low-down. You know you're caught, and if you spill, it will save everybody a great deal of trouble."

"True, possibly," said Chung Hua, in a manner which seemed to consider a passably important controversial matter in which he was but slightly interested. He flicked the ash from his cigar into a tray. His hand did not tremble. He looked at the glowing end of his cigar. "But you've forgotten something, Dorus Noel. This room is soundproof. The last man in closed the door. I'm the only person here who can open it. Of course you could pound on it, but that would be contingent upon one thing which will not come to pass."

"I understand," said Noel coldly, "it's contingent upon whether I'll be able even to reach the door. As to that there may be a difference of opinion."

"I think not. You have five shots left that you will be able to use, Noel. I don't mind losing five more men. What I plan to do is worth that many. The other two clips which you had in your pockets are of no use to you. . . ."

"Which I *had* . . ."

Noel started to thrust a hand into his pocket. Instantly many right hands moved slightly. He straightened a bit more, smiled grimly, looked at Chung Hua with approval.

"I almost fell for it, Chung," he said. "If I'd got my hand into my pocket your men would have nailed me before I could have got it out again. I suppose one of them got my clips while I was outside, fiddling around the table where Barry Hymer was murdered. Your men have facile fingers, Chung."

"They were carefully selected," said Chung, "because of that very fact—

no surprise to you because you already know it, and too much else besides."
Chung Hua sighed a little.

"Might as well get it over with, Noel," he said. "It starts now."

Noel wasted one of his five precious bullets. It went into the wall back
of Chung Hua's chair. Had Chung remained where Noel had last seen him
it would have gone through his shoulder, smashing it, rendering the Chinese
helpless. But where Chung Hua had been there now was—merely an empty
swivel chair. Chung Hua had vanished as though the floor had swallowed
him. It had.

And his going had been a signal.

The remaining Chinese moved with unbelievable speed, but Noel was
expecting that and moved ever so perceptibly faster. He hurled himself at the
door near Chung Hua's desk. Knives buried their blades in the wall against
which he had been leaning. Two men spun toward him, their hands snaking
forth. He fired twice. That left him two bullets. He started banging on the
second door with his left fist, yelling . . .

"Hartigan . . . Morrison . . . Flannigan . . ."

He was using the names of police officers who had patrolled Chinatown
for years, who must surely be known to every man here. If, for even a fleeting
instant, he could make them believe that he had officers planted beyond
that door, he might have a chance. Every second of life was precious to a
man who's mind worked with speed and precision. Whole schemes could be
laid out, under stress, in a heartbeat. By the time they guessed that he was
bluffing . . .

The Chinese guessed it almost at once . . . and he wasted one more shot.

Then he used the last one . . . and the cluster of lights over Chung Hua's
desk smashed out under the impact of his bullet and the soundproof room
was in utter darkness. He banged on the door again . . . then jumped to his
right, knowing that the Chinese had charged. As he felt for the chair Chung
Hua had quitted he tried to remember something. . . .

"Where were his hands the last infinitesimal instant I saw him? Where
were they?"

He remembered Chung Hua moving his right hand forward to flick the
ash from his cigar, remembered how his eyes had followed the movement, as
had those of Chung Hua himself. He cursed himself for a fool.

"He did that deliberately," said Noel to himself, "to keep me from seeing
what his left hand did. Where was it?"

He tried to take the position in the chair, without moving it to make it
squeak, Chung Hua had last taken. His left hand fell to the edge of the desk,
palm downward. That brought his left thumb free of the desk edge entirely.

To his right, while he concentrated fiercely on what he did, yet could not
help hearing his enemies, the Chinese were all entangled with one another

at the door. They must have thought he had performed a miracle to escape them. Had he, they must have thought, somehow managed to get through that door in the infinitesimal moment since the lights had been shot out?

His thumb played along under the desk edge. He knew that the Chinese wouldn't come to the desk for several moments. It would be inviolate for a brief time, because it belonged to their master. Even in little things, Chinese—even the minions of a master of murder—were respectful to their bosses. Noel's thumb found a button, pressed it.

The chair edge slid forward with the speed of light. Under his feet was only space. He felt himself falling. He went limp. He heard something click into place above him, knew that the floor section under the desk, and the chair itself, had jumped back to their normal positions. He fell, at a guess, ten feet. He plunged into something soft. Instantly he covered his throat with his left forearm, expecting a knife thrust.

But nothing came. There was no sound. If Chung Hua were here anywhere, he gave no sign. There was a musty odor in the place. He judged he had fallen into a basement. He rose to his feet, taking stock of himself. No bones broken. With all the knives that had been thrown he was fortunate to be alive. He thanked his gods for quick hands and feet and excellent coordination of both with his brain. These only had saved him, as they often had in the past.

He began to feel around him. Yes, it was a basement. There should be some way out of it. Probably Chung Hua didn't give him credit for being able to reach this place. Perhaps that's why the man hadn't waited to see whether he followed him into the pit. He had fallen on what seemed to be a feather mattress or a pile of rugs.

His hands came in contact with a damp wall. He began to feel his way along it. The hair at the base of his skull shifted oddly. He had the feeling that even in the darkness eyes were on him, that at any moment knives might slice into him from behind. But his fingers kept on inching along the wall, his feet made no sound as he edged forward to keep pace with his hands. His fingers finally touched wood and he breathed a sigh of relief. It took him half a minute to find the knob of a door. It gave under his hand . . . and straight ahead of him he saw a dull glow of light.

There was a shadowy form near the light. A man sat there in a scholarly pose, chin in hand, apparently reading. He could make out several of the strands of the five-strand beard. The old carver was dozing over some Chinese volume, he decided. The old, usually, were rather deaf. If he could get out past this man . . .

He closed the door behind him. He could just make out a further glow of light beyond the old man, where lights from the street sought to pass through the debris of the old man's back room. There somewhere was the door leading out. Noel gritted his teeth. He'd go through that door and back into Chung Hua's to continue the battle. From somewhere came the sounds of men laughing loudly, the voices of men telling bawdy jests.

The pool room was still going full blast. Probably nobody had heard a sound from the room he had just escaped. Only Chung Hua, he remembered, could open that door. The men against whom he had just fought were prisoners until Chung Hua appeared again, or the door was cut through by the police. Noel grinned to himself. It was a race between himself and Chung Hua as to who would act in the pool room first.

He guessed that when one crew of men had entered Chung Hua's office, they had instantly been replaced by another . . . all so deftly done that the players hadn't noticed. Chung Hua could be trusted not to overlook anything so obvious.

Noel's foot touched something. It made a sound. A voice in English came softly to Noel.

"What are you seeking, my son?"

Noel, almost past the stooped, seated old man, whirled and looked. The old man's face was bland, but Noel looked deeply into his eyes, thought he caught a glimpse of mockery . . . and came instantly to a decision.

He grabbed the old man by the back of his gown, dragged him from his chair with a brief command to keep his mouth shut . . . and hurried him to the door, half dragging him. He banged his way through, disregarding the old man's request that he not break the door, and climbed the five steps to the street. There he yanked the police whistle which he always carried, from his pocket, and blew it shrilly.

His answer was the banging of several nightsticks at various points around the place . . . that and the instant keening of several sirens on what he knew to be police radio cars. His superior out on Park Avenue, then, was overlooking no bets.

But simultaneously with the coming of the coppers—cars began to stream into Pell Street, together with motorcycles ridden by men in uniform, and lumbering harness bulls on foot—a stream of Chinese poured from Chung Hua's place and raced toward Noel and his prisoner.

They yelled as they came . . . and Noel shouted to the coppers.

"Get them! Shoot to kill!"

In the forefront, brandishing a weapon, came Chung Hua. His face was a mask of horror . . . and Noel chuckled, knowing exactly why, in one of those brief flashes of inspiration which sometimes came to him in moments of need. Chung Hua cried:

"Release him before they reach you! I shall take his place!"

As Chung Hua came within jumping distance, Noel hurled himself forward, knocking Chung Hua out with a straight right to the button. Then he jumped back, grabbed the old man by the collar just as the old fellow would have darted back into his basement.

The police rounded up Chung Hua's men with their usual proficiency.

Then, with two detective lieutenants in attendance, Noel returned to the pool room. The players stopped when the mob entered and ranged themselves along the wall. Noel strode to the table where Hymer had been playing . . . looked at a solitary Chinese who stood as though turned to stone. Noel extended his hand. It was noticeable that it was covered by a leather glove.

"Give me the ball!" he snapped.

This he held up to the two detective lieutenants. He shook it. It rattled slightly.

"Chinese carvers take pride in this sort of thing," he said. "This ball is really two, one inside the other. That's simple for a good carver. They have been known to carve twenty ivory balls . . . inside one another! They carve the outer one first, then cut a hole of pinpoint size, through which they carve the next one, using instruments no Occidental would understand. Then they pull the second ball close against the orifice, and bore into it as they bored into the first, carving out another ball. And if you think that sounds tough, listen . . . they can work all sorts of designs on each successive ball . . . though what good they are when nobody ever sees them is a mystery.

"Well, this old man did the carving. Chung Hua ordered the balls, one ball inside the other, to make it simple. The holes which made the carving possible were then plugged up . . . and when a Chinese carver plugs a hole it's almost invisible, even to a microscope. But the plugging *will* come out, especially if it is intended that it shall, when some drinking pool player *bangs* the cue ball hard against fifteen others that are solid. The player notices that the ball is different. He hefts it. The poisonous substance inside the second ball, released when the plugs are knocked out, runs onto his hands. Even the best kept hands have abrasions on them unknown to their owners. You see? The stuff—probably some deadly derivation from *ma huang*, a heart stimulant when properly used, a heart paralyzing agent when too strong— gets into the blood, and the victim dies of heart failure.

"Nimble fingers take his money sometime during the festivities. Later, when the victims have 'died of natural causes,' their deaths can be alluded to in furtive threats which may make their friends and relatives cough up plenty of money to keep from suffering a like fate. Only, we caught this deadly racket before it got to that stage. Look, here are the tiny plugs which fell out of the cue ball that killed Hymer. I got them from his table. The attendant who palmed the ball when he got suspicious, substituting one that was all right, overlooked these little items. Don't be surprised at the palming; Chinese have been known to produce bowls of goldfish, and even half-grown mulberry trees, from the folds of their gowns."

"But where does this old man come in, did you say?" asked Lieutenant Hawkins.

"He didn't do anything!" It was the voice of Chung Hua, now keenly alive to what was going on.

Dorus Noel grinned.

"He's sending you to the chair, Chung Hua," said Noel. "If he hadn't spoken when I stumbled over something in his rat's nest, I wouldn't have looked around and seen a certain billiard ball, tinted with crimson, and with some of my own hair clinging to it, on a shelf beyond his table. Naturally I connected billiard balls with this place . . . and grabbed him. Your flying to his defense can mean but one thing: He's your dad, isn't he? You chaps, even when you are murderers, are loyal to your parents. Oh, I know he didn't throw the ball at me. He's too old and too nearly blind. If it's any comfort to you I'll see that his expenses are defrayed back to China, where he can leave his bones in the soil of his fathers.

"Now, fellows, get the rest of this gang. They're in Chung Hua's office. . . ."

"Listen," said Chung Hua earnestly, "send the old man back soon, will you? I don't want him to wait until . . ."

"Until you burn, eh? I know. I will, on one condition . . . that you come clean."

Instantly Chung Hua nodded.

"Beats all," said Hawkins, shaking his head, "how even Chinks like this buzzard will die to save their parents from inconvenience."

"Not at all," said Noel quickly. "Not when you know Chinese! To them family is everything . . . greater even than greed of money . . . or fear of the electric chair!"

DESIGN FOR MURDER

*The officer threw up his weapon
for a quick shot at the Chinese boy.*

**Dorus Noel and the Sinister Master Used Mysterious
Chinatown for Their Chessboard and Human Lives as
Pawns; and Though the Master Had Many Pawns, Noel
Held a King.**

IT WAS RATHER A STARTLING THING, even to the mind of Dorus Noel, who should
never really have been startled at anything. And yet, after all his time in
China, it was a wonder the thought hadn't occurred to him. In five years in
China it had almost ruined him—destroyed his ambition, made him utterly
lazy. Chinese servants, in their homeland, were perfection, especially when
"foreign" trained.

In Tientsin, Shanghai or Peking, when one was served by Chinese "boys" one was never allowed to light one's cigarette, find carpet slippers, flip the ash from a cigar, find a chair, or open a door. One's servants did absolutely everything. One wished for something and there stood the perfect servant with the thing in his hand. They were amazing.

Five years of Chinese servants and an American man or woman found all others impossible enough to murder, and themselves unable even to breathe without help. So Dorus Noel thought of the matter. Perfect servants. Where, any place else in the world, could perfect servants be found? Yellow servitors almost ate, slept and bathed for their masters. If their peculiar arts spread . . .

And now it seemed that their arts were to spread. Some enterprising American, Noel thought, must have figured out a new way to become wealthy. But no, the man who initiated the idea, if observation meant anything, was a Chinese who just happened to be a graduate from Harvard. He did a very simple thing. He opened an employment agency in Chinatown.

He must have had the Chinese government backing his play to have worked the thing out as he was apparently working it out. Two hundred handsome young Chinese men had been brought into the country, under heavy bond for a period of six months, with option for two renewals for the same period.

And Dorus Noel stood looking into a long building on Mott Street, where Tsa Liu, the Harvard graduate, was working out his inspiration. The young Chinese he had imported were all from Peking and Tientsin, husky, upstanding young men. And Tsa Liu was teaching them better English.

Noel guessed that all of them had served in "foreign" homes in China, where they had picked up just enough English to serve. Tsa Liu was perfecting them. Their sing-song repetition of certain phrases, coming out through the open door, were what had attracted Dorus Noel's attention to the "school." He smiled as he listened, heard the young Chinese repeating after Tsa Liu:

"Dinner is served, master."

"Cocktails, master?"

"Is the dinner satisfactory, missy?"

Tsa Liu was being thorough. He was teaching his prospective servants to ask every conceivable question they might be called upon to answer as servants in American homes. And teaching them the proper answers to those questions. He was carefully teaching them the exact translations of the English words in their own dialects. The Tientsinese and Pekinese varies but slightly from the once official Mandarin. Dorus Noel moved closer to the building as he listened, his eyes glued to a huge red poster on the wall, covered with Chinese characters in black. He could read Chinese readily. In effect, the poster set forth as follows:

> Chinese servants are the best in the world. Tsa Liu, master of servants, is the world's best teacher of servants. Make your choice from among the pupils of Tsa Liu for the small sum of forty dollars weekly, and you may dispense with your cook, your valet, your butler, and even your chauffeur, for the servant of your selection will undertake all those tasks for you, and do them faster than all the servants to whom you now pay, in the aggregate, many times that sum.

The statement spoke the exact truth, Noel knew, provided these handsome young men were even approximately as efficient as the "boys" who had once served Dorus Noel during his sojourn in China. He made a mental note to hire one of them himself, and at once. It would give a sort of completeness to his life in New York's Chinatown. He wondered, though, just what Tsa Liu expected to accomplish with a sign in Chinese. He came to a decision, entered the place. Instantly Tsa Liu stopped his lecturing. Two hundred pairs of almond eyes turned on Dorus Noel. Tsa Liu came forward smiling.

"Ah," he said, "the famous Dorus Noel. This is indeed an honor. I shall do myself the honor of selecting your servant myself. It shall be Lung Fao, whom I had intended reserving for myself because, of all these perfect servants, he is easily the best. And for you I shall make a price of thirty-five dollars per week. Lung Fao!"

A young Chinese came forward to stand before Dorus Noel, his eyes respectfully cast down.

"Yes, master?" he said softly, addressing Noel.

"The man is yours, Dorus Noel," said Tsa Liu.

Noel spoke to his new servant.

"My house is just off the intersection of Pell and Mott Streets. You will go there, inform my Cantonese boy that I shall pay him well for discharging him, when I return home, and you will take complete charge. Here are my keys."

"Yes, master," and Lung Fao was gone. Tsa Liu kept on smiling.

But Dorus Noel was troubled, without in the slightest understanding why. All this was too open and aboveboard, he felt, to be as Chinese as it seemed. Nor was his doubt alleviated when, leaving the servant school, he purchased a newspaper from a Chinese newsboy. In the want ad section he found, in English, practically a word for word copy of what he had just read on the poster in Chinese. Tsa Liu was going after candidates. Dorus Noel knew very well that Tsa Liu probably paid his boys something like fifteen dollars a month out of their own salary, retaining almost a hundred and fifty dollars for himself.

Two hundred times one hundred and fifty—why, Tsa Liu, if all his servants found positions among the wealthy, would himself be wealthy in a very short time! And yet everything was legal. Dorus Noel even felt a bit of admiration for the enterprising Tsa Liu.

But just to be on the safe side, he went to his usual telephone, in a cigar store on the corner of Canal and Lafayette Streets, and called his superior out on Park Avenue—the unknown police official who had given Noel his undercover job in Chinatown, to see that the Chinese kept the peace. The unknown one had scarcely recognized the voice of Dorus Noel than he spoke excitedly, not waiting to discover why Noel had called him.

"Noel, just what do you know about Chinese porcelain?"

"Considerable, sir. Their manufacture dates back before Christ. Their cobalt blue, their gold, their celadon or jade green, their peach bloom, their variously tinted rose porcelain . . ."

"That's enough, Noel. I can see you know something about porcelain. What, for example, would a porcelain vase of the authentic Kang Hsi period, bearing the imperial stamp, be worth to an American collector?"

Noel gasped, wondering whither the question was leading.

"At a conservative estimate," he said, "fifty thousand dollars in cold cash!"

"And now suppose that the Kang Hsi vase were of the eggshell porcelain variety . . ."

"Impossible!" The eggshell stuff didn't come in until Ch'ien Lung—"

"But if there *were* such porcelain, not one specimen but scores, what would they represent in money?"

"There isn't any such porcelain. I wouldn't believe it even if I saw it stamped with the imperial seal of Kang Hsi."

"Well, you're wrong. Somehow, somewhere, at least sixty pieces of eggshell porcelain, stamped by Kang Hsi—or with his stamp so expertly faked that not even our most brilliant collector would dare pronounce it counterfeit—have entered the country. It is duty free because of its great age. Tough as times are, the pieces are being bought up by Park Avenue at fabulous prices."

"But why all the excitement about them?"

"Just this. There is record of sixty pieces, but in each case where Customs men have checked on the ultimate purchasers of the stuff, additional pieces have been found to a total of almost a hundred and fifty. And these pieces also seem to be genuine."

"I still don't see."

"Well, Chinese are in it. And thousands upon thousands of dollars are involved. In this day and age you know what that can mean?"

"Yes. Robbery. Blackmail. Extortion. *Murder!*"

"Right! I've nothing to go on, but if anything unusual happens in Chinatown—"

"Something *is*," retorted Noel as he quickly retailed what he had discovered about the servant school of Tsa Liu. His boss gasped. His voice rose to a fever pitch of excitement.

"Noel, you've got to be on your toes. Something is going to happen. Something that will shake New York City to its foundations. I feel it. And you can't take steps until something happens. It's no crime to sell porcelain on which duty has been paid, nor to teach properly entered young Chinese how to be good servants, but just the same . . . well, what else is there?"

The connection was severed. Noel walked thoughtfully back to his quarters. As he approached the "school" of Tsa Liu he noticed fully a dozen huge cars, driven by chauffeurs in livery, waiting in line before what amounted to a Chinese employment agency. Wealthy families uptown were already answering the ads of Tsa Liu, and pouring their dollars—all quite legitimately—into the pockets of the graduate of Harvard. Noel swore softly. He entered his house. Lung Fao took his hat, thrust a cigarette between Noel's lips, lighted it. Noel grinned. It was good to have so much attention again.

He entered his favorite room. It was filled with Chinese bric-a-brac which he himself had collected. Clocks of strange design, tapestries beyond price, feather screens, jade ornaments, cloisonné, porcelain. He thought of porcelain and stopped. For there resting on a shelf back of the feather screen was a porcelain vase whose sides were as thin, almost, as tissue paper, a gorgeous, beautiful thing.

But Noel had never seen it before! He whirled on Lung Fao.

"Where did that come from, Lung?"

Lung Fao's eyes widened.

"It was here when I entered the place and kicked out the Cantonese, master," he said.

"Do you know what it is?"

"Yes. An imitation of Ch'ien Lung eggshell porcelain, stamped with the seal of His Imperial Majesty, Kang Hsi. It is worth perhaps two dollars."

Noel moved to the shelf, gingerly took down the piece, stared at it. He knew something of porcelain, but as he studied this vase his mystification deepened, became something bordering on fear. He turned to Lung Fao.

"Lung," he said, "you may be a smart servant, but you don't know porcelain. That vase is worth all I could earn in fifty years of working without sleep if I were paid ten times what I am actually worth."

Lung Fao shrugged. Obviously he didn't believe it. He changed the subject:

"Tea ready, master."

Noel partook of tea in an adjoining room, but the Kang Hsi vase stuck in his mind, and when he had finished he came back to finger the priceless, useless ornament . . . and uttered a shout of dismay, almost terror. Lung Fao came running. Noel was holding up the vase.

"Lung," he said, "when I handled this last it was worth . . . it was priceless. Now it is worth even less than the two dollars you mentioned!"

"My have tell you!" said Lung Fao imperturbably, relapsing into the pidgin of his servitude with foreign masters in his home land.

Noel thrust his face close to that of his boy and said, "If anything the least bit out of the way happens here," he said, "I shall kill you without the slightest compunction."

The statement seemed uncalled for. Noel thought he could see the mockery in the eyes of his servant. Yet he wouldn't send him back to Tsa Liu, for here was a clue to the mystery.

That evening a late edition of the biggest newspaper reported the death of Gerard Servis, a wealthy Wall Street manipulator. He had just left his downtown bank for home. He was stricken with apoplexy just as he stepped into his car.

Servis' picture was shown and there was a long story because the man had been wealthy. There was also the picture of his car and chauffeur. That same car and chauffeur had been before the servant school of Tsa Liu that same afternoon. Noel's first act was to telephone the home of Servis, where he asked for the butler.

"Did Mrs. Servis hire a Chinese servant this afternoon?"

"Who calls? Who wishes to know? There are no Chinese here."

The receiver clicked up. Noel had listened too often to English on the lips of Chinese to be mistaken. The man who had answered him was Chinese! Noel had a feeling of great urgency, so for the first time he called his Park Avenue superior from his own telephone.

"Tell me," he said, "did Gerard Servis buy one of those Kang Hsi vases?"

"Yes. Two days ago. Why?"

"He's dead, isn't he?"

"My God! I had a hunch . . ."

But Noel had clicked up the receiver. He now dialed police headquarters.

"Hold everything," he said, "including the doctor who diagnosed apoplexy in the case of Gerard Servis. Servis was murdered. I don't know how, but—"

"We know he was murdered," came the grim reply, "but who are you? Nobody is supposed to know except the doctor—and the murderer! Who are *you*?"

Noel clicked up. The coppers would trace the call but drop any investigation when they found his name. Noel turned and found himself staring into the black eyes of Lung Fao.

"You remember what I said!"

"Yes, master. But I give you no reason!"

The answer was strange, startling, for Noel had been intending to remind the boy of his intention to kill him in case anything went wrong. Noel hadn't completed the wording of his thought but the boy had answered anyway, as though he had read Noel's mind. It was uncanny, frightening. In spite of himself, Noel gave the boy a wide berth as he went past him into the room which held his Oriental collections. Noel's eyes went to the vase on the shelf and a startled oath leaped unbidden from his lips. The eggshell vase had taken on a delicate rose color!

Noel whirled on Lung Fao.

"Has anybody been in here? What makes that vase change color? Is it the same vase? It must be. You couldn't have changed it. Lung Fao, what does it mean?"

"Maybe message from long-dead Imperial Master!" Lung Fao's almond eyes were narrowed. The boy seemed poised as though for a spring. Mentally Dorus Noel tensed. It was damned odd that Lung Fao should have put into words the odd fancy which had come to Dorus Noel when he had read of the death of Gerard Servis.

Nothing made sense, and yet—Noel waited, fully expecting to hear extras cried in the street, to hear of the deaths of other wealthy men. But nothing happened and the tension grew until it seemed to Noel that all Chinatown, all New York, were holding its breath in readiness—for what?

Noel wiped the sweat from his brow. Something was awfully wrong, dead wrong, and he didn't know which way to turn. Something had to be done to break the spell. He did the first thing that came to his mind. Suddenly, he stepped in close to Lung Fao and drove a savage right fist into the Chinese boy's stomach.

Lung Fao fell backward. Wearing the Chinese gown of the regular servant, his hands had been in his sleeves. As he gasped and fell backward, his hands shot from his sleeves.

Out of the right hand of Lung Fao came a slender knife with a green jade handle. It clattered on the floor. Noel jumped forward to grab the knife. He heard a crash, and something hard struck him on the back of the head. He thought he heard Lung Fao laughing. His blurred eyes showed him that he fell toward Lung Fao, whose right hand groped for the knife he had lost. The hand started up and Noel tried desperately to fling himself aside, to escape that blade. Another shock, then oblivion.

His very first knowledge on returning to consciousness was that the

Kang Hsi vase had been smashed into thousands of infinitesimally small pieces, on the floor under the shelf where it had thrice undergone miraculous metamorphoses. His next knowledge was that his room of Chinese curios, sacred hitherto to himself alone, was defiled by the presence of two strapping coppers in uniform. He rose on his elbow and stared at them. One was staring down at the shattered vase. The other was looking out the open window. Lung Fao was gone. So was his knife.

"What the devil happened?" asked Noel of the coppers.

The man at the window turned.

"We're of the radio patrol," he said. "Just got a call to come here and see what was happening. Something about a telephone call. We came on the jump. We looked through the window, saw you fall and just miss getting knifed by a Chink boy you probably had just knocked down. He was twisting around to get a fresh crack at you with his knife when I took a snap shot at him through the window.

"Listen, Mr. Noel, is everything screwy around here? I missed that Chink clean. My partner and I came into this room through the window there"—he indicated a window opposite that at which he was standing—"because if we'd taken time to come through the door the Chink would have knifed you. But fast as we were, that buzzard was chained lightning. He got to his feet, holding onto his knife, and flung himself at this window. But on the way he jumped aside just long enough to grab that gadget off the shelf and smash it against the floor. He used both hands, holding them at arm's length above his head, to make sure he busted the vase plenty. Now tell me how I happened to miss him, where he went between the time he jumped through the window and when I looked out, and I'll prove to you that two and two make five!"

"That," Noel said grimly, "is just about what I have to prove. But I've got an idea now. If Lung Fao hadn't broken the vase I might never have got the answer. Thank God headquarters believes in tracing strange telephone calls. Thank God also for the radio patrol. And say, I don't know what's going to happen next, but I've got a police whistle. You may hear it in Chinatown sometime during the course of the night. Please be around where you can get to me. You're right. This is screwy. And if it weren't for the apoplexy of Gerard Servis, they'd have got away with it, instead of stubbing their toes just as they started."

"What the devil are you talking about?"

"If I told you, you'd take me to the booby hatch."

"We would now, if the chief hadn't told us to lay off you! We're not good at riddles! Give us something to start on, won't you?"

Noel grinned a tight grin.

"Sure," he said "you have to know a hell of a lot about Chinese servants, and have some inkling of at least the rudiments of chess. Only this chess game is played with the lives—or fortunes—of human beings at stake."

The two coppers looked at Noel queerly. But he had a reputation for success in unraveling strange crimes, else he wouldn't have been in Chinatown. They shook their heads. The spokesman agreed that his patrol car would cruise within the limits of Chinatown until they heard further from Dorus Noel.

He looked behind him. His back had been squarely to the window through which the coppers said Lung Fao had gone. Somebody had thrown something at him just as he would have done something drastic to his boy with the mocking eyes. He'd got that servant from Tsa Liu, and Tsa Liu must give him some further hints as to the answer to the rapidly growing riddle. If it were as bizarre and unusual as Noel thought, it was unbelievable, required more proof, more evidence—each bit of evidence unbelievable in itself. The whole would make up proof that even an Occidental jury would accept as good enough to send a man to the chair!

Noel deliberately went out and down the street to the school run by Tsa Liu. He entered, his face very grim, and asked a single question:

"Have you a list of the people who hired servants from you today?"

Tsa Liu, whose face was utterly expressionless, arched his black eyebrows, then nodded and gave the list to Noel without further words. Noel thought he saw the same mockery in the eyes of Tsa Liu he had seen in those of Lung Fao. He opened his mouth to ask Tsa Liu point blank about Lung Fao but Tsa Liu answered the unspoken question.

"He's dead. Suicide caused by sorrow that he had failed his master!"

Dorus Noel understood and shuddered inwardly. Tsa Liu had actually told him that Lung Fao had been murdered for bungling. And when Tsa Liu used the word "master" there was a double meaning to it. Tsa Liu, if he were not in turn the underling of some one unknown to Noel, had killed Lung Fao for bungling his job. What that job was Noel could only guess.

He strode back to his own residence. As he went he was thinking of the strange experiences he had had with his servants and of experiences of Occidentals in China told to him. The resources of Chinese servants were inexhaustible, They could furnish meals on order for one guest or twenty, formal or informal, with every piece of table silver in place, in any given period of time.

His own servants had furnished such meals, piping hot, when Noel knew very well that his icebox was, or should have been practically empty. But he knew how they did it. Servants exchanged things. Let one of them have a sudden need for food and table service, and he called on his fellow servants in the neighborhood and the iceboxes of neighbors, and their silver cabinets were sacked to provide the unexpected feasts.

"And there," Noel said to himself, recalling, "is the key to the riddle. But I've got to unwind the cord leading out of the labyrinth step by step."

Noel's first step was to check the list Tsa Liu had given him. He discovered that the twenty uptowners who had taken servants from Tsa Liu that afternoon lived within a radius of four city blocks of one another, out on Park Avenue. Noel smiled inwardly, wondering if his own boss might not live within the very heart of the section in which Noel was so vastly interested.

Noel's next step was to plan his campaign carefully. He waited for darkness. Then, thrusting a key-ring containing many keys into one of his pockets, he approached the now silent building where Tsa Liu taught his pupils. Noel's heart pounded with excitement. He might draw an utter blank. Or perhaps a dagger through the heart.

Tsa Liu's building seemed to be deserted. It was utterly dark. He glanced right and left along the street, then darted into the doorway, where he searched his key-ring until he found a key which opened the outer door. He left the door ajar, opened a side window and ducked inside. He stepped swiftly aside so as not to be outlined against the faint light which came through the window. One never could tell who or what might be waiting in the shadows of the building with drawn knife ready for hurling.

Dorus Noel waited for a long time, holding his breath to listen, but heard nothing. Then far away, he heard a faint roaring sound. He started moving toward the back of the room where Tsa Liu held "classes." And as he progressed the roaring sound became perceptibly louder. Noel's heart beat high with excitement, for he knew the meaning of that roaring sound. It came from a muffled blast furnace somewhere in the earth under the building. To another investigator that would mean a private crematory, where a mass killer destroyed the gruesome evidence of his crimes. To Noel it meant something vastly different—though he hadn't the slightest doubt that Lung Fao might have been thrown into the furnace.

He hesitated, then pressed his ear against the floor and gasped. Yes, the sound came from far below. Somewhere in the back of the place, or perhaps even in some Chinese-occupied building a full block away, there was a way which led down to the mysterious furnace room. Noel might go directly to it from here, or search for weeks to find it. Such a visit, at this stage of the game, he decided, would scarcely be worth the risk, since it would only confirm his suspicions. His one desire was to get out.

And at exactly that moment men piled onto him out of the darkness. Noel grinned as heavy bodies crashed against him, and was thankful that he had left the outer door open. He started for the rear of the building with the silent Chinese hard on his heels. Now and again he turned to fight furiously for a few seconds, then would dart on. He made his attackers believe that he was en route to a stairway leading down. And they redoubled their efforts to head him off. Then there was an entrance in this building which led to the furnace room! That was all he wished to know, and the efforts of the Chinese attackers to prevent him reaching it were all the proof he needed. So now he did what they could least expect. He doubled back on his tracks, lashing out with feet and fists, and charged directly into the thick of his attackers. They were thrown into turmoil for just the few indecisive seconds he desired. He was through them, and running with his best speed. He gained the door and was out onto the street, racing toward the Bowery.

He looked back, but there was no pursuit. He laughed to himself, circled about until he reached his own quarters, to find the radio patrol car parked at the curb, both officers sitting there, patiently waiting for something to happen.

"Can you leave your cruising area to take me uptown?" asked Noel. "Or shall I call headquarters?"

"We've called, Mr. Noel, and another car has taken our place. We are at your disposal."

"Good! Take me to the home of Gerard Servis."

The coppers gasped. One of them swore and said, "screwy," but neither offered any objection to his suggestion. He sat between the coppers on the race uptown, left them at the curb and entered the foyer of a cooperative apartment house. He felt in his pockets for his keys, looked about for the doorman or the elevator boy. The boy came forward. Noel gave the name of Gerard Servis. The colored boy's eyes widened.

"I have to find out if they'll see you, sir. Whom shall I say?"

"Nobody. I'll go up."

But the boy wouldn't have it. Noel, apparently much disappointed, withdrew. But fifteen minutes later he was inside the building, via the fire escape, and stalking along a hallway two floors below that of Gerard Servis. He went softly and silently up the stairs until he came to the proper floor, utterly silent. He peered along a hallway to make sure he was not observed. A copper dozed in a chair at the far end. Noel knew that he risked a bullet if the copper wakened and spotted him, but he had to risk it. He was careful that his keys made no sound as he tried them in the door of the Servis apartment. He entered.

There was darkness. He guessed that Servis would probably have a huge suite of rooms. From the sound, or lack of it, Servis believed that most of the family had left the place for the time being. He started moving silently through the darkness, feeling his way with hands and feet.

Doors opened softly under his hands. There were times when he heard the voices of coppers outside, wondered what they would say, think and do if they knew a skulker walked so close to them, in the home of a man who had just died under peculiar circumstances. But he shrugged away irrelevant thoughts and went on.

A thin pencil of light showed under a door at last, and Noel pressed his ear against the panels to listen. A gentle sing-song, as of a person thinking half aloud, half to himself, came through the panels. But the part of the sing-song which was audible was in Chinese . . . and the words were these:

"I hear . . . master . . . I obey . . . master!"

Noel suddenly stepped through the door into a brightly lighted room, obviously the quarters of the servant. A man whirled on him, startled. A Chinese boy, dressed in the habiliments of his native land, stared at Noel with widening, startled eyes. In his hands he held one of the eggshell-thin porcelain vases.

When Noel surprised him, the boy had been holding the thing up to the light, staring at it with the concentration of a connoisseur of fine porcelain. Now, as though by accident, the boy dropped the vase to the floor, which happened at that particular place not to be covered by a rug. It broke into thousands of fragments, with a sound as of many eggshells breaking.

Noel hurled himself forward, glancing right to make sure of the window, however, as the boy dashed toward a door which obviously gave onto the hall, screaming at the top of his voice. But Noel didn't even swerve toward the boy. As the banging of heavy fists on the outer panels came through to him, he dropped on his knees and placed his hat beside the fragments of broken vase.

With his palms together, cupped, he began to scoop up the broken fragments, keeping at it until the door was about to open—almost too late to make good his escape. Then he hurled himself through the partially raised window, his hat all but filled with the fragments. Very few remained behind on the floor when he had left.

In a second he knew that the coppers would be firing at him on the fire escape, so he dropped down one floor only, swung over to a window ledge—unmindful that the pavement was fourteen stories below—and crashed through a window into what must have been a bedroom, for a woman screamed and a man swore savagely. But Noel was against the far wall, feeling for a door, which he found, opened. He rushed out into the hallway and started down the stairs at breakneck speed. Shots sounded behind him, but he rushed on, carrying his hatful of broken fragments surely in one hand.

One floor above the pavement he entered another hallway, at right angles to the first, and opened a window. The drop was not a long one or difficult for a man of Noel's attainments. He scarcely felt the jar, nor did he lose a fragment of the broken vase when he struck the pavement on the balls of his feet. He raced up the street, crossed over, came back on the side opposite the apartment house, then crossed quietly to the radio patrol car. He startled the coppers into surprised oaths as they whirled on him.

"Back to Chinatown," he snapped. "As soon as you are well away from here, however, stop at the first cigar store where I can get to a telephone."

Mystified but obedient, the patrol officers shifted gears and darted away. Noel looked back to see coppers boiling onto the sidewalk from the apartment house. He grinned as the radio in the car began to speak . . .

"Calling all cars . . . calling all cars . . . disturbance at home of Gerard Servis on Park Avenue. A burglar at the home of Gerard Servis . . . calling all cars."

The two coppers laughed uncertainly. The one who had done all the talking so far spoke again.

"You really are Dorus Noel, aren't you?"

"Stick with me until this is all over and I'll prove it to you," said Noel, grinning. "Meanwhile I won't get far away from you, and never out of your sight."

The car stopped at a cigar store some twenty blocks from the Gerard Servis home. Noel telephoned his superior.

"Noel talking," he said when he got his sleepy boss on the wire. "I want you to get this information for me from the Customs officials. Find out if Chinese are cooperating with them in trying to find out about the excess Kang Hsi vases. I'll call you back from the usual phone in fifteen minutes. You'll have to pull strings in a hurry."

His superior was wide awake now.

"I'll do it, Noel. Got something?"

"Yes, the answer to the case if the Customs officials say yes."

"Then I *will* pull strings. I'll be ready for you."

Fifteen minutes later Noel called back. His superior excitedly told him that the answer was yes. Noel then spoke distinctly and earnestly.

"Have the building where Tsa Liu holds his school-employment agency raided at once. Round up everybody you find. Search for a back stairway which should lead the raiding party to a kiln, probably many feet underground, or blanketed by asbestos or some soundproofing material to keep the noise it makes from the ears of the curious. When you've done this, bring your prisoners—or have the chief bring them in person—to my home on Mott and Pell Streets. There I'll have something to say to everybody. It should be of interest to chess players—and educational in things Chinese, with special reference to Chinese servants!"

The radio coppers went into the house with Noel. Noel's first act was to glance toward the shelf where the vase had rested. The shelf was empty. But what was more to the point as far as Noel was concerned, not one scrap of the broken vase could be found on the smooth floor beneath.

"That saves me trouble," he told himself. "I don't have to piece it together. I can guess the rest of it."

Sirens raged through Chinatown. Revolvers and Tommy guns clattered, while Noel sat unmoved at a table, while the coppers stood behind him watching, and carefully laid out before him the pieces of vase which had been broken by the new servant of the Servis family. The pieces all laid out, Noel moved a reading lamp over the jumbled mass—which looked like a disjointed jig-saw puzzle, and began swiftly to hold various pieces up to the light.

Now and again he exclaimed with satisfaction. Each time he did this he placed the piece he held in his hand aside.

And when the Chief of Detectives, herding some ten or twelve frightened Chinese, with Tsa Liu, imperturbably smiling, in their midst, Dorus Noel grinned his satisfaction. Tsa Liu stared at the egg-thin shards on the table. His face went pale. He screamed and whirled to bolt. He was struck down by a club in the hands of the copper.

"That settles it even more," said Noel quietly. "And now I'll tell the story, as soon as you've manacled Tsa Liu and brought him back to consciousness. It is vital that he hear me. What I have to say will make his confession easier."

Tsa Liu was sullen when he finally was himself again. The look he bent on Noel was murderous. Noel began to talk.

"I got the first hint," he said, "when my own vase, which appeared so mysteriously in my house, changed from a thing of vast value into a two dollar fake . . . and then into a vase of delicate rose color. I knew that one vase couldn't do that, that, actually, there were three vases, shifted by some one who came through the window to make the changes when I was out of the room. It didn't make sense, until Lung Fao, the servant I got from Tsa Liu, tried to kill me.

"He broke the vase when he escaped, which told me something vital about the vase. It came to me, knowing something of porcelain, that the vase held a message, not for me, but for Lung Fao, my boy, I knew that the rose-tinted one gave him instructions to kill me. He failed only because police headquarters traced a telephone call of mine and coppers got here in time.

"My experience tonight in the 'schoolhouse' of Tsa Liu, told me he had a kiln in a deep basement. You found it? Fine! There, I knew, he turned out the fake vases. You probably found plenty of them. Right! There's nothing miraculous in the way this stuff was figured out. Chinese are logical. I merely had to have a starting point, but I confess I wasn't sure until Gerard Servis' boy broke another vase. I gathered up the fragments and brought them here.

"Here's how the rest of it was done. The shipment of sixty reputedly Kang Hsi vases—which were actually of the period of Ch'ien Lung, when eggshell porcelain was the vogue, but stamped with the seal of Kang Hsi as a tribute to his activities in advancing the art of porcelain making—was bona fide. But Tsa Liu wasn't satisfied with that. He decided to use the real vases for juggling purposes.

"He sold the fake vases for the regular price . . . and it was his idea to have his own minions in the homes of the purchasers in case they got suspicious and called in experts to look at the additional vases. They, of course, would instantly have spotted the fakes—which, however, the purchasers would scarcely be able to do. And here's where the chess problem came in:

"With Chinese apparently helping Customs to run down the excess vases in position to know every move of the officials, it was a simple matter for them to do a bit of shifting. They could get into the homes of other purchasers, exchange fake vases for good ones and show the experts bona fide vases in each case. They shifted back to the fakes after the experts left. So, though there never were more than sixty vases, the seeming hundred and fifty were always the same ones.

"Tsa Liu then started planting his servants to make the shifting of the porcelain pawns easier. . . ."

"But what good," began the Chief, "did the servants do? I don't see any sense in what you said about messages."

"Simple," said Noel. "In Ch'ien Lung's time infinitely small designs were worked into the eggshell porcelain, so skillfully that one had to hold the designs up to the light to see them at all. Tsa Liu used this idea. But the designs on the fake porcelain he planted in the homes which interested him, were messages in Chinese to his servants. The vases gave them careful instructions as to what to do next, where to exchange fakes for authentic pieces and vice versa.

"In this way he could sell the authentic ones over and over again. When the hue and cry died down, any number of rich people would possess 'Kang Hsi' vases which they believed to be genuine, but which were worth something like two dollars each. Tsa Liu would become fabulously rich on this alone, to say nothing of what he would drag out of the salaries of his servants."

The chief stared at the pieces of broken vase on Noel's table.

"And what do those pieces say?" he demanded.

"They outline a design for murder," said Noel. "Tsa Liu should have stuck to his own people. They are more skilled. He got through a message to one of his men, who was instructed to contact a certain Doctor Bridges with an offer of one hundred thousand dollars in cash—"

"Doctor Bridges? That's Gerard Servis' physician!"

"I know it. The good doctor accepted. Tsa Liu had been warned by his servant that Gerard Servis wasn't the fool Tsa Liu had thought him. He had discovered he had purchased a fake vase for fifty thousand dollars. On the point of making a row which would have made all other purchasers regard their acquisitions with suspicion, and thus ruin Tsa Liu's schemes for the future, Gerard Servis was murdered—by his own physician. Did you hold him, as I suggested?"

Grimly the chief nodded.

"Yes."

"You'll find, I think, that Servis didn't die at the bank, as the papers said. He did have a stroke. But he was alive when he got home and called Doctor Bridges, who simply gave him a dose of medicine, signed the death certificate!"

"He admits giving Servis a hypo, but stated that he always gave him the same hypo when his heart cut up capers. . . ."

"But not quite so strong," said Noel grimly. "The fact that he admits it is enough. The autopsy will show the rest. What Tsa Liu will tell, to keep himself from burning, will probably be plenty. But don't forget, Tsa Liu, that by the laws of this state, the accomplice is equally guilty with the principal. Especially when the apparent accomplice, yourself, actually procured the murder! You should, my friend, have been less open and aboveboard in your activities, though we'd probably have got you in either case. It just happens, though, that this way we got you faster. Good day, gentlemen. Let me know when Tsa Liu sees fit to confirm what I have told you."

It was as though a monster had awakened inside Noel, and the Chinese complacently watched his torture.

TINKLING BELLS

Encoiled in That Serpentine Chinese Scheme, Dorus Noel Didn't Weigh His Life Against a Pork Chop Until He Discovered That "One Man's Meat Can Be Another's Poison"—Even in Chinatown.

DORUS NOEL LEANED FORWARD.

"You interest me strangely, Gordon," he said. "I know something of Manchu royalty. It's plain that this host of yours—as I'll find out for sure when I see him—is a Manchu and not a Chinese."

"Right, with six Occidental languages and nine Chinese dialects at the tip of his tongue," Gordon replied. "He's class, Noel, which is why I'm here, and why I considered his meal worth five hundred dollars."

"Then what is the complaint?" asked Noel. "If you are satisfied to pay five hundred dollars for his meal, there is certainly no reason for making charges of any kind against Lung Chur."

"No," said Mory Gordon slowly, "there isn't, and I couldn't make them stick if I did. I could hale him into police court and still get nowhere. His crime is the perfect crime, crazy as it will sound when I've told you about it. No, I wouldn't mind the five hundred dollars. But when I had to go back to him, five hours after the meal, and pay him an additional twenty thousand dollars—well, maybe I'd better tell you about it."

A statue of Kwan Yin (his story ran) stood on a dais at one end of the room in which we dined. It was flanked by a huge scroll of the famous legendary trio, Kwang Kung, Hsiang Fei and Liu Bey, the former, the Chinese God of War. There were statuettes on shelves about the place. The odor of "Buddha's hands" filled the place with a soft fragrance. Feet sank deeply into red carpets of great richness.

The table was circular, without a cloth covering—after the Chinese fashion—and its top was covered with myriad intricate designs done in the most beautiful of Chinese paints, and obviously the work of the best artisans. The table itself was worth a fortune. Perhaps, after all, this meal was worth five hundred dollars.

There were jade chopsticks at each place. Lung Chur seated himself and quickly explained the use of the chopsticks, easily understood by Westerners really desirous of learning. Knives and forks were obviously taboo. The guests were thus transplanted from a Chinatown street, in a twinkling, to the innermost culinary secrets of the Manchu Court. New York City was instantly as far away as the moon.

Lung Chur was a marvelous conversationalist, the easy flow of his English a joy to hear. He merely glanced at the servitors, who instantly got into motion toward a swinging door opposite the dais of the statuettes. Lung Chur was dressed in imperial yellow, minus only the five-toed dragon design of an Emperor. Dorus Noel, even in fancy as he listened, pinched himself to make sure that he was not dreaming.

The food began to arrive. Dorus Noel knew his Chinese foods, but he had never heard of any of these. And certainly they—and Lung Chur—must have made a vivid impression upon Mory Gordon, for he was able to describe each dish minutely, to remember even the intonations of Lung Chur's voice, and to recall—at least closely enough for Dorus Noel, who knew his Mandarin dialect—the Chinese names of the food.

"You will shortly understand," said Lung Chur, "why this meal is worth all you spend for it, and very much more. As a matter of fact, it costs me almost as much as it does you. You wonder then how I am able to have in perfect strangers as guests? I shall explain. You will not long remain strangers, and there shall be payment. But let us not speak of plebeian matters like money when there is choice food to be enjoyed."

Lung Chur paused as though for effect. He lifted the filigreed lid from a silver tureen, and sniffed the steaming contents of the container.

"Ah," he said, and there was rapture in his voice, as though he were a worshipper before a shrine. "I shall tell you what this is. It is *ying tao jo*, or 'cherry pork.' But I have—being something of a gourmand—improved the dish by the addition of rare mushrooms from Szechuan, so that it is even superior to the court dish, which no European has ever eaten to my certain knowledge.

"You will note the rich gravy of the *ying tao jo*, on top of which float several globes, at least two for each of you. The globes are called *ying erh*, and they are a fungus which grows on certain pine trees in Szechuan. I brought many boxes of them with me. It is not, you understand, that I wish to remind you of the richness of this feast. But the boxes which hold these *ying erh* are valuable creations in themselves, being the work of erstwhile craftsmen of the court, paid by myself, and the contents of each box cost me, in China, fifty *taels*—almost as many American dollars at the present rate of exchange.

"I shall spare you the cost of the other things. But eat, and enjoy."

Lung Chur, like a good host, smiling, jovial, helped his guests to their food, working his chopsticks rapidly, and placing two each of the *ying erh* on their yellow plates. After this he instructed his Number One Boy to pass the dish from guest to guest, so that each might help himself of the succulent pork, mixed with fresh cherries.

"It takes four hours to cook this dish," said Lung Chur, "and it must be most carefully done."

His guests were properly silent in the face of such magnificence. But they tasted the mushrooms somewhat doubtfully—to find that they had no taste whatever.

"No, they have no taste," said Lung Chur, "but they have always been considered great delicacies in the Middle Kingdom."

"Some mushrooms," said a guest doubtfully, "are poison."

Lung Chur laughed, reached into the dish and plopped two of the mushrooms into his mouth very rapidly. Then—and the guests noted that he did not eat of the pork or the cherries—Lung Chur devoted himself to an entirely different sort of food: pork rinds which had been cooked to a crisp, and crackled when eaten. Lung Chur, as his guests looked at him, laughed in high enjoyment.

"It is called 'tinkling bell,' this pork rind," he said. "The Chinese are nothing if not imaginative, as you will see."

If there were a hint of threat or promise in his words his guests did not notice. They were too deeply absorbed in the marvelous dish called *ying tao jo*. One noticed that he ate only the *hsiang ling*—tinkling bells, but he quickly explained that.

"We Chinese and Manchus are prone to obesity," he explained. "I must keep a sharp eye on my girth."

One by one the dishes came on, and Lung Chur explained each one.

"This mushroom which looks like a baseball," he said, "is *ho to*. It comes from Szechuan, also, and you will note how it expands when steamed. It is delicious, you will find. Its cost . . . but I said I would not speak of cost, else you will think me mercenary. It is best sliced, and steamed, as I serve it to you now.

"This long stringy growth is called 'hair vegetable' in English, *to fa tsai* in Mandarin, and you will pardon, me if I again serve you pork, since *to fa tsai* is best when served thus. However, the dish is so different that I doubt you will mind additional pork. It might be served with *jo mo*, which is meat dust, but I have been unable to get that in Chinatown, properly prepared.

"Your Cantonese are atrocious cooks, which is why I pay heavy Federal bond to bring in my own chefs. These greens are not spinach, though they resemble it. There is no English equivalent. If you are able to remember it at all, think of it as *hsien tsai*, 'vegetable from the south.' It comes from South China. Nice, isn't it?"

Many Mandarin words fell glibly from the lips of Lung Chur as he entertained his guests at a dinner which ran the full thirty courses. Some of the names were familiar, some were unknown even to Dorus Noel, but just to smell the marvelous cooking, to taste the food of the world's best cooks, was a treat which not one guest had ever experienced before and—though none knew it then—would ever experience again.

Wo sun was a salad, like salad romaine, *hsi kua* and *tung kua* were candied melons. The greatest dish of all was called "eight precious vegetables and fruits." It was the rind of a huge watermelon which had been divested of its meat, to leave a melon container which was filled with chicken, ham—both chopped very fine—pine needle seeds, lotus seeds, apricot pits, almonds, walnuts, and a Chinese fruit called "dragon's eyes." All this had been steamed, together, for many hours. Its taste was beyond the vocabulary of any of Lung Chur's guests.

"I felt," said Mory Gordon, suddenly bringing Dorus Noel back to the fact that he had never, actually, left his house on Mott and Pell Streets, "as though any meal I might ever eat afterward must be an anticlimax. The whole thing was so delicious as to be indescribable. When we had finally finished, after seven hours of feasting—during which Lung Chur had eaten nothing but the 'tinkling bells,' but had eaten these in great quantities—I would have died with the knowledge that life had nothing left to offer me. Then Lung Chur's smile faded. . . .

" 'You gentlemen may go home now,' said Lung Chur, his eyes very narrow, 'but each of you will return to me. You, Mory Gordon, will come to me at five in the morning. You, Carl Jaydick, at seven-thirty. You, Leslie Canavan, at eight. You, Peter Morgan, at eight-thirty. Each will bring his checkbook. . . .'

"We all thought it a joke," said Mory Gordon sadly, "but when my time came I was only too glad to return at the time he had stated—and to take my checkbook. I telephoned Lung Chur first and he was very grim, and insistent on the checkbook. I took it and, as I told you, paid him twenty thousand additional dollars for that meal."

"And the other nine men?" Dorus Noel's voice was scarcely above a whisper. He couldn't really believe his ears, yet he knew something of each of the ten men Mory Gordon had named, and they were not the sort to perpetrate jests, certainly none as fantastic as this one. Noel realized that he was perspiring. Gordon hadn't told him exactly why the additional money had been paid.

"Each of them has paid, or is paying at this moment," said Gordon grimly, "twenty thousand or more dollars into the hands of Lung Chur—and glad to do it, understand? My wealth is less than that of several other men at that feast, and I think he scaled his prices carefully to fit the fortunes of his guests."

"Which means," said Dorus Noel in amazement, "that his ten guests paid Lung Chur somewhere in the neighborhood of a quarter of a million dollars for food?"

"Exactly that."

"Why? Give me some inkling, for it comes to me that I myself may wish to eat of this marvelous food."

Gordon opened his mouth to speak. A low laugh came from the door. Both men, so deeply engrossed in the strange narrative that they had heard nothing, turned to see a well-dressed Chinese, carrying a cane, standing in the door which gave on Noel's reception room. He would have passed for an Occidental, from a back view, so impeccably groomed was he. But when he faced his audience there was no mistaking his nationality.

"Ah, Mister Gordon," he said silkily, "you remembered your promise in time, didn't you?"

Gordon gulped and swallowed.

"That's right, Noel," he said. "If you hadn't told me you might be a guest I would have told you the truth. Now my word has been passed, and I can tell you nothing beyond what I have—nor would I have been able to speak of the twenty thousand dollars had I thought you might sit down at Lung Chur's table."

Noel stared at the Chinese, a total stranger to him.

"This is Lung Chur?" he said.

The Chinese himself answered.

"No, Dorus Noel, merely one of his many cousins."

"And what would happen to Mory Gordon if he broke his word? Promises given under duress are not binding."

The face of the Chinese became stern for a moment.

"He would die," he said simply. There was mockery in the eyes of the Chinese. He thrust a well-manicured hand into an inside pocket and brought out an engraved card, which he tendered to Dorus Noel with a smile. It was an invitation to be a guest of Lung Chur, on Mott Street, that very night. "There is nothing you can do, Dorus Noel," said the Chinese. "You could fill the dining room with police and Lung Chur would laugh at you."

"But if I spoke of the twenty thousand dollars . . ." began Dorus Noel. "It sounds like extortion, you know."

"I should be forced to deny having told you anything," said Mory Gordon miserably. "Yes, Lung Chur foresaw something of the kind, and that is part of my pact with him. You'll have to go through what I went through, and depend on your wits—whose fame brought me to you—to checkmate this Lung Chur. You'll find him more than a match for you, I'm afraid."

"But if I compelled his arrest . . ." began Noel again.

"None of us would bring charges," said Mory Gordon. "Sorry, but that's how it is. Our lives would hang in the balance if we did otherwise."

"You mean *murder*?" asked Noel of the Chinese.

"Ugly word," the other answered. "No, my friend, even extortion does not fit it, and my master has never slain a human being. Nor will he, because all men prefer life to money, are always willing to exchange the one for the other, with usurious interest. Good day, my friends!"

The Chinese bowed mockingly to Dorus Noel and departed. Mory Gordon, entreaty in his eyes, spread his hands helplessly.

"I can't do any more," he said. "From here out it's up to you."

"It's the screwiest thing I ever heard of!" exploded Noel.

"Yes, but every word true. Well, Noel, I'm pulling for you, and terribly sorry that I can't help further."

"But a promise given under duress . . ." protested Noel desperately.

"Wouldn't protect my family if I broke the promise," said Gordon. "I know that when Lung Chur told me that members of my family might die— note that he said *might*, not *would*—he meant what he said. The only answer is to win in a game of wits."

"And if I lose?"

"Plenty of others have lost before you, and will continue to lose."

Mory Gordon departed. Dorus Noel sat for a long time in a deep study. Then he went to a telephone booth on Lafayette Street and called his superior out on Park Avenue—a man he had never seen, but whose voice he knew, and who had procured his assignment to Chinatown in the first place. Noel told him what had happened as far as he knew it.

"There's nothing the police can do," said his superior regretfully. "It's extortion, but the victims won't testify for themselves and can't testify for one another because they don't witness one another's payments, and their testimony wouldn't be evidence, but hearsay. Mory Gordon is right. It has to be a battle of wits. We've go to do something about it, or the police had better close up shop, or make Lung Chur mayor or something."

"But it's ridiculous! What did he say to his victims to make them come back to him and cough up?"

"Maybe he poisoned them."

"Mory Gordon didn't look very dead to me, and if anybody had died the newspapers would be shrieking. I've never heard of anything like it, and yet nobody can laugh off a quarter of a million dollars. I guess it *is* up to me, at that. What if I were also forced to pay a huge sum of money and saw no way out of it?"

"I would advance you what I could!" was the prompt answer. It was the most abject confession of defeat Noel had ever heard from the lips of a police official.

That night he dressed with care, ready to play out the strange farce to its logical conclusion. His brain had worked at top speed, finding no reason anywhere why ten men should pay one Chinese a quarter of million dollars for a meal for which they had already paid five hundred dollars—what power kept them comparatively silent, why the police were unable to do anything.

Of course he might look Lung Chur up, arrange for his deportation, but that seemed like an additional confession of defeat. Of course, if somebody actually were murdered . . . but nobody had been! Noel swore softly. In past clashes with Chinese criminals he had been able many times to win out against them by sheer brawn, to batter his way to a decision against them.

But no brawn was indicated here. Lung Chur, secure in his knowledge of a strange immunity, wasn't even putting up a fight. Else why had he invited Dorus Noel to be his guest at dinner?

The whole thing was utterly unreal, fantastic. But he would see it through, resolving as he came to the decision, that when the smoke cleared away he would have the right answer, and Lung Chur would be beaten.

Only yesterday new telephone books had been delivered. Noel, on a hunch, looked for Lung Chur in the directory, finally running him to earth in the professional "red book," under the heads of "doctors and physicians," which caused him to scratch his head. The whole thing was more muddled than ever.

Finally he grinned.

"Whatever it is," he said, "the fellow is good."

He had to appreciate a worthy foe-man in any game of wits. The men who had lost so much money could afford it, and probably deserved what they got for going in for exotic entertainment. Restaurants and medicine didn't seem to go together, Noel thought—or did they? He thought of that angle without arriving at any sort of conclusion.

At seven-thirty o'clock he strolled out onto Pell Street and made his way to the residence-office of "Doctor" Lung Chur. He rang the bell, which was set into a scroll representing one of the traditional "dogs of Fo," which Westerners usually regarded as stone lions. But he wasn't interested in Oriental niceties of name at the moment.

The door swung softly open. A slim young Chinese, lighter of color than any Cantonese, faced him, pleasantly smiling. Then the lad cast his eyes down, as became a good servant, as he said:

"Deign to enter, Noel *hsien sheng*," he said.

Noel shivered a little. This commonplace acceptance of him, the calling by name, got under his skin. It was as though Lung Chur held all the cards and knew it, as though the Manchu were laughing at him already. He stepped across the threshold. The servant led the way to a richly furnished room, where a man in a yellow gown, below which showed the fine leather of white-soled Manchu-noble boots, turned as the servitor murmured the name of Dorus Noel, and rose to his feet.

"You know my country, Dorus Noel," he said, bowing deeply, making it a statement instead of a question.

"Yes, real and adoptive. I know Manchuria, the birthplace of your race, and China, the land of your race's adoption."

"Then you must know how low our caste has fallen? They are very poor since the fall."

Noel found himself really liking the man. He had a smile.

"A man who can get over a quarter of a million dollars for a single meal, however lavish," he stated, "can scarcely be called poor."

Lung Chur, a handsome man, chuckled as he bowed deeply, hands in his voluminous sleeves. Noel never doubted, once he saw the man, the truth of his claims to kinship with the royal Manchu family. He was too light complexioned for any Chinese.

His right hand came forth from his sleeve finally, and Noel did not hesitate to grasp and shake it heartily. They were like fighters sparring for an opening, or meeting at the scales before post time. Lung Chur seemed serenely conscious of his own power, though he was too much the diplomat to, by word or look, indicate that he belittled the mental powers of Dorus Noel.

"We shall wait for the other guests, if you don't mind," said Lung Chur. "I am sorry you did not come earlier. There is so much we could find to talk about."

"We shall find the time, sometime," said Noel quietly.

Lung Chur arched his eyebrows.

"Perhaps," he said softly.

A bell tinkled through the house.

"My guests are arriving," said Lung Chur. "We'll be going in shortly."

Fifteen minutes passed. No guests came into the room where Lung Chur had received Dorus Noel. The Manchu was paying Noel a high compliment, setting him apart from his other guests. He excused himself at last, went out to greet the others. Then the boy came for Noel and he was ushered into the dining room, where Lung Chur, with the grace of a veteran courtier, introduced everybody to everybody else.

Mory Gordon had certainly not exaggerated the richness of that dining room. He had done it far less than justice. It was a throne room fit for an Empress. Columns upheld the roof, and around them wound the folds of five-toed dragons, done in gold. Brocades, rich embroideries, covered the walls. Feet sank soundlessly into the rich red carpet which could only have come from some storeroom of the Manchu royal house. The table was a masterpiece. The guests were awestricken by the splendor, and one spoke up quickly.

"I wondered what in the world could make a dinner worth five hundred dollars," he said. "Now I know."

"It is really," said Lung Chur quickly, "worth much more than that, Mr. Abbott, as you will discover. Boy, bring food!"

Dorus Noel did not need to be told how to use chopsticks. There had been months on end, in China long ago, when he had used nothing else. To him Chinese food was really tasteless if eaten with knife, fork and spoon. The sticks fell into his right hand with the surety of the master trencherman. Noel helped Lung Chur show his guests, of whom there were nine besides Noel, how to use chopsticks. When the first dish, the *ying tao jo*, with floating *ying erh* visible in the rich gravy, came on, Noel smiled at Lung Chur.

"It's poison, of course?" he said.

"Of course," said Lung Chur softly. "I invariably poison my guests."

They all laughed at the jest, but Noel was doubtful. Lung Chur had answered too quickly. Maybe he had told the truth in such a way that nobody—especially his victims—would believe it. But that couldn't be so, for Mory Gordon had eaten and lived, and so had nine other victims, last night.

Whatever happened, Noel had never before tasted such marvelous food, even in China, and nothing would deter him now. He might never again have the opportunity. Course followed course in silence, as the soft-footed servitors came in with tureens, bowls, casseroles. Remembering everything Gordon had told him, Noel recognized each dish as it came on.

Guests were served from each dish, which was then pushed to the side of the table to make room for other dishes. As each dish came on they were privileged to eat, not only from the new dish, but to go back and eat from all previous dishes. That everybody dipped his own chopsticks into the food did not trouble Noel, who knew the custom which disregarded the possibility of germs in someone else's eating utensils.

He noted that the other guests, at first, were inclined to be squeamish, but they forgot their feeling as the rich food warmed their stomachs and filled them all with a feeling of immense well-being.

Noel noticed that Lung Chur ate "tinkling bells," and when Lung Chur noted his glance, he explained why, just as Gordon had reported him to have done last night. He was, he said, on a sort of diet. He was a brilliant conversationalist. He answered questions relative to the possible restoration of the Manchu throne in Manchuria with the surety of a statesman conversant with the subject. He knew world politics and discussed them without the verbal circumlocutions which Westerners find so trying in Chinese.

There were beatific expressions on the faces of Lung Chur's guests, and Noel himself had never felt more sympathetic with all the world. Lung Chur even introduced a rare wine which everybody pronounced excellent. Over all hung the odor of the delicious food, mingled with the odors of incense and sandalwood. The room might have been the boudoir of an Empress—except that so many men made a jarring note.

The whole atmosphere made Noel think of a story he had heard about two Chinese generals, one of whom had invited the other to dinner, telling him, when he sat down, to eat heartily, that he would be decapitated immediately after eating. The story went on to say that the two ate in perfect amity, laughing and jesting, and that afterward the guest-general was duly decapitated by his host's soldiers.

This was much like that, he thought—for now and again he saw Lung Chur speculatively regarding his guests. When Lung Chur caught the eyes of Noel on him he smiled, his eyes vanishing under folds of flesh, as though he vastly enjoyed the situation. The meal went on interminably, as Chinese meals invariably did. There were many dishes now which had not been included in the meal Gordon had described—birds' nests, sharks' fins, bears' paws, ducks' lips, humming birds' wings.

No more lavish dinner could possibly have been devised.

But all good things must come to an end. Lung Chur finally thrust back his chair, signaled for cigars for his guests. The cigars were Corona-Coronas, and the guests sat back to enjoy them to the limit. Lung Chur glanced often at a clock on the wall, in the midst of many other clocks, set in between and among the scrolls, the brocades and the satins. The denouement would not long be delayed now.

Lung Chur glanced briefly at Noel, then spoke to his guests, and there was a steely glint in his eyes.

"Excepting Dorus Noel, the criminologist," he said, "I wish to bid the rest of you goodnight. It is one o'clock in the morning. However, each of you will return here at the hours indicated, and each will bring his checkbook. At least that is my suggestion."

Startled amazement showed on the faces of the guests. They stared from Lung Chur to Dorus Noel and back again.

"Checkbooks?" said one. "Why?"

"I told you all that you would find this meal well worth the price—and more," said Lung Chur. "In an hour or two, nearer two, you will understand why. Haggard, you will come back to me at seven o'clock. You, Blythe, at seven-thirty. You, King, at eight . . ."

"But why did you not mention checkbooks before?" asked Noel quietly.

Lung Chur smiled.

"I know rich men," he said. "Had I suggested that you gentlemen bring checkbooks with you, you would have scented something and would have remained away, leaving me with only the five hundred dollar reservations, which would pay me but poorly for the entertainment I have furnished. You are to go home now to get your books—remaining long enough to make the discovery that it will be extremely dangerous for you to fail to return."

"Just what do you mean?" asked Haggard.

Lung Chur studied each face in turn before replying, then said:

"Each of you has, at least, seven hours to live. During those seven hours you will be desperate—desperate enough, I fancy, to count the cost and find it worth paying, and to visit certain people who have served you in the past, to be told they can do nothing for you. Then you will inevitably come here. Dorus Noel, remain seated, please."

"If you," said Haggard grimly to Noel, "an officer of the law—as I take it—are in on some sort of a swindle . . ."

"There is no swindle," said Lung Chur sharply, "as you will find out at seven o'clock, Mr. Haggard. Even if there were, Dorus Noel is as helpless as you are, though he would never believe it. And a warning: any contact with the police on the part of any of you, any attempt to thwart my plans, may mean a considerable lessening of the seven hours of life I have mentioned. Good morning, gentlemen!"

Noel stared at Lung Chur after the guests, their faces suddenly white, had left. He sank back in his seat.

"I swear I can't see any sense in it," said Noel. "But there must be something, or your guests last night would not have paid through the nose and protected you afterwards."

"Wait!" counseled Lung Chur, looking again at the clock. "Let us talk of the Manchu court, a subject close to my heart."

If the man were bluffing, his bluff was magnificent. Noel could not allow himself to be found wanting in meeting the challenge of his adversary. He entered with enthusiasm into the discussion on a subject which interested him no little because of his own acquaintance in China. Now and again Lung Chur glanced at the clock. He smiled, nodded, held up his end, and scarcely seemed preoccupied, save for that periodic glance at the clock. Finally his face went grim and he faced Dorus Noel.

"How," he said softly, "do you feel?"

As though the matter had been timed to the second, a hard savage hand seemed to grasp at Noel's innards. It was as though a monster had wakened inside him, turned over and begun to gnaw cruelly at the walls of his stomach. He knew that his face had gone white. He doubled forward, moaning, hands at his stomach. His eyes seemed bursting from his head. He gasped for breath as he stared at Lung Chur, and all the strength seemed to go out of him, as the pain, bitter and excruciating, gripped at his vitals.

"Blow poison!" he rasped.

Lung Chur chuckled.

"About this time every one of my recent guests is experiencing the same torture, Noel," he said. "Each will send post haste for his own favorite physician, not one of whom will be able to do anything for his patient, because none will know what ails him. There will be questions and answers. The food will be analyzed.

"The physicians will say that the patients will die, unless—unless they come to me, and pay to have their lives returned to them! As for you, however, I have no quarrel with the police. I had you here, without charge, you'll remember, to show you my power—and to prove that there is, really, no crime in what I am doing. Here is the antidote for what tortures you."

Lung Chur indicated a small jade box to Noel, in which were several little white pellets. Noel, his hands shaking, plopped two into his mouth as Lung Chur named the dose. Then he waited. In a few minutes peace came to Noel.

"It's still extortion," said Noel.

"From you?" snapped Lung Chur. "I have asked you for nothing, not so much as a penny."

"Then from the others."

"I have made no demands on them—yet."

"Your guests of last night?"

"Will not bring charges."

"You threatened their families."

"I merely said that something *might* happen to their families. And something might, even though no member of those families ever heard of Doctor Lung Chur! Something is always liable to happen to any family."

"But you intimated, suggested . . ."

"I merely spoke the truth. What construction my guests placed on my words is no concern of mine!"

"You meet attack at every point with rare skill," said Noel with grudging admiration.

"I planned far ahead," said Lung Chur softly.

"I shall stay," said Noel grimly, "to see you make demands upon Haggard, and those who come after him. Then, Lung Chur, you lose—for I shall certainly place you under arrest."

"You are welcome to stay."

And stay Noel did, until Haggard came, his face twisted with pain, his body drenched with perspiration.

"My doctors can do nothing," he moaned. "They don't even know what is wrong. They suggest growing bamboo shoots in the stomach."

"Stuff and nonsense!" snapped Lung Chur. "Western conception of Chinese cruelty. I can cure you of your pains, Haggard, but there is a fee . . ."

"I refuse to pay extortion."

"You'd rather die?"

In the end Haggard paid, and promised to say nothing of any of this, in addition to signing a check for twenty-five thousand dollars. Lung Chur took the check, tendered Haggard one of the pills. He gulped it down. Noel stepped to Lung Chur.

"I arrest you in the name of the law for extortion, Lung Chur," he said. "Come with me."

"Arrest me, Noel," said Lung Chur, "and I shall sue you for every cent you possess, for false arrest."

"You just took twenty-five thousand dollars to furnish Haggard with an antidote for poison which you gave him."

"I simply cured him of his pains. I am licensed to practice medicine in New York State. I will show you my papers. The law does not prescribe the size of the fee."

"But you administered poison!"

"I did not, or at least you can't prove it."

"You frightened your guests into paying by suggesting, before they left, that they had seven hours to live."

"I told the truth. They'll all live more than seven hours—if they come to me on schedule."

"If they don't?"

Lung Chur grinned.

"Does the law deal in suppositions?"

Noel was again stumped.

"Do you deny you administered poison?"

"I deny nothing, nor do I affirm."

Haggard left. One by one the erstwhile guests of Lung Chur came.

When the last had gone, and Lung Chur was richer by almost another quarter of a million dollars—fruit of mankind's fear of death—Noel played his trump card. A snub-nosed automatic appeared over the table, pointing at Lung Chur.

"Lung Chur," said Noel calmly, "I tell you in all sincerity, that if you do not eat of the same food that your victims ate, I shall shoot you between the eyes, understand?"

Lung Chur's face went blank with amazement at this sudden move of Noel's. Noel shoved the dishes on the table closer to Lung Chur, who suddenly burst out into laughter, pulled the plates close to himself and began to eat. He ate swiftly, portions of every food his victims had tested. Noel, afraid that even his new idea was a failure, stared at Lung Chur in silence— ready to spring his prize bluff.

"There's no poison in this food," said Lung Chur. "I merely fed my guests different types of mushrooms—each one harmless in itself—which are extremely inimical to one another. The resultant pain is terrific, but would pass away of its own accord in twelve hours. I can stand the pain twice that long for half a million dollars, Dorus Noel!"

Noel leaned forward.

"That is where you are fooled, Lung Chur," he said softly. "When I pushed the dishes toward you—having a hunch of the truth—I dropped poison into two dishes. I have its antidote in my pocket. You may have such antidote, but if you move to get it I shall slay you. I shall allow you to die, here and now, Lung Chur, if you do not do as I bid you."

Lung Chur's face went dead white. He stared long into the eyes of Noel, and Noel could read sudden growing respect in Lung Chur's black orbs.

"You wouldn't," Lung Chur almost whispered it.

"Try me," stated Noel.

Sweat began to bead the face of Lung Chur. His hands moved to his stomach. Imagination could do great things to men gripped by fear's hypnosis. Noel knew.

"What do you want?" asked Lung Chur.

"A promise from you never again to have guests to dinner."

"I promise readily. I already have enough to last me, in money, the rest of my life."

"No," said Noel inexorably, "for you will return every last penny to the men you mulcted, save only the five hundred dollars each paid, of his own free will, for dining with you. And allow me to say that the meal was worth the money. I'd have paid it myself, gladly, even after the meal."

"Leave me some of it," said Lung Chur desperately. "Certainly it is worth something . . ."

"No. Write out the checks. Hurry, there isn't much time."

Lung Chur writhed, twisted. Noel almost pitied him. Finally Lung Chur said:

"If I give you my word, will you give me the antidote?"

"Of course. No Manchu of the royal house would break his word."

Noel thrust a round pellet at Lung Chur, who grasped it eagerly, swallowed it, and sat back, waiting. Finally, when his face began to smooth into calmer lines, he mustered the courage for a sportsman's grin.

"You've beaten me fairly," he said. "I'll carry out my compact. We might even be friends?"

Noel grinned in return.

"Maybe. I'm sorry I had to prove to you that sauce for the goose is sauce for the gander."

Lung Chur answered gamely. "I must confess at the moment, Dorus Noel, that right now I wouldn't even care to partake of Peking duck!"

"And you'd like it even less," said Noel to himself, out on the street a few minutes later, his hands filled with letters addressed to nineteen men, the envelopes containing nineteen checks of varying sizes, "if you'd guessed that I didn't use poison at all, but merely a mild irritant. Funny what fear does to people—even Dorus Noel. Before he gave me that 'antidote,' I wouldn't have taken fifteen cents for my life."

BLACK SNOW

*"What is the black kiss? What is this
stuff in my hand?"*

**Only From Chinatown, Where Fate Creeps on Silent Feet,
Could Have Come the Black Kiss, Which Dorus Noel
Gave When He Kept That Rendezvous With Death in the
Graveyard.**

GOLDEN SAND DRIBBLED THROUGH THE HOUR GLASS. Dorus Noel, watching
it, could hear its soft whispering as it measured off its little fragments of
eternity. It was, oddly enough, something out of China.

It almost was China. For the sand was yellow. It had come from the
Imperial Gardens in Peking, where some had remained in a certain building
which had been locked against the world since Her Majesty Tzu Hsi had

ascended the Dragon Throne.

In Her Majesty's time the yellow sand had been scattered on any road over which this last of the important Manchus had ridden outside the palaces of the Forbidden City. And now an infinitesimal portion of it whispered through the hour glass in Dorus Noel's "China Room," speaking softly of the passage of time.

Dorus Noel shivered a little. When he speculated on the little things of China and her past—especially as it was linked with New York's Chinatown—its spirit seemed to enter into him, whispering like the golden sand, hinting of dark mysteries, deep in the heart of Chinatown, deep in the hearts of her people.

"For ways that were dark and tricks that were vain." But to Dorus Noel they weren't "heathen Chinee." He knew them too well to regard them as heathen. He had a healthy respect for their strange powers, which was why he sometimes shivered unaccountably and wondered if coming events didn't really cast their shadows before—especially in Chinatown.

For when he felt like that, things invariably happened. The whispering of the sand seemed to grow louder, as though his growing dread had caused it to cry out a warning. He was hypnotizing himself into—what?

As though in answer to the question his prized clock—he had over a dozen in his China room, all different, all somehow Chinese—began to sound the hour. It did this by rolling a golden ball out of a notch in a winding stairway, visible because the casing of the clock was of clear glass, and bouncing it down enough steps to make the sound coincide with the hour.

Noel shivered again.

It was eleven o'clock at night. The ball had fallen down eleven steps. Noel looked toward the door which led to his "boy's" room, where Hsiang Liu held forth. Hsiang Liu was a perfect servant. When you didn't want him he wasn't there; when you did, he was, arriving in catlike silence. From his room came a sound of gentle breathing. If coming events were casting their shadows before at this moment, Hsiang Liu was not affected.

Then, out of the smother of sounds which came from Pell and Mott Streets, Noel picked out one that troubled him. It came from the corner of his house. It was a scratching sound, as though a cat were testing its claws. But it moved along the wall toward his window, and the sound of it grated on Noel's nerves.

He twisted his chair to look toward the window—and something caused him to step swiftly to the wall and snap out the lights. Then he stood up, several feet from his chair. His window was open a few inches from the bottom.

There was nothing at the window. Or was there? Suddenly something moved there. Just a flashing shadow. It might have been a hand. But he caught less than a glimpse of it, as though it had been jerked into view and withdrawn immediately. Something struck the chair in which he had been sitting. Noel had too many times listened to a knife striking wood not to know the sound. But he gave no sign that he had heard. He kept his eyes on the window.

He held his breath as a shadow moved into the window again—then the shape of a head, topped by a queue. Chinatown Chinese didn't wear queues. The head rose higher. It rose until Noel could see a face. And what a face!

He had last seen its like in the Yellow Temple at Peking, where devil masks were set to frighten away the devils of a *feng shui*. It was a horrible grinning mask with glowing amethystine eyes and phosphorescent, slavering jaws. Below the mask was an expanse of yellow throat. Watching this, Dorus Noel wondered if he would ever fasten his fingers in that throat.

On the point of hurling himself through the window, to catch and hold this apparition in order to ask it some questions, he decided against it. Instead, he raced as close to the window as he could, knowing that the man outside could not see into the total darkness of the room, and stared at the mask and the neck, especially the neck.

Then the face was gone.

Noel knew that if he went into the street this minute he'd never see the mask, that any Chinese face he would see might well be that which the mask had hidden. He shrugged. He was glad that his eyes seldom missed anything.

Then, there came a long pealing at his doorbell. He snapped on the lights again, turned and looked at his chair before answering the bell. He heard Hsiang Liu mumbling in his bedroom, roused by the bell. Hsiang Liu was coming, in his sleep, to answer. A knife with a flame-shaped blade and a green jade handle was sticking in the back of his chair. It wasn't deeply driven. Whoever had thrown it hadn't thrown it to kill, but to leave the message which he knew he would find inscribed on the red piece of paper which surrounded the haft of the knife. He tore off the piece of paper, went to answer the bell.

The man who came in was an American. His face was white as death. He was laboring under such ghastly fear that he couldn't control the working of his face. It writhed and twisted like that of a madman.

"You're Noel? Dorus Noel?"

"Yes," said Noel, stepping aside for the man to literally fall into the room. "Why? And how did you get my name?"

"I telephoned the police. They gave me a number on Park Avenue to call. I called it. The man who answered gave me your name, as soon as he had heard mine, and swore me to secrecy about your connection with the police. He said I was to come to see you."

Noel nodded. His superior out on Park Avenue, whom Noel had never seen, often sent people to him on mysterious missions, if their discretion could be relied upon. It was necessary to Noel that he be publicized as little as possible. Some regular police officer always got credit for his coups among the Chinese. Few Chinese, even, knew his connection with the police.

"Won't you sit down, Mr. Charleson?" said Noel.

"You know my name then?"

"Of course. I read the newspapers. The name is nationally known. I'd be ignorant indeed if I didn't know it. You'd have to be that influential for the man on Park Avenue to pass you along to me. I don't even know his name myself."

"Nor do I. Noel, I'm in desperate straits! It's . . . it's . . ."

And then the man's eyes suddenly widened to their fullest extent. Noel started, looked at his own right hand, at which Charleson was staring. Charleson almost frothed at the mouth. His eyes were fixed in a hypnotic stare. But it was several seconds before he could find words. He gulped. His Adam's apple moved up and down rapidly several times as he struggled to find words.

"God almighty!" he finally managed. "They know I'm here, or that I was coming. They've warned you already! They know everything I do. Now there's no chance at all. You won't help me!"

"They?" repeated Noel. "Whom do you mean by *they*?"

Charleson pointed at the red piece of paper in Noel's hand. Noel excused himself while he studied the ideographs on the paper. He knew many Chinese characters, far more than the number at the command of the usual foreign student of Chinese. He could read these few as easily as though they had been written in English.

They said, translated to English:

"If you would live, have nothing to do with the Black Snow!"

Noel looked up at Charleson, his eyes narrowed. He debated with himself a moment before speaking to Charleson again. Charleson seemed sure that the piece of red paper had something to do with his own visit tonight.

In Hsiang Liu's room there was silence. Noel knew that beyond the panels Hsiang Liu was drinking in every word. The door stood open, so slightly that only Noel himself could have been sure that it wasn't tightly closed. He grinned to himself. Hsiang was loyal to his master. He was making sure that Noel was in no danger from this nocturnal visitor.

Then Noel decided to plunge. He knew nothing so far, and anything he could surprise out of this man would help him. His superior out on Park Avenue had known it was in Noel's line, else Charleson wouldn't be here now.

"I wonder what this thing means about Black Snow?" said Noel casually, as though he were talking to himself.

The result of his question, spoken aloud, was curious indeed. Charleson choked off a scream in his throat, and it sounded as though invisible hands were throttling him. The bedroom door banged open with a sound like a pistol shot, and Hsiang Liu, his eyes wide open, fully awake, catapulted into the room.

Charleson whirled at the sound of the door. An automatic, blue of barrel, snub-nosed of muzzle, had leaped into his hand. It spoke flatly, but Noel had jumped, thrusting the muzzle aside. The bullet went harmlessly into the floor. If Noel hadn't jumped Hsiang Liu would have been dead.

But Hsiang Liu scarcely noticed what had happened. He was on his knees at Noel's feet, hands clutching Noel's garments, yellow face lifted beseechingly. He chattered away in Tientsinese.

"If it deals with the Black Snow, oh my master," begged Hsiang Liu, "have nothing to do with it! For it is the kiss of death—the black kiss of death! Black Snow brings suffering and death to everyone who hears the very words of it."

Noel stared at his servitor.

"And to you, too, Hsiang Liu, because you have warned me?"

"It is already written that I shall die of the Black Snow," said Hsiang Liu, "because of this warning. But I die gladly if my warning saves your life, master!"

Noel patted the shoulder of the coolie. There was a little choke in his throat. He could never understand the loyalty of the Chinese servant. Such a servant quitted his homeland, his wife and his children, even his parents— than whom the world contained nothing to which he was more loyal—for the master who paid him wages. And now, if Hsiang Liu spoke truly, he had deliberately thrown away his life to save his master.

"I won't let you die, Hsiang," said Noel soothingly.

"There is nothing you can do, master," said the servant with an air of fatalism. "Sooner or later I shall die of the black kiss, the kiss of the Black Snow. Nothing anybody can do will save me. I wouldn't even run away."

"Get up," said Noel.

The servant rose, backed against the wall, his beady black eyes turned toward the window through which Noel had seen the apparition of the devil mask. The servant didn't blink. When he turned his face back toward Noel he cast his eyes down, as became a good servant. Noel turned again to Charleson.

"If you had killed my servant, Charleson," he said quietly. "I should probably have killed you in turn."

Charleson was trembling like a leaf.

"It wouldn't have mattered, master," said Hsiang Liu. "I shall die anyhow. This was the first attempt of the Black Snow, but fate saved me to give you warning—which will make my death doubly sure."

"What did he say?" asked Charleson. "Believe me, Noel, I didn't mean— you see, Chinks—I thought—well, I'm afraid of all Chinks, since—"

"Since you first got one of these?" Noel held up the piece of red paper. Charleson nodded, licking dry lips.

"Tell me about it," said Noel softly.

"There isn't much to tell. My daughter, Maida, disappeared three days ago. I thought she was kidnapped. I waited for the snatchers to contact me. Nothing happened. I didn't tell the police, fearing they would kill her. Each day I received a red piece of paper. I couldn't read any of it, was afraid to ask a Chinese for a translation, until tonight. Then I asked my laundryman. He shrieked and ran. I thought he yelled something about Black Snow. That reminded me of something I found in Maida's bedroom. Here it is."

Charleson took something out of his pocket, a black pulpy mass, tendered it to Noel. Hsiang Liu hurled himself forward, clutched at the black stuff.

"Do not touch it, master," he cried. "Its touch is death! This man will die for having touched it."

A queer chill ran along Noel's spine, but he said "Nonsense!" louder than the occasion demanded, and put out his hand. Charleson, keeping his eyes on Hsiang Liu, dropped the thing into Noel's hand. It had a familiar feel, somehow. Noel stared at it closely.

"It's just a flower," he said, letting his breath out in a sigh of relief. "It's an Ink Chrysanthemum—"

Then he noticed something else, and his breath caught sharply again. The blackness of the flower was coming off on his hands. It looked like soot. Noel's eyes widened. He stared at his spread fingers. Then he looked more closely at the flower.

"No," he said slowly, "it's a chrysanthemum, all right, but it's the kind known as Jade Girdle, whose petals touch tips across the top of the flowers, while the petals of all other royal 'mums' bend down under and touch the stem of the flower. But the Jade Girdle is white. This is black."

He looked at Hsiang Liu again. The coolie was visibly trembling, staring at the black stain on Noel's hand.

"It is the kiss, master," he said. "And not even my death can save you now!"

Noel shrugged, trying to disregard the chill along his spine. He held out his hand to Charleson, smiling slightly.

"If it meant death you'd be dead, Charleson," he said. "Let's see that last piece of red paper you received."

• • •

Charleson fished in his pockets again, his hands shaking so that he could scarcely find the pockets. He brought out a piece of paper. There was an address on it, an address unfamiliar to Noel, in Brooklyn. Slowly he read the number. Hsiang Liu gasped and muttered two words:

"*Feng shui!*"

"Nonsense!" snorted Noel. "Wind and water spirits have nothing to do with this. What does the address mean to you, Hsiang?"

"It is the Chinese cemetery in Brooklyn, where the honorable dead repose, master, awaiting return to China. The wind and water spirits sigh and moan there, troubled because the honorable dead cannot sleep until they return to China."

"There's a time indicated on this. Why, it's two o'clock in the morning of the seventeenth. That's about an hour and a half from now. It probably means that you're to go there, Charleson, to make contact with the kidnappers!"

Charleson looked at the window. Streaks of water ran down the panes now. None in the room had noticed the rain. There had been none when Noel had last looked. Utter blackness, through which street lights glowed as though from a far distance, held all of Chinatown in its grip.

"I can't do it!" groaned Charleson. "Not even for Maida."

Noel stared at Charleson in disgust. The man was as yellow as hell, held his own skin as of more value than that of his own daughter. Noel studied Charleson, then looked at Hsiang Liu.

"Pull the curtains, Hsiang!" he snapped. "Cover the windows with heavy scrolls besides, so that there won't be a chance we'll be observed. Then get busy with Charleson and me."

Fifteen minutes later and two men stood side by side, staring into a mirror. They were the same two men, yet not the same, for now Dorus Noel was Charleson, Charleson was Dorus Noel. Hsiang Liu had worked wonders with make-up at the behest of Dorus Noel, working much against his will.

"Now, Charleson, I don't know how safe you'll be here, for I've been warned, too, and they'll think you're me, just as—I hope—they'll think I'm yourself. But you'll have to risk it. And don't be too quick with that gat. It may be me coming back."

"I go with you, master," said Hsiang Liu simply.

Noel didn't even argue. He knew it was useless. Hsiang wouldn't stay behind even if he bound him. What loyalty was this, that Hsiang dared even the spirits of *feng shui* for his master! Noel shrugged. He let himself out a back way. He went into the Bowery, walking many blocks from his residence. Then he telephoned his superior on Park Avenue.

"Noel speaking," he said. "You sent Charleson to me? Describe him.

That's tight. That's the guy. Now, do something for me. I'll be calling you again in a couple of hours, or less, from Brooklyn. I want you to find Maida Charleson, or news of her, to pass on to me when I call. I'd believe she were kidnapped but for one thing—Charleson is too damn' fast with a gat. Yes, and one other thing. He won't risk his life for his kid. That sounds screwy to me. And find out if there's a skeleton in his closet. Yeah, a woman."

Noel clicked up the receiver on his superior's questions. How could he answer them when he didn't know what came next? He caught a taxicab, gave an address in Brooklyn within several blocks of the cemetery. When he dismissed the cab it was still raining. He pulled Charleson's coat around his ears, dragged his hat down to keep rain from going down his neck, started walking.

"Shall I wait, Mr. Charleson?" asked the cabby.

Noel almost stopped. The cabby had called him Charleson. He wondered what else the man might know about the rich broker. He was half minded to go back and ask. Instead, he burrowed deeper into his coat and went on—on until he reached the cemetery.

He glanced at his wrist-watch. Half an hour to wait. He shivered, went on, found a telephone, called his superior again.

"Maida Charleson seen at Kindy's night club tonight at twelve, came crackling over the wire. "What's up, anyhow?"

"I wish I knew," said Noel crisply. "And I'm going to find out. 'Bye."

He clicked up, deliberately went back to the cemetery gate. It was closed, locked. The street lights did not penetrate this far through the rain. The cemetery itself was a black splotch in the ebon gloom, surrounded by trees through which distant lights were like stationary fireflies.

Noel looked around him, went up the cemetery fence, feet fitting easily into the mesh of the tough wire. He went down the other side, was in the cemetery. He shivered again. A sudden chill had come sweeping out to him across the graveyard. He thought of wandering yellow ghosts, fancied he could almost see shadows, there through the gloom. Something warned him away from the black walls of the trees.

He started straight across the cemetery. His right hand was in his pocket, grasping the butt of an automatic. His left hand caressed and crumpled the black flower Charleson had given him. He didn't realize what he did until after he had stumbled over several grave mounds, had barked his shins against the simple markers.

The stale odor of incense assailed his nostrils, coming damply through the rain. He could smell burned firecrackers, too, and the decaying remains of food left at the graves for the spooks to eat. It was as though he were in another world entirely.

The chill rain ran down the markers, whispering, oddly like the whispering of the golden sand in Noel's hour glass. It skittered into puddles at the bases of the markers. Lightning streaked the skies to the east. Thunder rolled its chariot wheels across the sky. The lightning brightened the cemetery in orange, yellow and blue, like flashing phosphorescence.

Noel, feeling as though he stood out in sharp relief in the light, felt very much alone, felt the near presence of all the gods and demons out of China. It was so easy to feel them there, knowing Chinese beliefs as he did, and how the dead must lie so restlessly under those markers against the time when their relatives could afford to return them to China. He wouldn't have been surprised had graves opened here and there for the dead to arise and walk slowly through the rain.

He walked on through the cemetery's center, eyes searching the surrounding walls of the trees. A man might yell here, in the sound of the drumming rain, and not be heard. A man might be slain here and not found for days, if he happened to fall behind a mound. The silent city of the restless dead! Certainly a strange place for an after-midnight rendezvous. It was so easy for the dead to rise. . . .

A thin wavering cry came out of the black shadows of the trees to the west. It was the voice of a woman. Noel stood stock-still to listen, not realizing that his left hand in his pocket was ripping the black flower to shreds. His right hand gripped that automatic with all his power.

Deliberately he turned now toward the sound. He knew that it hadn't been Maida Charleson who had called to him, and that Charleson had lied about her snatching. But why? Noel intended to get to the bottom of the affair as quickly as possible. He turned and walked straight into the west, ready for any eventuality.

The lightning flared again. He saw something, a mere glimpse, to his left, out of the tail of his eye. It was the fence over which he had climbed, and somebody else was climbing over it now. He had seen the shape of a climbing man, sharply etched by the lightning flash—as though the man had been crucified against the wire.

Fire ran along that wire. Noel shuddered. If the man hadn't dropped clear, he had, at the very least, been terrifically burned by the racing of high voltage along the wire. He stood, waiting for the lightning to flare again. Long minutes passed before it flowered once more in the sky. Then he saw a bundle against the wire. He shrugged, fighting off a growing fear he could not explain.

Then he started on—and his eyes almost popped from his head. Coming toward him from the woods, scattered out, bending forward, moving without sound like so many cats, were five men. He knew by their manner that they were Chinese. Then the lightning showed him their faces and proved his belief. They *were* Chinese. And they were dressed in white, the color of mourning! God, were these the restless ones, now risen from the dead?

His automatic came out. His thumb found the safety catch. He stopped, listening. He heard the sloshing of feet through muddy puddles, and grinned. Ghosts didn't make noises like that. These who came to meet "Charleson" were not ghosts. They were men, who had selected a cemetery for—what? Murder? Perhaps. He'd soon know.

And then, as the woman's cry came again, they were upon him. They attacked with silent ferocity. In the first instant of contact he knew one thing for certain. They weren't out to slay, but to capture. Why? He fought at them savagely. They evaded the lunges of his automatic muzzle. He kept his thumb on the catch. He wouldn't shoot unless he had to, unless they shot first, or flashed knives.

He clutched at one man who came in low. His fingers, the fingers of his left hand, found, not the man's throat, but his face. His fingernails bit in as he tried to shift his grip to the throat, bringing his automatic over for a smashing blow to the skull. The Chinese gasped. Then he shrieked. The lightning flashed again. Five faces stood out in sharp relief—and Noel's hand came free of the one man's face. Noel started. The print of his hand, in black, showed plainly on the face of the man he had clutched. That man's mouth was wide with horror. His face twitched.

Four Chinese voices shrieked in unison: "The Black Snow! We are dead men!"

But Noel hurled himself forward, suspicion of the truth coming to him. The man he had clutched had suddenly gone crazy. He seemed to forget Noel. He plunged past Dorus, staggering all over the place—doing an inconceivable thing for a Chinese, staggering over the mounds of his people's dead, something no Chinese in his right mind would think of doing. Noel heard him fall, rise, fall again, try to shriek—but his voice was locked in his throat.

Noel, hurling himself at the other four, heard the one he had touched go down again, and remain down, heard the tattoo of his beating heels in a puddle of water. Then even this ceased. Yet Noel knew he hadn't dealt a fatal blow—but the man was dead by the absence of sound.

Noel thrust his automatic into his pocket, lunged forward. He grasped another man by the front of his shirt, and while the man shrieked as though he were being murdered, rubbed his stained left hand over the fellow's face and mouth. It didn't surprise him when the second Chinese broke free, staggering as the first had done, in among the graves, to fall at last and kick his life out in turn among the puddles of water, while the rain hammered down upon him, sounding a wild requiem which seemed somehow fitting.

The three remaining Chinese started to run.

He covered them with his weapon, called upon them to halt. They did, turning, their hands raised.

"Do not touch us," said one in broken English. "Do not touch us or we die."

"Run, and you die anyhow, of bullets," said Noel grimly. "Come here!"

And he held up his blackened hand. They shrieked. They were trembling like crazy men. Certainly all of this must have been horrible for these men, with the beliefs Noel knew they harbored about this time and place—especially the place. He halted them again.

"Stop!" he said. "Give me your names, instantly!"

The names they gave were not Cantonese names, proof that these men were not the usual Chinese sojourners. Bei Shuh, Li Fung, Kai Ling. And they could be found in Chinatown. Noel waved them on. They raced for the gate. One got over, running madly down the street. But the other two were caught in the wire, by the streaking fire of the lightning—never, reputedly, striking twice in the same place. He whirled, racing again for the sound of the woman's voice.

Finally he heard someone running, ahead of him, running and sobbing. He flashed his light on the ground, after he had entered the woods. He found a woman's footprints. He raced after her. Water was dribbling into the holes her feet had just made. She was running for the fence which surrounded the cemetery. Noel caught her just before her extended hands would have touched the wire. She struggled with him, fighting like a tigress. She swore deep oaths, not words which might have come from the lips of any Maida Charleson.

Noel fought back at her, striving to imprison her hands.

"So you're the skeleton," he said. "The skeleton in Charleson's closet. What night club do you work at?"

Then he saw her face, and almost lost her in his surprise. Her face was Chinese, yet not Chinese, American yet not American. His prisoner was an Eurasian—of exquisite beauty. He gripped her more tightly.

"So," he said, "you meant to snatch Charleson, eh? Wasn't he paying you enough hush money to keep you away from his wife? You were ready to do anything, even murder, to make him kick in, weren't you? Swell idea, bringing him here, and fixing things so you could charge the wire in case he was trailed. The papers *did* say rain tonight, didn't they? The rain fit right in, for there would be lightning to explain the dead ones on the wire. But who worked the juice? Another American lover?"

"Let me go!" panted the girl. "Let me go! Charleson deserved anything we might have done to him—anything. He forced me to give up all my

Chinese associates, he kept me a virtual prisoner of his passionate whims in a retreat far from his complaining wife. In return he taught me to live like a white woman of wealth, covered me with jewels and clothed me in gorgeous gowns.

"Gradually he tired of me and finally, because of his wife's suspicions, ordered me to leave the country. Imagine! What place would there be for me, an Eurasian, in any land but this? It would have been condemnation to death.

"I merely meant to get my money from him, and a promise to let me live alone to enjoy it. That was all, I swear it!"

"And he got me to help in his dirty business by telling me it was his daughter!" exploded Noel. "Well, I wonder what he'll have to say when I take you back with me?"

"Nothing, you fool! Nothing, ever!"

And beyond the wire a snarling figure rose from the shadows, bearing a heavy burden—the apparatus, Noel instantly knew, by which this woman's accomplice had accomplished the destruction of the Chinese on the wire. The stooping figure raced for a car at the curb, jumped in, gears were meshed, the car was gone.

"And that's your *real* lover, eh?" said Noel. "What does he mean by what he shouted?"

"Charleson has been trailed all evening. Your house is being watched by my men. If anything went wrong here you were to be killed to keep you from meddling. If you changed clothes with Charleson and left him in your place, it will be Charleson who will die. My man would already have telephoned, after he heard the first shrieks in the cemetery, giving the word for 'your' death. Now, you see?"

"Only that two of your men died on the wire, and someone else I don't know . . ."

"A man who followed you," said the girl.

"Hsiang Liu, my servant!"

"Perhaps," the girl shrugged.

Noel was suspicious of her apparent resignation to capture. He had been staring into the cemetery, to see whether the two who had staggered away from his clutch had risen again. They had not.

"What," he asked suddenly, "is the black kiss? And what is this stuff on my hand?"

He dared to release his grip on her with his left hand, which he held up before her face. She didn't answer. Her eyes widened. She suddenly clutched at his stained hand, held it against her mouth and nostrils, breathed deeply. Then she laughed, long peals of crazy laughter. This time when she tried to break away he didn't try to stop her. She staggered into the cemetery as her two men had done, and fell as they had. When Noel reached her she was dead.

He went back over the wire, for a brief glance into the face of Hsiang Liu, the servant who had died to help his master. He could do nothing for the boy, so he left him, telephoning to the police at the first place he could find a phone. Then he called his superior, out on Park Avenue.

"Yes, the flower," he said, "was a Jade Girdle chrysanthemum, smeared with a coat of black stuff that was deadly poison if breathed or tasted. I might have got it myself, if I hadn't remembered that an Ink Chrysanthemum turns its petals down, against the stem—and that only a Jade Girdle touches the tips of its petals over the top of the flower. But the Jade Girdle, naturally, is *white*. You see? A black Jade Girdle spelled something phony. So I didn't taste or smell.

"Queer people, the Chinks. Now, get the dragnet out for Bei Shuh, Li Fung and Kai Ling. Two of 'em are dead, but I don't know which two. The one you find, if I hold a 'black kiss' in front of him, will squeal plenty. He proved that by running out on his mistress. He'll tell us who she is, who turned on the juice—which chap will get some juice turned on in his turn— and the whole story of Charleson's skeleton in the closet. He'd probably rather die than have the truth told, but men have died and the truth must come out."

"That's strange," said his superior. "I got word, just before you called, that you had been stabbed to death in your residence."

"In that case," said Noel grimly, "I guess Charleson won't care much how the story breaks. Let it ride like that, then—and send the dead wagon to the Chink cemetery in Brooklyn to pick up the other pieces of the case!"

And Noel clicked up the receiver.

THE BLOOD SCREEN

Feeling the black horror of the place alive with menace, Noel crept forward.

Only From the Sinister Depths of Chinatown Could Have Been Spawned a Mystery That Was Screened With Human Blood.

DORUS NOEL ENTERED THE CIGAR-STORE TELEPHONE BOOTH on Lafayette Street and telephoned his unknown superior out on Park Avenue. No sooner had he given his name, than that superior heaved an explosive sigh of relief.

"I wanted you to call, Noel," he said, "for I hated to get in touch with you other than in the usual way. We are always more effective when our connection is not definitely known."

"Why, chief, what's up?"

"I don't know exactly. Something all-fired queer, I should say. It probably isn't anything for you at all, and I wouldn't even think of you and your Chinese knowledge but for one thing: the victim bought some Chinese things the day before he died."

"Victim? What victim?"

"Thaddeus Courtin, the race-track man."

Noel whistled softly. He'd just read all the police knew about the matter in the morning papers. At his next question, his superior told him to hop up to Washington Square North and listen in on the police investigation. Noel clicked up the receiver, and twenty minutes later was in the death chamber.

Thaddeus Courtin had died in bed. Noel, on viewing the corpse, was struck by the alabaster whiteness of the skin. His eyes narrowed thoughtfully. The lieutenant in charge of the investigation regarded Noel with a certain degree of animosity.

"It's a queer go, all right, Noel," he said, "but I figure I can handle queer cases as well as the next one."

"Maybe," said Noel. "Nobody denies your ability, Marquiss. What does the coroner say?"

Marquiss' face sagged.

"That's the queerest part of the whole thing. He reported a small incision in the neck, and the fact that less than a third of the normal amount of blood remained in the body of the victim after death!"

Noel whistled again.

"Incision in the neck, loss of blood. If we believed in vampires, or vampire bats . . ."

Marquiss lifted his eyebrows, startled. Then he walked to the window and looked steadily out into Washington Square Park. He flirted the clammy sweat from his forehead as he came back.

"Jees, Noel," he said, "you certainly gave me a turn for a minute. I fully expected to see a flock of vampire bats hanging from the trees in the park. Hell, if anything like that got loose in New York City, you know, even if they were one one-hundredth as thick as the recent invasion of white moths . . ."

Noel interrupted the talkative lieutenant, with a wave of his hand.

"He bought some Chinese things yesterday, down in Chinatown. Where are they?"

Marquiss led the way to the first floor, two floors below the death chamber, and pointed.

Courtin hadn't been very selective. There were some queer clocks, a few pieces of eggshell porcelain, some bronzes of the Ming Dynasty, several pieces of rare brocade, some silken garments of yellow which must have once been worn by royalty, and various ornaments of jade, including a plaque covered with Chinese, Manchu, and Tibetan characters—official pronouncements from some vanished Manchu throne thus indelibly set down so that all who ran might read.

Noel turned the plaque over and over in his hand. He deciphered the Chinese with little difficulty. It said:

"Hear, tremble, and obey. It is decreed that hereafter, throughout the Celestial Kingdom, only eggshells from the egg of the pheasant shall be used in the manufacture of lacquer ware."

The characters of the signature were the name of one of the Ming Emperors, whose rule ended some fifty years before the advent of the Manchus. Noel puckered his lips in a soundless whistle.

"A good graft," he said, half aloud, "for probably all pheasants were the property of the throne."

"What's that?" asked Marquiss. "Found something?"

"I've just uncovered a crooked deal," said Noel with a twisted smile. "This guy could be sent to jail for extortion—only trouble is that he's been dead for three hundred years or more."

Marquiss snorted. Noel went on.

"This all he bought?"

"No. There's a screen of some kind in his bathroom."

Marquiss led the way back. Courtin's bathroom was huge, fit for a king. The huge tub was masked from the rest of the room by a segmented screen which reached to the height of an average man's shoulders. It was of brilliantly vermilioned lacquer, with beautiful white feathers set into the wood. It was an excellent piece of work, Noel knew, one of the best outside of China.

"Funny," said Marquiss, "I'm not an emotional guy, but Chink stuff always gets me. This screen for instance; it gave me the creeps. Maybe it's the smell of the thing."

Noel sniffed.

"Incense seems to cling to everything a Chinese touches. It's nothing. Don't let it worry you. Know where Courtin bought this stuff?"

"Yeah. Lom King's, on Mott Street."

Noel knew that place, though he hadn't visited it more than once or twice. It made him fidgety just to watch the Chinese at work.

But he went down there now and entered the building where Lom King turned out his masterpieces. He entered by a series of three doors, passing through the second door only after the first had closed behind him, the third after the second had closed. He nodded with approval. Lacquer was supposed to be manufactured in dustproof rooms, Otherwise it caused workers almost as much discomfort as radium. Noel had seen some of the irritating boils caused by the juice of the lac tree.

Inside he found himself in the long room where the painting was done. A slender Chinese came forward, bowing from the waist, all Chinese hospitality. Noel guessed that he was probably a graduate from an American university. Chinese young men went in for plenty of education.

"I'd like to see Lom King," he said. "My name is Noel, Dorus Noel."

He watched the young fellow's face as he gave his name, wondering what effect it would have. The man gave no sign.

"May I ask the nature of your business?"

"Yes. I wish to buy some lacquer screens."

"I am sure I can handle your purchases, sir."

"I wish to see Lom King," insisted Noel, "and I'll find him myself, if you don't conduct me to him."

Ten minutes later Noel faced Lom King, an old man, stooped, wearing spectacles and the traditional long gown. Noel looked deeply into the old man's eyes, wondering at the malevolence he saw there. Lom King spoke before Noel had a chance.

"I resent this intrusion, Dorus Noel," said Lom King. "I have done nothing to merit your forcing yourself upon me. I leave menial details to my menials. An artist, a super-artist, like myself, cannot be annoyed by ordinary folk and do their best work. I am, sir, in process of introducing China's most beautiful things to America."

Noel arched his brows.

"Didn't you handle the sale to Thaddeus Courtin yesterday?" he asked. "Certainly a man so important would not have been satisfied to treat with your servants."

"Thaddeus Courtin? Thaddeus Courtin?" The old man's voice was waspish. "I never heard of the man. Please go."

"I want three screens!"

"See Chang Sing!"

"I am going to buy them from you, Lom King, here and now, or . . ."

Lom King stared at Noel. His black eyes narrowed suddenly.

"I sense a threat in your voice, Dorus Noel," he said. "May I ask why?"

"Yes. There is a dead man whose soul is asking questions."

"So? Then let him ask of the police. An artist cannot be troubled."

"And the three screens?"

"Will be sent to your dwelling-place within the next twenty-four hours, during which time you may wish that you had not threatened Lom King."

• • •

Noel went back into the room of the screens. There were dozens, hundreds of them, scattered all through the room. Coolies, more coolies than there were screens, stood before the screens, working on their tops, or squatted before them, working below their middles.

Since Chang Sing made no objection, Noel walked among the screens to watch the work, about which he already knew something.

The lac tree was tapped for its juice after seven years of age, twice a year in middle and late summer. Wood to receive the lac was highly polished, then covered with thin paper or fine silk, over which was smeared a layer of lac mixed with emery powder, red sandstone, and vermilion.

When this dried, the dose was repeated, anywhere from three to eighteen times, depending upon the quality to be desired. If designs were to be worked into the lacquer they were first drawn on heavy paper, pricked in with needles, transferred to the lacquer piece with chalk, then pricked into the lacquer again.

Powdered eggshells were used in the best lacquer for consistency.

Memory of that caused Noel to jerk his head sharply, remembering what he had read on the jade plaque at the home of Thaddeus Courtin.

But, the devil! What connection could a three hundred year old plaque have with a present day murder? Not one of the working coolies looked at Noel. They worked in silence. Some smeared on the lac. Some worked the designs on heavy paper, some transferred the designs in chalk, some pricked them into the finished lacquer. All worked in the strangest kind of silence.

When the coolies moved—and only their eyes and facile fingers seemed to move—they made no sound whatever. It was as though the place of lacquer-making was a cathedral where they did not dare even to speak in whispers. They would probably kill to preserve its sanctity. Kill?

A strange feeling was coming over Noel. He whirled to look about him, almost knocking over a screen to which a fresh coating of lacquer had been applied. Some of the stuff stuck to his coat-sleeve. The coolie working on the screen twisted his lips in a silent snarl, but when he caught Noel's eyes, he cringed and went on with his work.

Near one end of the room Chang Sing stood, and Noel fancied he caught a look of hatred on the man's face. He looked at the door, beyond which he knew that Lom King labored over his artistry, producing designs out of his ancient imagination. He thought he saw eyes peering at him from a slit in the door. He shivered.

This place somehow felt like a morgue, he told himself. He couldn't explain it And then he remembered what Marquiss had said about the queer feeling which had been his in the presence of the screen in the bathroom of Thaddeus Courtin. Noel started for the door, walking on the balls of his feet for silence. Chang Sing hurried to let him out through the three doors.

"You have made purchases?" asked Chang Sing.

"Yes. I go now to await their coming, and to clean this coat of mine. Awkward of me, wasn't it? I often think, when I get something on me like this, how such things so often point the finger of accusation at a murderer!"

Chang Sing arched his brows, but said nothing. Noel could read nothing in his eyes. He passed through the three doors. At his home he gave his coat to the boy, ordered him to keep it in the closet without cleaning it, and sat down to some deep thinking.

He couldn't get over the strange sensation he had had in Lom King's place—that it was like a morgue. Silly, of course, but when one deals with Orientals even queer impressions may mean more than a man can guess. He hesitated, then went out and called his superior again.

"Anything new?"

"Yes!" There was excitement in the voice of the other. "It didn't seem to be important at first, but now it does. A bum was found dead in Washington Park this morning and was taken to the morgue for identification. Marquiss checked on the autopsy, and the poor fellow's body had all but been drained of blood, exactly like Courtin's. Washington Square Park at this moment is being turned upside down for vampire bats, seven of which have escaped from the Bronx Park Zoo!"

"Nonsense!" snapped Noel. "Vampire bats are over-rated. Seven of 'em couldn't kill two men that way, with two or three nights in which to work. Besides, they'd be easily found. They sleep in the daytime, hanging upside down from tree limbs. However, there may be something in it somewhere. When did the bats get away?"

"Sometime yesterday. No trace of them has been found, and there is something else queer! The man responsible for their care has vanished!"

Noel's heart hammered with excitement.

"Listen," he said, "have all the zoo attendants questioned about any Chinese who visited the zoo yesterday. Get the best descriptions you can and send them to me right away. Find out the name of the missing zoo attendant and have a dragnet thrown out to bring him in. The best thing would be to search the grounds of the park, Bronx Park. I'll call you back in an hour!"

Noel hung up. He literally raced back to his quarter. At the door he snapped a question at his boy.

"Chang Sing here? Or Lom King?"

"Chang Sing, master, yes."

Noel gulped. His guess had been a good one.

"And the lacquer screens?"

"No screens. He say must have money first."

Noel went into his reception room, where the slender, immaculate Chang

Sing rose to greet him. The man's face was expressionless. His black eyes glowed. He stood with his hands folded behind him.

"I come for confirmation of the order for three lacquer screens," he said. "Do you still wish them?"

"Of course," said Noel in exasperation, "more now than ever. Why should I change my mind?"

"Lom King has other orders to fill. He does not wish to be hurried. He tells me . . ."

"To try to talk me out of buying, eh? Well, I want those screens, and the fastest way you can bring them here will be too slow! If he won't sell I'll know the reason why, or he goes out of business. Understand?"

Chang Sing bowed deeply, departed. At the door he looked back. His eyes played over the room as though he wished to remember every detail of it, and Noel caught himself shivering again. This was the queerest thing he had ever run into. Then Chang Sing was gone.

By nightfall the screens had not come. Noel had telephoned his superior as arranged. The zoo attendant, one Lemuel Haslup, had been found in a clump of tropical plants, in one of the hothouses, dead, with an incision in his neck, and most of his blood missing!

A cold sweat broke out on the body of Dorus Noel. Horror was somehow being heaped upon nameless horror in a way which made for madness. He telephoned Lom King's and got no answer. He went to the lacquer place to find it closed and locked. No way to get in unless he forced the locks.

He went back to his residence on Pell and Mott Streets, sat down in his favorite chair in his "Chinese Room," as though he would get some inspiration there which would supply him an answer to the riddle, and listened to the interminable ticking of the half-dozen clocks—all from China—which held position in various parts of the room. The hours dragged along until it was almost midnight.

Nothing had happened. His superior hadn't communicated with him. Yet he felt that all through Chinatown strange forces were being mustered against him, strange undercurrents were flowing through the rabbit warrens, strange alliances to combat his investigations were being arranged. And he could still see the eyes of Lom King, the maker of lacquer ware, the "artist" of the lac tree.

If this hunch were correct, what was the motive? Money? Courtin had plenty. The bum in the park had been just a bum. The zoo attendant had been making a wage of twenty-one dollars a week. No, it couldn't be money. But maybe, he decided, there was a different motive behind the slaying of the last two named.

He called his superior once more, to be advised that there was nothing new anywhere along the line. Returning to his quarters he noted the furtive behavior of the Chinese he met. They looked at him, then looked quickly away when he caught them at it—looked away and hurried their steps as though it were absolutely necessary for them to quit his vicinity as soon as possible. He knew the signs. He was somehow a marked man. But how?

He went to bed and dreamed of vampire bats settling on his neck, and sucking the life from his body. He fought out at the furred, stinking horrors, and wakened to find that his hands, flailing the air, actually touched something furry, something that squeaked in terror, something musty of odor. He leaped from his bed as the thing escaped him with a flash of shadowy wings toward his open window.

He hit something and knocked it over with a clatter. The winged thing escaped through the window. Noel turned on the light to make a queer discovery.

His three lacquer screens had been mysteriously delivered. They had surrounded his bed, one at the foot, one at either side. Two of them still stood at his bedside. He had knocked down the third when he had chased the furred horror to the window. Cold perspiration bathed his whole body.

He studied himself in the brilliant light, after pulling the window blind. In knocking over the lacquer screen he had covered the knees of his pajamas with fresh lacquer.

"Odd," he muttered to himself, "damned odd. I never heard of a lacquer screen being delivered before it had thoroughly dried. Lung Tze!"

Lung Tze was his boy, or servant. Lung Tze didn't answer. Noel raced to his bedroom. Lung Tze would never answer again. He was thoroughly and completely dead, and the yellow of his skin had turned to old ivory, almost white ivory. Noel knew without being told that Lung Tze's blood had been drained.

Noel gritted his teeth. There was just one thing to be done, and he meant to do it right now. He dressed quickly, first hanging his pajamas in the closet where he had left his stained coat. He donned clothing, using another coat, and fastened automatics at his waist. Then he telephoned a friend whom he sometimes used in his mysterious, often fearful, work.

"I'll leave the door open, Jack," he told that friend. "You can't miss the place. Have the dope for me by morning, will you?"

Then he clicked up the receiver, dashed from his house, heading straight as might be for the lacquer manufacturing place of Lom King. Neither locks nor bolts should deter him this time.

He entered the hallway of a building adjoining that of Lom King's place, went up black, silent stairs as far as he could, found a ladder leading up to a trapdoor, went out onto the roof, crossed to the roof of Lom King's place, hunted over it for a skylight. But there were only chimneys.

Finally, however, he found the inevitable trapdoor. Its hinges creaked as he swung it open. If there were anyone inside, he must certainly have been heard. If Lom King was as frugal as most Chinese, he probably lived somewhere in the bowels of this building with his family.

It took him fifteen minutes, after the closing of the trapdoor, to get down into the room of the screens. He hadn't heard a sound save the creaking protests of timbers, the whisper of his own breathing, and the hammering of his own heart.

He stood in the black room of the screens, and saw the countless screens stretching away from him like an army of queerly-shaped soldiers and shivered. More than ever the place seemed like a morgue.

Everything, or at least almost everything, depended on the work of his friend, Jack Larkin, between now and morning. Larkin would have reached his quarters by this time. He hoped Larkin wouldn't find the dead Lung Tze and call the police. He wasn't yet ready for the police.

Noel, fairly certain he was alone in the shadowy confines of the screen room, started edging his way through the screens. He brushed against one. It trembled. He caught it to keep it from falling down. If it fell it would, like cards piled against one another on end, take down a score of other screens with it—and rouse the whole neighborhood. The screen he touched was wet. He rubbed his hand on his handkerchief before going on.

He touched another screen, playing his hand over it. It was then that Lom King's men struck, coming at him without sound. Noel grinned as the first man catapulted himself from behind a screen he was approaching. Noel's hands instantly went to his automatics. He could handle unarmed Chinese.

This first one seemed to have only his fists. Probably a *ta chuen* man, a *jujitsu* artist. The word "artist" made him think of Lom King and his claims.

His automatics leaped out. The muzzle of the gat in his right hand cracked down on a skull. The man fell at Noel's feet, squirming, his legs threshing. Several screens toppled. Instinctively Noel thrust out his hand to keep them from falling, even as other Chinese came at him from all sides, materializing from behind the screens as though every screen had been the hiding place of a coolie.

Noel stood his ground as screens crashed down. From the back room came shouting in Cantonese, a few words of which Noel understood.

"Take him alive if possible. Otherwise slay him quickly before someone comes!"

Noel knew that voice, would never forget it, the voice of Lom King. He whirled toward it, intent upon reaching the lacquer master. The Chinese coolies redoubled their efforts. Noel surged forward. Men grabbed at him, grappled with his legs. He kicked out, glad that he was a fair master of *savate*. The muzzles of his automatics were reddening with the blood he drew from the faces and heads of the coolies, not one of whom cried out as his gats smashed down.

Screens were falling in all directions with a fearful clatter. Noel knew how Lom King must feel about all this. Manufactured lacquer was not so terribly valuable, but this stuff Lom King was making, entirely with the skilled hands of heavily-bonded coolies brought in from China, where their ancestors had also labored in lacquer, was worth thousands of dollars.

A man like Courtin would pay ten thousand dollars for the best lacquer, such as Lom King was making. Noel swore at himself that he had forgotten to ask the price Courtin had paid. On the three screens delivered to himself he had seen no characters indicating their price. But that scarcely mattered, he now understood, for it had never been intended that he should possess them.

Only the fact of his waking had kept him from going as Courtin had gone, and the bum in Washington Square Park, and the zoo attendant.

Coolies clung to Noel. He hurled himself forward. Desperation gave him the strength of a madman. He hammered away with his gats, cracking down with all his might.

"I'm coming for you, Lom King," said Noel. "Too bad your operatives failed to slay me tonight. And the touch of the vampire bat was an excellent one. I give you full credit."

Lom King laughed, brittle, metallic laughter.

"You still may not live until morning, my friend."

The brittle laughter came again. It made Noel's flesh crawl. The coolies seemed to redouble their efforts, but with that laughter in his ears nothing could stop Dorus Noel. He pushed forward. He stumbled, almost fell, knew that if he once went down he would never rise again.

He saw Lom King standing in a door, ready to duck back if he came too close.

Outside the building, attracted by the smashing clatter inside, policemen were banging with nightsticks and yelling for admittance in the name of the law. Noel debated with himself whether to put a bullet into Lom King. But a coolie might strike his arm at the moment of firing and cause him to kill Lom King, and he didn't wish to do that. He grasped his opportunity, just as Lom King turned to flee, and hurled one of his automatics with all his power. He saw it fly swift and true to its mark. It struck Lom King in the back of the head. Lom King went down, kicking.

Dorus Noel jumped astride the lac master, standing there, battling like a Trojan against the desperate attacks of Lom King's coolies. They were piled around him, none dead, but with many skulls fractured, when the coppers finally came through the door and took command.

They turned on the lights to survey the wreckage. Noel was a mess. His clothing was covered with wet lacquer paint.

"You look," said a sergeant, "as though you'd been through a slaughter house."

"If you knew," said Noel grimly, "how true that is, you would quake in your boots."

The sergeant's eyes widened. Noel went on.

"Take in Lom King and all of his men you can gather up," he snapped. "I'll press charges against them before noon tomorrow morning."

Noel went to the cigar store on Lafayette Street as soon as he had changed clothing, carefully hanging the clothing he had worn in the lacquer place in the closet. His superior answered. Noel spoke swiftly.

Have you any information relative to the disappearance, in the last twenty-four hours, of a surgeon of importance?"

"Why," gasped his superior, "it's strange you should ask. Word came in just before midnight that Dr. Lancing, of the Manhattan Clinic, had been kidnapped thirty-six hours ago. His people, expecting a demand for ransom, which they could settle with safety to Lancing if the police weren't called in, didn't report it."

"What about him? He a strong character?"

"Not exactly. Anemic chap, horn-rimmed spectacles, all brains, rather weak . . ."

"And a nut on blood transfusions?"

"Yes; how did you guess?"

"Because it couldn't be any other way. I think I've got the goods on who murdered Courtin, the bum, and Haslup, and maybe before them a whole slew of people who never got reported because they were all bums and not worth the expense of an autopsy. We'll have to trace back on that. Send Marquiss to me in the morning, will you?"

"Of course. And congratulations on your good work if you've actually wound up the case."

Noel slept the rest of the night, deep untroubled sleep.

The next morning, Marquiss, looking mystified, entered his house on Pell and Mott Streets, bringing Lom King and several of Lom King's men, among them Chang Sing. All wore manacles. Noel looked at each of them in turn, and shuddered a little. Marquiss noticed and his eyes went even wider.

"The charge against Lom King is cold-blooded murder," he said. "The most cold-blooded I ever heard of. Three killings we know about, with maybe others to look into when we start checking back. You know what sort of work he does?"

"Yeah," said Marquiss.

"Note the brilliant redness of his lacquer work?"

"Yeah."

"Jack!" Noel raised his voice. Jack Larkin came in from an adjoining room. His seared fingertips and dirty nails, the stains on his clothing, told the story of his profession. He was a chemist, the best one Noel knew.

"What were those stains on my clothing you got from the closet, Jack?" he demanded.

"Lac juice," said Larkin promptly, "mixed with human blood."

Marquiss gasped. Noel went on.

"See? Lom King finds out what doctor is the best on transfusions. He kidnaps him and under threat of death, maybe after doping the doctor to dull his scruples, forces him to take blood from his victims. And he'd probably not have been caught if he hadn't picked on Courtin, a man with money. Vermilion is a necessary part of lacquer work. It decides the color.

"The next best thing is blood. In old Chinese red paintings, pig blood was used. Lom King couldn't be bothered with pig culture, and human blood was the next best thing. So he went after it. But he didn't want to burn for murder, so he made his plans.

"Vampire bats would be suspected if some escaped from the zoo. That took money to bribe an attendant. Every Chinese who entered the zoo the day seven bats disappeared has been described after a fashion. One description fits Chang Sing. The bribed attendant might talk when he knew what was being done—so he died.

"While investigating Courtin's murder I naturally thought of vampire bats, as Lom King had foreseen—foreseen so efficiently that he had a bum killed in Washington Square Park for us to find. Being frugal, he took the man's blood. Too bad, Lom King, you didn't turn loose one of the bats in the park, as you did at my place last night, when you surrounded my bed with screens before putting Dr. Lancing to work. Too bad I wakened so quickly before you could get under way.

"I don't know how you got away so quickly—which reminds me of a fourth murder, that of Lung Tze, my servant. You had to get him so you could reach me. Am I right in all this, Lom King?"

"The wise man, accused, says nothing," replied Lom King sonorously.

"You don't have to," said Noel grimly.

"But how could they get the doc into Courtin's house without being heard?" asked Marquiss.

"If you'd ever watched Lom King's coolies at work, in silence so deep you could cut it with a knife, you wouldn't need to ask," said Noel. "They move without sound. They can almost go through keyholes. They probably carried Dr. Lancing in. You will, after a bit, start turning Chinatown upside down to find the kidnapped doctor. Is there anything else?"

"Yes," said Marquiss, unwilling even now to give Noel too much credit. "I don't see any motive for all this."

"Easy," said Noel, "the queerest kind of extortion you ever heard of. Lom King ran out of vermilion and needed blood. He needed it because he had to make the kind of lacquer that would bring thousands of dollars for each of his beautiful screens. Men have killed for less money than this meant to Lom King. Money, however obtained, is always motive enough for murder."

Marquiss sighed.

"I have to hand it to you, Noel," he said. "You win hands down. I don't even figure in this case."

Noel grinned.

"Yes, you do. You're the whole case. If you hadn't told me how queer that lacquer screen in Courtin's bathroom made you feel, I might never have had the right hunch. But you gave it to me, and when I saw the other lacquer screens, and they made me feel as though I were touring a morgue, I couldn't miss. Take the credit, Marquiss. I'll take my pay in remembering the excitement. So long, Lom King, I'll see you at the little green door."

OFF-TRAIL PUBLICATIONS
Specializing in the era of American pulp fiction

THE WEIRD DETECTIVE ADVENTURES OF WADE HAMMOND
By Paul Chadwick
Volume 1: 10 stories, 180 pages, $18
Volume 2: 10 stories, 172 pages, $18
Volume 3: 10 stories, 202 pages, $18
Volume 4: 9 stories, 232 pages, $18

The Wade Hammond stories complete in four volumes. In these chilling adventures, all from the classic 1930's pulps, Detective-Dragnet *and* Ten Detective Aces, *freelance investigator Wade Hammond battles a series of weird enemies. Some of the best of 1930's pulp fiction.*

DOCTOR COFFIN: THE LIVING DEAD MAN
By Perley Poore Sheehan • Introduction by John Wooley
8 novelettes, 178 pages, $16

Weird stories from Thrilling Detective, *1932-33. A former character actor who faked his own death, Doctor Coffin runs a string of mortuaries by night and fights crime at night. One of the strangest detective series.*

SUPER-DETECTIVE FLIP BOOK: TWO COMPLETE NOVELS
From the pulp *Super-Detective*:
"Legion of Robots" (November 1940) by Victor Rousseau • Introduction by John McMahan •• "Murder's Migrants" (March 1943) by Robert Leslie Bellem and W.T. Ballard • Introduction by John Wooley
2 short novels, 174 pages, $18

Super-Detective *started as a Doc Savage-like adventure pulp, then changed format to hardboiled detective. The* Flip Book *features a novel from each of the two phases with intros exploring the historical background. Exciting!*

PULPWOOD DAYS: VOL 1: EDITORS YOU WANT TO KNOW
Edited by John Locke • 180 pages, $16

Numerous articles from the writers' magazines by and about pulp editors, with ample biographical profiles. Editors include: Frank E. Blackwell (Detective Story, Western Story), Ray Palmer (Amazing Stories, Fantastic Adventures), Edwin Baird (Weird Tales, Detective Tales), and many more.

GANG PULP
Edited by John Locke • 19 stories, 294 pages, $24

Hardboiled stories of the criminal underworld from the first year (1929-30) of the gang pulps: Gangster Stories, Racketeer Stories, *etc. These violent tales came under immediate censorship pressure; the history is explored in an in-depth essay. "A remarkable work of popular-culture scholarship"*—MYSTERY SCENE, *Fall 2008.*

THE GANGLAND SAGAS OF BIG NOSE SERRANO
Volume 1: DAMES, DICE AND THE DEVIL
Volume 2: HORSES, HOBOES AND HEROES
Volume 3: HELL'S GANGSTER
By Anatole Feldman • Introductions by Will Murray
Each: 4 novels • **Volumes 1-2**: 266 pages, $20 • **Volume 3**: 224 pages, $18

The complete Big Nose Serrano novels from Gangster Stories, Greater Gangster Stories, *and* The Gang Magazine, *1930-35. Feldman was the best of the gang pulp authors, and Big Nose was his most inspired creation, the berserking king of Chicago gangsters.*

THE CITY OF BAAL
By Charles Beadle • Introduction by John Locke
7 stories, 240 pages, $20

Authentic stories of African adventure from an author who had traveled the lands he wrote about. Lost cities, strange tribes, jungle magic. Six stories from Adventure *(1918-22) and one from* The Frontier *(1925).*

CULT OF THE CORPSES
By Maxwell Hawkins • Introduction by John Locke
2 novelettes, 150 pages, $13.95

Two weird detective stories from Detective-Dragnet *(1931) by a forgotten master. Introduction discusses the weird-detective trend of the early '30s, and the career of Maxwell Hawkins.*

THE OCEAN: 100TH ANNIVERSARY COLLECTION
Edited by John Locke
20 stories, 234 pages, $18

Munsey's The Ocean *(1907-08) was one of the first specialized pulps, a sea-story magazine. The best adventure stories are included here, along with 30+ pages of nonfiction material: a history of the pulp, and extensive author profiles.*

FROM GHOULS TO GANGSTERS
THE CAREER OF ARTHUR B. REEVE
Edited by John Locke

Vol 1 (fiction): 21 stories, 264 pages, $20 • **Vol 2 (nonfic):** 260 pages, $20

*Reeve was the leading American detective-story writer of the early 20th Century, with his scientific detective, Craig Kennedy. The astonishing breadth of his career is explored for the first time here. Vol 1 includes a cross-sction of fiction from all phases of career, including many never-before-reprinted pulp stories. Vol 2 provides a 40-page biography; an extensive Art Gallery of cover repros, interior illos, ads, etc; a 75-page guide to Reeve's work in all media; and more. An "excellent piece of scholarship"—*MYSTERY SCENE, *Spring 2008.*

AMAZON STORIES
Volume 1: PEDRO & LOURENÇO
Volume 2: PEDRO & LOURENÇO
By Arthur O. Friel • Introductions by John Locke
Vol 1: 10 stories, 222 pages, $18 • **Vol 2**: 10, stories, 286 pages, $20
Collects Friel's first twenty stories from Adventure *(1919-21), following the strange experiences of two Amazon Basin rubber workers as they explore the jungle. The best of pulp adventure fiction.*

Shipping: $3.00 media mail; $6.00 priority
Check or MO to:
Off-Trail Publications
2036 Elkhorn Road, Castroville, CA 95012
Paypal: offtrail@redshift.com

www.ingramcontent.com/pod-product-compliance
Lightning Source LLC
Chambersburg PA
CBHW030503260626
47157CB00005B/1623